AIN'T NOTHIN' DOWN ABOUT IT

AIN'T NOTHIN' DOWN ABOUT IT

P.R. HAWKINS

www.urbanbooks.net

Urban Books
1119 Straight Path
West Babylon, NY 11704

ISBN-13: 978-1-60162-078-1
ISBN-10: 1-60162-078-0

First Printing January 2008
Printed in the United States of America

10 9 8 7 6 5 4 3 2 1

Submit Wholesale Orders to:
Kensington Publishing Corp.
C/O Penguin Group (USA) Inc.
Attention: Order Processing
405 Murray Hill Parkway
East Rutherford, NJ 07073-2316
Phone: 1-800-526-0275
Fax: 1-800-227-9604

Dedication
To Rickey Rodgers, who said I should, and to all of those
who knew I could . . .

Acknowledgments

Sisters, Sistaahs, Girlfriends, and Divas! Sorors, confidants, and sounding boards! Thank you, thank you, thank you! And thank you! To the extra special people in my life who provide support, support, support and don't even know it: Angelicque, for inspiration; Becca, for unwavering confidence; Carol and Georgia Mae, for being my other mothers; Chevelle, for being real; Linda, who always supported me; Stephanie, for being there even when it was hard; Roz, for being so very supportive and listening to my crap; Andre, for being his multi-talented self and telling me I could do anything; Dion, who I love like family; Joann, who has once again become my friend; Lisa Jason, who always makes time for me; Lisa Holly or Lisa Smith, whichever one you are, for just being available to listen, listen, listen; Charla, for helping me see the light; Tammy Anderson, for being cheerful; Ann Young, for coming through when others wouldn't; and Cydney. You guys hold up my head for me when I just can't do it anymore. To all of you, a big fat THANKS. What a party we are going to have!!!!!! And yes, I will pay for it.

CHAPTER ONE

They moved together in a rhythm familiar even in sleep. Easy, slow, that's the way to do it, gently bringing each other to a shuddering climax and falling, glistening in sweat, into each other's arms. It had never been so good . . . so right. Sighing with contentment, Val reached for David's mouth for an all-consuming kiss, only to grab David's lower lip playfully and tug and nibble until they were both ready once again. Laughing softly, Val got on top of David and the magic started all over.

"What are you doing?" David moaned, thrusting his hips uncontrollably against a body that was, after years of exercise, lean, muscular and athletic, without an ounce of fat.

"I'm making love to you," Val replied.

"That's fine. I like the aggressive type."

"Me too."

Soon they were too busy to talk. Val gloried in the feel of David's hard body. There was the perfection of muscle moving beneath skin. There was the easy way they fit against each other in harmony, as if there were no others capable of creating the song of love.

Val knew that David loved getting his nipples licked and was susceptible to light pressure on the head of his penis. Val knew this and took advantage of it. Soon, Val had David where he loved to be, back arched, face strained, hips thrusting in ecstasy.

"I love you," David groaned.

"I know," Val said and swallowed David greedily. Val loved the feel of David's powerful, straining body. Val loved to make David feel good. Val loved David. Their love was all-consuming and unconditional. They had been roommates before they became friends. Friends before they became lovers. Lovers before they knew they were in love.

It happened a long time ago. Back then, before David's first book had sold, they lived in an old apartment. It was their first apartment after four years of campus life. The neighborhood wasn't the best, but their building was clean, spacious and most importantly, cheap. They picked it because it was the only thing David could afford at the time, and it was essential for him to pay his way. Money wasn't an issue for Val, but Val wanted David happy. That said, they moved into the apartment.

There was only one bathroom in the apartment, and Val was in the shower. On that particular morning, David had awakened late. David had just graduated from the police academy, and it was his first day on the job.

"Come out of there, will you? I'm going to be late," David said as he knocked on the Plexiglas shower door.

"I'm taking a shower," Val called back.

"Well, hurry up."

"If you are in such a goddamn hurry, get in here with me," Val said and opened the shower door. Not giving much thought to it, David slid out of his pajamas. He only wore the bottoms. Val lounged in the tops. Before either of the two knew it, David stepped into the shower with Val.

David had seen Val naked and Val had seen David naked. But they had never been naked *together*. Suddenly, there was not enough room in the shower. They could not attempt to get clean without touching. Arms, legs, hips, thighs, and buttocks fought for space in the shower, which suddenly seemed only large enough for one. Like most men, David had awakened with an erection. Embarrassed, he tried to hide his condition from Val.

"Do you have to keep the water this hot?" David asked.

"Look, I'm just tolerating you," Val replied, reaching around David and adjusting the temperature of the water.

"Give me the soap."

"Turn around. I'll wash your back."

David followed Val's orders and Val began to wash his back. Smooth hands, soapy and wet, glided over David's skin.

"That feels good," David said.

"Uh-huh." Val continued washing David's back.

Val hadn't planned on seducing David, and David hadn't planned on being seduced. But when David presented that body, hard, masculine and morning-time erection, Val was shocked by the foreign emotions that came into play. Until then, Val had not thought of David as a sexual being. David was just David, friend, confidant and pal. David with a penis and a perfect body was something else.

Slowly, Val's hands traveled over David's body, soaping under arms, chest and thighs, avoiding buttocks and genitalia, but in a sensual caress just the same.

During Val's ministrations, David's penis developed a mind of its own, throbbing and straining for release. It was as hard as steel and pointed toward his navel.

"What are you doing, Val?"

"I don't know."

Val's hands slowly glided from David's thighs to his ass. They soaped, caressed and separated the cheeks gently, oh so gently. David thought he was going to die. The tip of a soapy finger grazed his opening. Quickly, he reached behind him and grabbed Val's hand in an airtight grip before Val could move another finger and embarrass them both. But Val had another hand. While David held the original offending hand, Val moved the other one. The urge to explore David's body was stronger than the urge to breathe.

"What are we doing?" David asked again in a voice growing hoarse with desire.

"You know, David. You know."

And David did know. They had been traveling down this road, taking this inevitable journey since the day they met. So, the only thing David was able to do was release Val's hand. Val turned David around so that they faced each other.

Hazel eyes stared into dark brown ones, trying to convey the message, "I'm digging you." Val was tall, but David was taller. That didn't stop Val. Val kissed David and then David did the unthinkable. He kissed Val back.

With the touch of their lips, the interplay of their tongues, it started. Val blazed a trail of fiery kisses from David's lips to his hard nipples and down his well-defined stomach. Then faced with David's penis, Val did the only thing there was to do. Val's mouth opened and swallowed the whole of David.

David braced himself against the walls of the shower

as he gave in to the sensation. He was big, bigger than he had ever been, and filled with wanting—wanting only Val and the sensation of that sweet, sucking mouth. He didn't want Lequita or Brandy or Helen. He didn't even want Patti, his first love, who was the model to which he held all others. David wanted only Val. So, when it was time, Val swallowed David's seed because it was meant to be.

Afterwards, the only sounds heard in the room were those of their heavy breathing and the running water. David didn't know what to do with his hands, which were entwined lovingly in Val's shoulder length auburn tresses. Val didn't know where to look. Val wanted to look at David, but did not want to see in David's eyes the hatred, the anger, the denial, and the contempt. *COCKSUCKER!!!!*

It wasn't there. None of that was there when David pulled Val up to face him. In David's eyes, Val saw only David. There was no hatred. There was no anger. There was no denial. There was no contempt. There was only love.

"You had better hurry or you'll be late," Val said, stepping from the shower.

"Yes, I'd better hurry."

Neither one of them mentioned what had happened between them. They knew that everything had changed.

VAL

Watching him get up and walk to the bathroom, I marveled at how sexy he still was to me. Tall, six-four, built solid but lean, his muscles were well defined and flowed with his movements. A configuration of browns, he had just shaved that coal black, tight curly mass atop his head, and was now sporting a bald dome. Eyes the color of coconut hull, with skin a smooth maple syrup, he was a fine ass.

I remember the first time we touched like lovers. I was as shocked as he was. I couldn't believe that the initiator of the act was me. Me! Until that morning, I had been secure in my heterosexuality. I had indulged in the desires of the flesh by finding my gratification between the thighs of so many women, so many women, so many, many women, always women. There had been Felicia, May, and my personal favorite at the time, Angela, petite Angela, my dark little nymphet with the pointed breasts and greedy, greedy mouth. But when I found myself getting hard as my hands glided over David's skin, I wasn't thinking of Angela. I was thinking of David, only David, and I wanted him with an intensity that made me weak.

Yes, I remembered the first time David and I touched as lovers. I stood in the bathroom as he walked away from me, head held high, back straight, refusing to turn around and see me. I wanted him to see me like he had when he came deep in my mouth. Wanted him to look at me erect. See me wanting. See me wanting him. See my hand grasping my penis, stroking it, calming it, and trying to ease the tension in my flesh. I was twenty-one years old at the time. David was twenty-two. We had just become men. Now, being with him seemed so natural, I knew our meeting had been fate, not happenstance.

"What are you smiling at?" he asked as he crawled back into the bed.

"You, baby. Only you," I said as I pulled him to me and kissed him. I could think about our meeting at another time. Right now, I was too busy to think.

CHAPTER TWO

Up on point. Leg kicked high. Back arched. Silhouette tense. Even after living together for more than a decade, David didn't know all the technical terms for the movements Val performed with such fluidity. He just knew that he liked to watch Val whenever he was experiencing writer's block. After three and a half unproductive hours at his computer, David had gotten up from his desk in frustration and wandered up the stairs to Val's dance studio. The house that David and Val shared was high in the Hollywood Hills and had been built in the 1930's. Prior to moving in, they had done extensive renovations on the six-bedroom Mediterranean. Now, housing a complete gym and dance studio, it was better suited for their lifestyle.

Low jazz was playing over the speakers while Val exercised by the bar against the wall. David took a seat at the baby grand piano and watched his lover. Val was in his element when he was in the studio. He was an extension of the music, a visualization of the song.

At thirty-three, Val had moved into his prime gracefully. He was a good-looking man, possessing the kind of supermodel attributes that turned heads. Standing a shade over six feet, he wasn't as tall as David, but he was still tall. He was the color of freshly baked Mrs. Baird's bread covered in melted butter, with hazel eyes that sometimes looked more brown than green and vice versa. Possessing the best features of both his West Indian mother and French father, he was a study in contrast; straight Caucasian nose, full, sensual, generous mouth. His smile was perfect. He wore his shoulder length auburn hair long and unbound. He was so handsome that he was pretty, but there was nothing soft about him. He was muscle and sinew with sculptured veins. He was a very pretty man.

"Don't stop," David said.

Val grabbed a towel and wiped at the layer of perspiration covering his body. Dressed in a pair of tights, his washboard abs were well-defined underneath the slickness.

"You don't want me to stop?"

"No."

"Sure?"

"Yes."

"Positive?"

"Yep."

"Really?"

"Enough already. Dance," David said, amused at Val's silly teasing.

"Dance?"

"Yeah, dance for me."

Without another word, Val dropped his towel and began a dance of seduction for David.

The first time he and Val had done anything sexual, David walked away conflicted, confused and afraid. He hadn't wanted to admit how much he liked what they had done, because to admit it would be to make a confession he didn't want to utter. As a young man, he had achieved more than was ever expected of him. He had not been to jail. He did not have any illegitimate children. He was not on drugs, selling drugs, or around people who used drugs. He wasn't unemployed. He had graduated cum laude from S-fucking-M-goddamn-U, the Harvard of the Southwest. He was a macho, dark-skinned warrior, symbolic of all that was phallic, with a nine-inch dick and a prowess with women because he was "packin'."

So, to come from all that to now, a man who accepted what turned him on and made his dick hard without conflict or remorse, was saying a lot. David dug Val. Val turned him on. Not men. David didn't dig men. David dug Val. Val was the only man David could be with because with Val, the fact that they were both men was irrelevant. Had there been another man in the shower so many years ago, the outcome would have been different. David might just have ended up in jail.

As Val danced before the mirror-covered walls of the studio, he watched himself watch David watch him. He'd had a hard-on ever since David sat down at the piano. He had known that David was on his way up to the studio. He could feel it. Sometimes it scared him that they were so closely in tune with each other. He knew what David wanted before David asked for it. David knew what Val wanted before Val knew he wanted it. They were like an old married couple, and even completed each other's sentences. They were that close.

David got up from the piano and stood behind Val. How did David want to play this? Val wondered, continuing to watch him in the mirror. Who would lead? Who would follow? Fuck, did it matter? Smiling, David reached around Val and cupped his balls.

"What is this?" David asked as he squeezed Val's hard-on.

"Man, if you don't know what it is, you'd better let it go," Val responded.

"Oh, I know what it is all right. I've got one too." He rubbed himself against Val's ass.

"Mine is bigger," Val teased.

"You wish." David breathed against Val's ear before Val turned to kiss him.

Sighing as the kiss deepened, Val cupped David's ass and ground himself against David.

"Let's fuck," David growled low in his throat.

"I stink. Let me go take a shower."

"You're sexy sweaty."

"I'm disgusting sweaty."

"I like you disgusting."

"I like you." Val liked to kiss David. Teasingly, he tried to swallow David's tongue and eased his hand between them and unzipped David's jeans. The sexiest sound in the world was that of a zipper being undone.

Val eased out David's hardness and began to work on him. He did it slowly because David was so hot. He knew David was hot because he had made him that way. Val's studio had mirrors on three walls. The way he was angled, he could see himself; it excited him even more.

"Damn." David moaned, thrusting himself into Val's palm, which had become slick with his passion.

Val's strokes picked up speed as he shifted his body so that David could see himself in the mirror.

"Feel good?"

"Yeah." David sighed.

"How good?"

"Damn good," was what David tried to say. Instead, what came from between his lips was a sexy moan before he came, watching himself watch Val watch him.

Afterwards, they stood. David slumped, and Val supported him.

"Let's take a shower."

"I am too weak to walk." David eased himself back into his jeans. "What the—?" He was taken by surprise as Val swept him off his feet.

"You are one heavy son of a bitch," Val said, straining. David outweighed Val by a good forty pounds.

"What are you doing?"

"I'm taking you to the shower."

"You're going to break your back, man."

"Then you had better help me. Go on a diet," Val joked with him. David didn't need a diet. He was muscular perfection.

"Put me down."

"We're almost there." Val was carrying David easily now.

"What are we going to do when we get there?"

"I think I might let you suggest something." Laughing, the two headed into the bathroom.

DAVID

It was 3:00 A.M. and I couldn't write. My computer screen glared at me like a one-eyed monster. I hadn't written anything in so long that all I could see was the screen-saving neon message that scrolled across it in an antlike crawl. It read: DAVID'S SHIT. It was the only light in a dark room. I hadn't been able to write for two days and thirteen hours. It had been that long since I was told that my novel, *Cake Walk,* was being made into a movie. I was excited about that. Really. This is what I had been working for, for so long.

Cake Walk was my first "real" novel. It wasn't the first book I had ever written. It wasn't the first book I had ever published. The first book I ever wrote was called *Black-Eyed Peas are Good.* I was eight years old when I wrote it. The first book I published was *Heart of Stone.* It was published back when I was a young cop in my early twenties. My days as an officer of the law seemed like part of another life now. Now I can't imagine having worn that uniform. Now I can't imagine having lived that life.

Heart of Stone introduced the world to Noah Drake, private investigator. He was a compilation and then some of all the great movie detectives. With that said, Noah was more suave than Bond, more sarcastic than Spencer, more innovative than McGyver, harder than Shaft and had more women than Matt Helm. He was bigger than life. He was badder than a motherfucker.

My detective series—correction—my *black* detective series, *The Drake Chronicles,* had been fun. They were successful mass market paperbacks that I pumped out at the rate of four a year until there was nothing else for Noah Drake to do. So, twenty-four books and a lot of money later, I was able to write what I had always wanted to write. I veered away from the formula that had made me very, very, very rich, obscenely rich, to do what I had always wanted. And I became even richer. I wrote about my Nanna, my mother's mother, who raised me and Patti, my first girl, my first love. Thus, *Cake Walk* had been born.

My second novel was called *Real Dance,* and my last one was *Down Went Jonah.* My last three books made the *New York Times* bestsellers list, and gained for me the respect, recognition, and accolades that *The Drake Chronicles* never did. It didn't matter that *The Drake Chronicles* had a cult-like following and had spawned a *Star Wars-*like fan club. They were trashy, fun paperbacks, not great literature.

So now, many years later, I found myself successful, happy and stumped. It was 3:15 A.M. and still I sat, unable to find the words to write. Blocked. Fucked. Shit. I knew this book, *David's Story,* would be my best work, but I couldn't get past my first page. My introduction read:

I never knew that I was poor or that we lived in the ghetto until Scott, the son of the white woman Nanna worked for, called me a nappy-headed nigger and declared that I would probably end up in prison like my father.

Those were the only words I had written in a brief descriptive paragraph. I knew if I got past those few words, then words and phrases that should only be shared by lovers and spoken in rooms far from curious glances would find their way to the page.

David's Story was our story, Val's and mine. It would be my best work to date. I knew this. I feared this, because as my best work, I would want to hand it to the world on a silver platter, but as my own personal story, I could not without cutting too close to the bone, leaving me exposed and baring my soul. I did not know if I would be able to show it to anyone, thus my dilemma. Forced to write and purge my system, yet fearing what disclosing little secrets would do to me, I sat stumped. *Shit.*

I saved what I had written and got up from my desk. It was so late. I realized that I should get some sleep or I wouldn't be good for anything. Yawning and stretching, scratching my ass, I started for the futon so that I could grab a quick nap.

My office was decorated in blues and greens. The furniture was chosen for comfort and convenience. There was a lot of soft leather. It was a very comfortable room with a minibar and partial bath. When I was writing, I lived in this room. Sometimes I came out for food, air, Val.

Stretching my long frame on the futon, I thought of him as I tried to drift off. Val slept in paisley silk boxers. I thought they would be too pretentious on anyone else. He was sound asleep upstairs. I knew because I had checked on him earlier. Soon, he would be dancing in a big charity event at the Wiltern Theater, and was practicing like a mad man. He didn't have to practice so long or so hard. He was a very good dancer. Like his mother, he was driven by the desire to be the best. He had to be the best. It was his passion.

As I finally drifted off, I thought about one of the first conversations we had as freshmen roommates at SMU.

"Track?" I said to him.

"Beg pardon?" Val replied.

"Do you run track?" I repeated.

"No, I am a dancer."

"Dancer?"

"Yeah, I'm a dancer."

I laughed. I couldn't help it.

"What's so funny?"

"A dancer named Valentine. Man, you better develop a big set of balls."

He laughed too. "Big balls or a mean left hook."

Together, we had laughed like fools, a friendship developing, a bond being formed. What God has put together, let no man put asunder.

VAL

It was 5:15 A.M. according to the pewter clock on the nightstand. I got up and peed. David wasn't in bed with me. When he was writing, he didn't take good care of himself. He didn't sleep or eat. I decided that I should go check on him to make sure that he hadn't fallen asleep at his desk. He did that sometimes.

As quietly as possible I opened the door to his room. I had chosen that room for him to work in because it was big and airy and facing the rising sun. He was stretched out on his back, slightly snoring and asleep on the futon. I sat at his desk, flipped on his computer and read what he had written. I was his biggest fan, and harbored a secret passion for *The Drake Chronicles*. I read them over and over. They were great trashy novels that offered hours of escapist fun.

After I read what he had written, I made a decision. I wouldn't tell him I had read *David's Story* until he presented it to me. This book was different. I could feel it. I crawled next to him on the futon. He mumbled but didn't awaken.

He really wasn't that much larger than I was. His

skin was not that much darker. Yet all it had taken was just these nuances of pigmentation to create a bridge I could never cross with him. To the world, he was black. To the world, I was "other."

Wide-awake, unable to sleep now that I had read his introduction, I pulled him closer into my body, wrapping my body around his, protecting him in his slumber. David and I didn't fuck all the time. Sometimes we just held each other, like now.

David's publicist had convinced him to go on a fifteen-city tour to promote *Cake Walk,* which was being re-released to coincide with its screen debut. The last stop on the list would be Dallas. David was from Dallas. Patti still lived in Dallas. It had been years since David had seen Patti. Nevertheless, she was a major influence on his life. He spoke of her with affection and nostalgia. As long as she was in Dallas, I didn't think about her. Now that they would be in the same city, I felt a twinge of jealousy. I convinced myself that I was being silly, and finally drifted off to sleep. I'd have to get up in an hour or so to take David to the airport.

CHAPTER THREE

As the resident choreographer of the very prestigious dance ensemble, The Troupe, Val had a schedule that was demanding. After dropping David off at the airport, he got stuck in traffic and was unable to make it to the studio in time to get a jump-start on the taxing day ahead. By the time he got to the impressive Beverly Hills offices, rehearsal had already started, thanks to his mother, Lola. She waited on no one. Not even her son.

At fifty, she was still an attractive woman. Her beauty was ageless and breathtaking. She stood six feet tall with a body that was lithe, supple and well preserved. She wore her hair void of permanents. It framed her face in a salt-and-pepper halo that was very soft to the touch. She avoided heavy, clunky jewelry, preferring simple strands of beads, pearls, or diamonds that glittered against her mahogany skin. Her look was exotic, erotic and sensual. Lola did not follow fashion trends, she set them.

"No!" Lola stated, emphasizing her displeasure at

the performance she had just witnessed with a shake of her head. "Watch me," she commanded without raising her voice. There were twelve dancers in the room. They watched, mesmerized, as she executed an intricate series of dance steps.

As she danced, she became one with the music. Anyone watching her would recognize her talent, respect her achievements, and visualize her fame. Val had grown up under the tutelage of this woman and emulated her in work ethic and desire. She *was* the dance.

Afterwards, she looked out at the troupe. Twelve faces looked at her with admiration.

"Not bad for a woman of fifty," she said with a laugh. She wasn't even winded.

"Not bad at all," Val said and kissed her cheek.

Lola accepted the kiss but didn't miss a beat as she continued instructing the class. "Now you, Kim. It is your turn," Lola said, acknowledging the young dancer who was to perform the piece opposite Val in their upcoming performance to benefit the homeless.

Val caught Kim's eye and winked at her, encouraging her from across the room while he slipped out of his jeans. Beneath them he wore tights and leg warmers.

Kim felt all eyes turn her way with the acknowledgment. Even though this was a rehearsal, Lola's performance would be a hard one to follow.

Gathering all the showmanship she could muster, Kim took the stage. She knew that she had been picked for this dance because Lola felt that she could carry it off. In the group of twelve dancers, six women and six men, next to Val, Kim was the best. Being the best of the best tended to keep her up nights before a big performance.

The music began and Kim danced. She danced as if her life depended on it. Kim always danced as if she had something to prove because she was a light-skinned girl with Caucasian features. With sandy brown hair and greenish-gray eyes, she looked more like a child born of Lola and Andre's union than did Val. Both her parents, unlike his, were black, Creoles from New Orleans. All her life, Kim had to prove so much. But just because she looked almost white didn't mean she had to dance almost white. Kim danced like a sistah. Kim danced like Lola. When she finished, winded and covered in sweat, she was met with thundering applause.

"Now, that's what I'm talking about." Lola gave her stamp of approval and continued with the rehearsal in earnest.

Two hours later, after everyone was long gone, Val and Kim found themselves still in an intense workout.

"I think if you make a half-turn then fall back into my arms, it would be effective," Val offered as a suggestion to Kim.

"Think so?" she replied, breathing hard. They worked well as a dance team because they were both perfectionists and didn't mind going the extra mile that separated the great from the good and the spectacular from the mundane.

"Okay. Let's try it."

Kim took her position a few paces in front of Val then followed his suggestions almost exactly. At the last moment, she had a sudden insight. Before she fell into his arms, she kissed him. It was a long, lingering kiss. Sensual. Realistic. After his initial shock, he kissed her back.

They had been dancing together so long that it

was impossible for one not to follow the other's lead. She probed with her tongue. He probed back. She ran her hands sensually down his body. He did the same to hers. But when she reached for his maleness, he broke off the kiss. Refusing to lose the momentum, she fell into his arms as they had rehearsed. Then he released her.

There was a deadly silence in the room. The air was heavy. They were both winded. Their bodies were shiny with perspiration. Their tights clung to them like multicolored skin against their faultless bodies. The room smelled like sweat and adrenaline, reminiscent of sex. They had worked that hard.

"Yes," Val pondered, "let's keep the kiss. I like it."

Kim could see the outline of his semi-erect penis through his tights.

"Do you?" Kim asked, hopeful that her improvisation would remain in the show because it gave her an excuse to kiss him.

"Yeah. It adds that missing element."

"I'm glad you liked it."

"I think we've worked ourselves silly, don't you?" He grabbed a towel and mopped at his sweat-drenched skin as if ignorant of his condition or the effect it was having on her.

"God, yes." She too grabbed for a towel, needing an excuse to look away from his perfection.

"Besides, I'm starving. Want to get something to eat?" It had been a while since they shared a meal outside the building commissary that served up salads, juices and protein shakes.

"Sure." Her mouth was dry. She needed something to drink.

"Josepha's?"

"Sounds good to me." Amazed that her voice didn't

crack with pent-up desire, she gathered her things and headed to her shower while Val did the same.

As the warm water cascaded over Kim's toned body, she thought about Val just one room over. He was magnificent. Dancing with him was as exciting as it was titillating and sometimes left her wet with more than sweat.

Val, on the other hand, thought only of David as the warm water caressed his skin and eased his muscles. He had been thinking of David throughout his workout with Kim. Thinking of David excited him.

DAVID

Were it not for Val's encouragement, I'd still be flying coach. I credited him with introducing me to first class. As soon as we hit the ground, I was going to call him and remind him of that. He'd get a kick out of it.

Dallas had changed considerably from the Dallas of my childhood. From my airplane window, I saw a high-tech conglomeration of glass and plaster so unlike what I had grown up with. The only familiar symbol was the neon red flying horse that belonged to the Mobil Corporation.

As we landed, I felt a mixture of excitement and dread. I was going home. The only thing I had left was Patti. She was a pleasant, comforting thought. Although there had been very little communication between the two of us over the years except for the sporadic Christmas and birthday cards, I knew I would see her. She was Patti. I was David. We had history.

We had been lovers. Before the publication of my last three books, before *The Drake Chronicles,* and before Val, there had been Patti. She knew me when we were Davey-Gene and Patticake forever.

There was a limo waiting for me when I picked up my luggage. The driver was a small Latino man. He weighed as much as a cloud and walked on the balls of his feet. He stood off to the side, holding a big sign with my name on it.

People were looking at me. It made me nervous. I didn't handle fame well. I was a writer, not a performer. I wasn't Val.

"Mr. Lincoln," he said as he smiled and held out his hand for my luggage.

"Hi," I replied.

He opened the door, and I got in the back seat. I'd been in limos before. It was always a smooth ride.

As he pulled into the airport traffic, I sat in the back seat thinking. If Val had been here, he would have insisted I relax and given me a massage if I could not. If Val had been here, instead of going straight to the suite at the Hilton Hotel, we would have gone dancing, drinking or carousing. If Val had been here, we would have made love. Damn, I missed Val.

I pulled out my cell phone and called him. I got the voice mail. Val's cultured voice, his accent not so pronounced after living with me so long and learning to say "y'all" and eat chitterlings, both very Southern things that I had taught him, comforted me. I left a quick message telling him where I was and where I would be. I didn't try to call his cell phone. There was no point. He rarely answered it, often leaving it in the car, and was quick to say nothing was important enough to give anyone twenty-four hour access to him, including me.

Then I called Patti. In all the years that I had known her, her number had never changed. She still lived in her mother's house. Her phone rang. She wasn't in either. I didn't have her cell phone number. Sighing, not really tired, not really hungry, not really sleepy, I got out my laptop and went to work. It was time for chapter two.

Her name was Patti, short for Patricia, but everybody called her Patticake. She was a pretty black girl, the color of dark chocolate, with an out-of-sight body and an ass to die for. She had a teasing way of licking a Popsicle that made me hot, and a way of walking that taught me that my dick was for more than pissing out of and jerking off with.

Patti taught me how to dream. When we were kids, we used to lie down and hold hands on the hill behind old man Thompson's store. We looked up at the clouds and picked out shapes. That's how I learned to dream, holding Patti's hand.

In each city, my book tour started with a guest appearance on the popular local talk show, maybe a few hours on the radio, then a couple of hours at a bookstore, usually a large one in the mall, where I smiled a lot, flirted a lot, signed a lot of autographs and sold a lot of books. I was used to the routine. In three weeks, I had done the same thing in twelve different cities. I was prepared for anything—crying babies, openly flirtatious advances made by fans, gushing bookstore clerks and overly nosy reporters more interested in my private life than they could ever be in *Cake Walk.* I was prepared for everything. I wasn't prepared for Patti.

I had just signed an autograph for someone named Helena when a copy of *Cake Walk* was pushed beneath my nose, opened to page thirteen.

"Say, Davey-Gene, this girl on page thirteen with

skin the color of plums and the bearing of a queen, is that me?" a female voice asked.

I looked up and there she was. Patti. The years had been kind to her. Her youthful beauty had blossomed into womanhood with curves that were plentiful but not abundant. She had shoulder-length braids and at least four pairs of earrings in her ears. I didn't know how she functioned with her nails so long or without damaging the miniature landscapes she had painted on each one. But it didn't matter. She was my Patti. I was her David.

Before I knew it, we were in each other's arms with hugs and kisses and "How have you been?" and "It's been a long time!" and "My God, look at you!" We caused quite a stir in the bookstore before I had to get back to "work."

I promised to meet her later that night at Turner's, an old juke joint in South Dallas. We had spent a lot of time at Turner's. I could find it with my eyes closed, and if not, there was always the navigational system in my rental car. I'd make it to Turner's. Patticake and Davey-Gene needed to play catch up.

Old juke joints and little hole-in-the-wall clubs that played blues and served collard greens, hot water cornbread and fried chicken littered South Dallas. I was hanging out in them well before I was old enough. I drank cheap wine, danced, fornicated and committed sins, as Pastor John Henry used to say, while I was listening to music so soulful that it made me laugh and cry and wail way into the night. I had fun. My early escapades with Patti in the juke joints later shaped my being. So, it was no doubt that I was hit with a rush of nostalgia when I walked into Turner's.

I arrived there about five minutes before Patti, paid my five dollars to get in and took a seat at the bar. I ordered a VO Scotch straight up and sat back to watch the show. There is no show like the show that goes on in juke joints. Asses were shaking, hips were moving, people were laughing, and the fashion show to end all fashion shows was happening on the crowded dance floor. The DJ was playing "Voodoo Doctor," a favorite song of mine. People were dancing, talking and eating. The people were so real. I felt so comfortable. I had come to the home of my memories.

I was on my second VO when I saw Patti come in. She had on a short, tight, black leather skirt, a fuchsia silk blouse over a braless chest, and three-inch "come-fuck-me" pumps. She was hot. She knew it. I knew it. Every man in the room knew it. I watched as she walked toward me, smiling, hips switching.

Damn! I thought. The Patti of thirty-three was so much better than the teenage Patti I had first known. She was a woman grown and comfortable in her womanliness. I felt my dick twitch in recognition of her beauty as it acknowledged the spell she cast.

"Dance with me, Davey-Gene," Patti said as she approached me. She held out one of her hands with the long, long nails and pulled me off the stool. My drink was forgotten as I accompanied her onto the dance floor.

"Come on, dance with me," she teased, sticking her tongue in my ear as we pressed our bodies tight and close to each other. The music, the heat, the people acted as an aphrodisiac.

I found myself out on the dance floor, hips gyrating, body moving sensually, meeting Patti's provocative undulations with body-rocking movements of my own. She put her arms around my neck and raked those long nails sensuously down my back.

Before Val, there had been so many women. So many. After Val, there had only been Val.

While I danced with Patti, I felt the familiar stirring of passion and the onset of desire that had been reserved for Val, only Val, for so long that I was confused by it at first. *What the hell?*

I don't know who suggested that we leave Turner's. I don't know who made the first move. I just realized as I was slipping on the extra thin latex condom and slipping into Patti that I was breaking my vows to Val. But it was too late. Lying between her thighs, belly to belly, chest to breast, her hard, chocolate nipples teasing me, her sensual lips kissing me and later her mouth swallowing me, I didn't care. I didn't care. I didn't care. I was unable to stop the movements of my body or the flow of my seed. I came, spurting big, copious globs of semen into the sheath that separated our most intimate parts. I came in Patti the way I had always come in her. I came in her like I came in Val.

VAL

I called David twice as I drove home from Josepha's. There was no answer at his hotel room or on his cell phone. With Dallas being the last leg of his three-week tour, I knew he was busy. The first thing he would do would be to find some little out-of-the-way place to soak up the ambiance. No matter what city we went to, David found the best spots for blues, jazz and food. He found these places with a sixth sense that was his own special talent. Deposited into familiar territory, he would be in his element.

It was only 11:00 P.M. Dallas time. I would call him again later. I was too restless to sleep and our house was too quiet. I didn't want to go home. I contemplated dropping in on Andre and Lola, but decided against it. My mother and father would talk to me, feed me and beg me to spend the night. In that sense, they were very conventional. I didn't feel like conventional tonight. I was anxious, restless and itching to do something.

As if to make the decision easy for me, my cell rang.

"Hello?" I answered.

"Where have you been all evening?" an annoyed voice startled me.

"Hello, Heathcliff," I said happily.

Heathcliff Garfield Swenson had been a friend of my family's all of my life. He was a cartoonist, very popular and syndicated. I hung the caricature of me he'd done when I was eight over the bed in the guest-room. I had been offered forty thousand dollars for it, but declined. Heathcliff was one of my favorite "uncles."

"Sounds like you're having a party," I said.

"Just a group of friends," Heathcliff responded.

"What do I have to do to finagle an invitation?"

"You know you're always welcome, Valentine. Always." Heathcliff was one of the few people who always called me Valentine.

"Good. I'll be there in a few."

"Okay, Valentine. Ta."

I turned my car around and headed toward Bel Air. When I pulled up, I marveled at the sheer audacity that was Heathcliff's castle. A loud pink monstrosity, it looked out of place in the exclusive neighborhood. I punched in the security code and drove past the gate. There were quite a few luxury cars present: Jaguars, Mercedes, BMWs and Cadillacs. A very conservative crowd was the only thing that occurred to me as I parked my vintage 450 SL and walked to the door.

Heathcliff answered the door, drink in hand and dressed in a floor-length silk kimono. He was fifty-eight years old, like my father, but looked 100. If he were six feet tall instead of five feet nothing, he'd still look like a gnome. His eyes were big, pale, water-blue bubbles that were intriguing, huge and expressive. I could pick him up with no effort, and had done so on numerous occasions because he'd lost both his legs in a car accident and wore prostheses, which he constantly complained about. I don't think there was anything wrong with the legs that he had. He just liked to complain. With the cane and his two state-of-the-art legs, he could get about rather well. It was only when he'd get drunk or was working on a project that he'd forget to put them on and I'd have to carry them to him or him to them.

"Hello, darling." He kissed my cheek. "Sampson tells me that gorgeous housemate of yours is away. You're all alone and you didn't call us."

Heathcliff always said "housemate" in reference to David as if he were saying a dirty word in a roomful of pious people and getting away with it. He was goading me to see if I would let something slip, but I didn't take the bait.

"How is Sampson?" I asked as if I didn't know Sampson was fine. Sampson was Heathcliff's young lover of eight years and a member of The Troupe. I saw Sampson almost every day.

"Sexy as ever," was Heathcliff's reply. "Now, come on in. We don't want to give the neighbors anything more to talk about."

He threw the door open wide for me to enter. Heathcliff's taste leaned toward the gaudy and bordered on the obscene. Although he wasn't able to do anything else to the outside of his house due to his neighbor's loud complaints, inside he was able to run amok, and decorated with sheer abandon. He loved the whole decadence of it.

"You know I love you, don't you, Valentine?"

"Yes, of course," I answered quickly as he ushered me into the foyer. I took his hand to steady his gait. He didn't have his cane.

"I've never hidden anything from you."

"No, never," I responded as I had a quick sickening thought. Before Sampson, Heathcliff's lover had been Kevin. He died of AIDS. I knew all of that.

"Are you all right?" I asked again, suddenly alarmed.

"Yes, yes," he reassured me.

"I mean physically?" I explained.

"Oh, yes," he reassured me again. "I just don't want you to hate me."

"What?"

He took a deep breath and said, "Look, Valentine, I would never set you up."

"Okay," I said, not knowing where this was going.

"Before you step through that door tonight, realize that what you see, who you see, you must be discreet."

"Are you drunk?" I reached for his drink, but he held it out of my grasp.

"Very, which is probably why I agreed to let you come over here tonight." Then he sighed. "Come on, baby." He opened the big double door leading into his study.

"Valentine! Hey, Valentine!" Sampson called as he swept me into a bear hug as soon as we entered. Sampson Stewart was a big guy. He was built like a brick wall, solid, with rippling muscles and a bone-crushing handshake. He looked more like a wrestler than a dancer, but a dancer he was. "I never expected to see you on girls' night out." He kissed me smack on the lips and released me.

The large room had been decorated very '70s, complete with disco ball. Everyone was dressed in retro fashions. There were fifteen people in the room. Most of them I knew personally, some only by reputation. There was a multi-million dollar quarterback for a professional football team, a guard for a popular basketball team, a network news anchor, a plastic surgeon who was a god to the stars, a tennis pro, a big-time lawyer and a star of a weekly hit TV series. All men. No women. I knew for a fact that several of the men were married, but none of their wives was present. Some were sitting. Some were standing. Some were drinking. Two or three couples—and that's what they were, couples—were holding hands. One gentleman had his arm draped casually around the waist of an Olympic gold medalist.

I was struck immediately by how comfortable everybody looked. All the hype and media personalities had been stripped away. In this sanctuary, devoid of women, some of the men looked more normal, happy, and comfortable than I had ever seen them. I felt the eyes on me, especially Heathcliff's.

"Well, Valentine?" he asked. I was confused by the hope I heard in his voice. "Do you stay or do you go?"

I had always been secure in my sexuality. Homosexuality, bisexuality, heterosexuality never were issues for me. Before David, there had always been women. After David, there had only been David. What I did for him, what he did for me, went beyond sex. Sex was just a part of our relationship. Did that make us homosexuals? Did that make us bisexual since we both found women mysterious and attractive, or did that make us heterosexuals who were having a homosexual affair? Were we on the down low? Were we in denial? I had never been with another man, only David. I never wanted to be with another man, only David.

Because of the life I led, there had always been the opportunity to experiment, to explore. I was a dancer, after all, and had been surrounded by male dancers all of my life. I knew what some men did when others weren't watching, and I knew what some did when others were watching. I had just never participated. I had never been interested, even after David. And once we were together, the life consisting of bars, parties and duplicity had been more than either of us had ever wanted. We lived our lives as we saw fit. We didn't have to answer to anybody. Occasionally, someone asked the question, a nosy journalist, a curious woman; we just never answered. We didn't have to. Our lives were very visible. Yet we often traveled in circles where there were so many people, who knew who was with who? There were times when an entourage came in handy. Entourage, camouflage . . . often they were the same thing.

"Well?" Heathcliff prompted.

I wondered what he was feeling, this friend of my father's.

"I think I'll get a drink," I replied to his inquiry.

"What'll you have, baby love?" Sampson called from the bar.

"Something strong," I answered as I walked toward him.

"How about me?" I heard a voice ask from behind me.

"Excuse me," I said as I took the drink Sampson offered. I think it was VO. I didn't drink Scotch, but I had asked for something strong.

"You wanted something strong." The man smiled

and I, like so many others, was pleased by that smile. It was a famous smile. There was the slightly crooked grin, the wholesome face, and the rugged good looks. He was Wayne Carey, star extraordinaire. One of the few to walk the thin line between television and movies so easily, he was an icon, like Will Smith, Tom Hanks or George Clooney. Lead actor in a weekly space western, he had women across the world offering to have his love child, and he was coming on to me in my uncle's house because he was in a place where it was okay to do that. Six feet two, sun-kissed blond, with eyes that were often talked about because they were striking and odd—one brown and one blue— he was the kind of good-looking that came from a combination of perfect genes and hard work. No one got a body like that without spending time in a gym. Dressed in black linen slacks and an oversized rough cotton tunic, he was arresting.

"No, thanks," I said as I tried to smile at him, but I believe I only grimaced. *Wayne Carey is gay. Damn.*

He held out his hand. "Wayne." He knew I knew who he was.

"Val." I shook his hand. He knew I knew that he knew who I was too.

"After your drink, would you like to dance?"

"No. I don't think so." *Wayne Carey is gay.*

"I can be very persistent."

All the men in the room are gay. "I can be very obstinate." *I am in the room.*

"What he's telling you, love, is that you're not his type," Sampson interrupted in his drunkenness and leaned over my shoulder to speak to Wayne.

"How do you know?" Wayne asked Sampson.

"He has a *housemate,*" Sampson whispered, but of course the words traveled across the room.

"Maybe he's looking for a lover," Wayne said to Sampson, but his eyes were burning into mine.

Alpha male. Conqueror.

"No, I have that too." He couldn't punk me. "I enjoy your show," I said and walked away, drinking the Scotch. *What am I doing here?*

Someone had changed the music from jazz to an old Michael Jackson song. I found myself perched precariously, as if poised for flight, as I watched the couples dance. Inside, I was fighting with myself. Should I leave? Should I stay? I was in the room! I had known homosexuals all my life, and none of them had been able to fool me like these men had. *Wayne Carey is gay.* Everyone looked so comfortable. I couldn't shake the feeling that I had been deceived. Some of these men were fathers. I had gone to college with the son of the plastic surgeon. His name was Sidney Feldman. His father's name was Sidney too. Did young Sidney know? I bet old Sidney's wife, young Sidney's mother, didn't know.

"Come on, Val. Dance with me," Sampson said, grabbing my hand and pulling me from my observation point. He was so silly, clowning and joking, trying to make me get over my discomfort.

Out of the corner of my eye, I saw Heathcliff remove his right "leg" and rub his stump. Before I could say anything, Sampson, drunk as he was, excused himself and went over to his lover. I watched as he picked him up and carried him to his wheelchair. Once Heathcliff was comfortable, Sampson kissed him and went to get him a drink. Sampson was good for Heathcliff.

"I see you've been left in a lurch," Wayne Carey said, joining me on the dance floor. "Come on, Valentine, dance with me. I'll behave." He looked so innocent, so harmless, and so silly.

I consented. Dancing with a man was different from dancing with a woman. There was no automatic assumption of who was going to lead. You had to figure it out. And like I said, Wayne was an alpha. So was I. Conflict. Laughing, a little nervously we both decided to just go with it. He couldn't dance at all. He had no idea where the rhythm started. He had no concept of the beat. He was funny.

"You're a great dancer," he said with a smile.

"It's how I make my living," I replied.

"So, tell me about your housemate." He rolled the word around on his tongue like he was tasting it.

"What about him?"

"Who is he? Where is he? What does he do? Where is he? How long have you been together? Where is he?"

"Wayne—"

"Really, I want to know."

"Why?"

"Because I've been watching you for a very, very long time," Wayne said with much sincerity in his tone. That caught me off guard.

"That's impossible. I just got here." I tried to play it off.

"That's not what I mean and you know it."

"No, I don't know it," I said.

The song stopped and a slow ballad came on. I stopped dancing.

"Come on," he coerced. "I'll behave. Trust me."

"No, thanks." I started for a chair.

He followed me. "Can I tell you something?"

"What?"

"I've been to every concert and performance you've been in for the past year. I tried to get on Leno when you were on last. I taped your performance at the Kennedy Center."

I hadn't expected that. "What are you saying?" I asked curiously.

"I'm saying that I think you're hot and I've been lusting from afar. I've asked anyone and everyone everything I can about you, and no one, no one was talking. Until tonight, I never knew for sure if I might have a chance."

Shit yes, I should have left, I thought. "Look, Wayne, I'm flattered. Truly I am, but I have a *friend.*" What was I supposed to say?

"He's not here."

"We've known each other for years."

"Are you married? I don't see a ring."

Fuck! This man is relentless. "Wayne."

"Have dinner with me," he said in an insisting manner.

"No."

"I'm real persistent."

"Yes, you are."

"You've got to love me."

"Wayne," I said, growing agitated. He was pushing a little too hard.

"Look, I'm not going to push you." As if sensing my mood, he backed off . . . a little. "At least not tonight. But think about me. Us. Our children."

Is this guy for real?

I was saved by the intrusion of the tennis pro who whisked Wayne onto the dance floor after saying, "Hey, Wayne. They're playing our song."

I watched him dance. He moved like a man who knew he was good-looking and used to people watching him. He hadn't moved like that with me. With me, he was being silly. With the tennis pro, he was being Wayne Carey. I noticed that he danced better with the slow songs, but of course, you didn't need rhythm for that. As I watched him, Heathcliff maneuvered his wheelchair through the bodies to my side.

"Am I still your favorite uncle, Valentine?" Heathcliff asked.

"Of course," I replied with a smile.

"I never hid anything from you. Ever."

"No, you did not."

"And you never hid anything from me. Any of us. We just never discuss it. And not discussing it makes it delicious."

After David and I graduated from college and still continued to live together, neither Andre nor Lola ever said anything to me. What they said to each other when I wasn't around was something else.

"They are very perceptive, your parents," Heathcliff said. David and I had been together twelve years. They didn't need to be perceptive.

"As is my uncle," I replied.

"Take some advice from an old queen, Valentine."

"I don't know any old queens." He laughed at my blatant lie.

"Always be comfortable in your skin."

I turned and kissed him on the cheek. "I always am."

I left the party, aware that Wayne Carey's eyes followed me out the front door. I was a little disturbed that I found his flirtations appealing. That was a first. Wayne was a man. Before David and after David, there had only been David. I couldn't wait to get in my car and call him. I needed to hear his voice to push thoughts of Wayne's million-dollar smile out of my head. I needed to talk to David.

CHAPTER FOUR

David didn't answer the phone because he was busy losing himself in Patti's soft flesh. She, on the other hand, heard it and took that moment to stop what she was doing and look up at him, smiling the smile of a vixen.

"Better answer it," she teased. "She might get mad. I know I would."

"There is no she," David managed to say before she once again engulfed him with her wetness.

Even though she didn't care whether there really was another woman—*I don't know that bitch,* was her thought—she just assumed he was lying. He was, after all, a man. *That's what they do—lie.*

So Val's call went unanswered while David cheated.

PATTI

I woke up the next morning feeling like I had swallowed sunshine. David was on his way back to Los

Angeles. I would miss him. Davey-Gene had always been one of the best I ever had. It was big, and he knew how to use it. Big don't mean nothing if you don't know how to work those hips and those lips. Damn! David was a considerate and kind lover. He cared a lot about if I came or not. Funny how we hadn't seen each other in so long, and it was just like we had seen each other yesterday. We fucked. And fucked. And fucked like rabbits. At first it seemed like he had something to prove, but I just didn't care. We played old blues songs, ate greasy chicken with hot picked peppers from Henderson's Chicken Shack in South Dallas, and visited old haunts. We had so much fun.

On the day he left, I got up at 2:30 P.M., like I always did. My momma, Linda, who I shared the house with, was out of town at a family reunion, so I had to fix my own lunch. I worked nights at the big post office downtown and didn't have to be there until 5:00 P.M. I always got up in time to get ready for work and watch the *Oprah* show that I had taped from the day before. I got up, flipped on the television and got the surprise of my life. David. David Eugene Lincoln, my Davey-Gene, was with Oprah-fucking-Winfrey. I knew he had written a book about being a cop or something. I had only read to page thirteen. But I didn't know he had written a lot of books. I didn't know that one of his books was going to be turned into a movie. A fucking movie!

We hadn't talked about that. We hadn't talked about tomorrow. We hadn't talked about our future together. We had talked about the old times, the good times and the back-then times. Davey-Gene was the first boy I ever loved. We used to play "married" and hide and go get it. We went to the same elementary school, the same junior high and the same high school. We knew all the same people and enjoyed all the same things. But when opportunity knocked, it wasn't at my door. I didn't know when Davey-Gene and I stopped being all and everything to each other. It had just happened. But last night when he was all into me, I was digging him all over again. Now, seeing him on TV got me wetter than his finger, tongue, or dick had. That boy was Somebody, and if I had my way, I was gonna keep sucking Somebody's dick.

CHAPTER FIVE

Due to an unscheduled rehearsal, Val was not able to meet David at the airport as planned, so David took a cab home. The $45 cab ride gave David additional time to think. He loved his life and what he had. He shouldn't have jeopardized it with drama and bullshit. He would have to make it up to Val. Had to. There was a slow pressure building behind his eyes, and he recognized it for what it was—guilt. It was guilt on so many levels: guilt for feeling like he had to have sex with Patti, guilt for having sex with Patti, and guilt for enjoying sex with Patti.

When the cab driver dropped him in front of their house, he gathered his luggage and walked through the front door just as Val rushed in from parking his car in the garage. For a minute, they stood looking at each other; then, unable to contain themselves, they were in each other's arms.

"I've missed you."

"Me too," was uttered against lips as they kissed and caressed each other through their clothes.

The three and a half weeks of long conversations, e-mails and text messages were nothing compared to actually being able to touch each other. The old saying that absence makes the heart grow fonder was true. They raced to get naked, stumbling over pants legs puddled at their ankles as they rushed, giggling like fools, to their bedroom. They tumbled into the bed, a tangled mass of arms and legs, happy to just touch each other.

Val rubbed his hard cock against David and licked his nipples, exciting himself as much as he thought he was exciting David. But when he reached for David's dick, it lay limp, dangling, and without character between his lover's legs.

Guilt, guilt, guilt makes even the strong impotent, David thought.

"What's wrong?" Val asked.

"Nothing," David said, distracting his lover by addressing the heat between Val's legs with his mouth. It happened so fast, Val wasn't prepared for David's insistent, wet mouth nuzzling his flesh.

"Ooooh." Val moaned. "What you doing, man?" This wasn't the way he had planned the seduction.

David didn't answer him. He worked Val's dick like he knew Val liked it. He worked it out of love. He worked it out of guilt. When Val had reached for him and he had not responded, he panicked. Had the sex with Patti been good because Patti was Patti or because Patti was a woman? Confusing thoughts raced through his mind as he worked on Val. No matter how much he wanted him, he wasn't able to complete the act unless he used his hands or his mouth.

But Val wasn't in the mood for a mouth or a skilled hand. He knew what he wanted. He knew what he had missed while he and David had been separated.

He eased himself out of David's insistent mouth and maneuvered his body so that he could work the fire into David. He straddled him, massaging, kissing and licking his lover's back and flanks. Then when he could take it no longer, Val eased himself into David. David let out a sigh. Satisfied that David was feeling all of him, Val reached around David for his dick and alas, it still was not inflated.

"What's wrong?" Val whispered in David's ear as he stilled the movements of his hips.

"Don't stop."

"Are you sure?" The tip of Val's tongue grazed David's ear. He loved it, laved it, and blew gently into it.

"Yes. Oh, God, yes." David was getting hard finally.

"That's it, David. That's it." Val rode David, unaware that David was filled with conflict and angst.

Afterwards, with Val still inside him, David said, "Forgive me."

Val kissed him long and deep, misunderstanding David's words of near confession, thinking it had something to do with his limp dick. He pulled David close, draping him with his body. If David couldn't get it up because he was tired or jetlagged or anxious, Val could get it up for both of them. Man, Val loved him some David. "There's nothing to forgive." He kissed David again before easing out of him.

Afterwards, they lay together, sated, both deep in thought.

When David awoke, he was naked and alone in the master bedroom. Sitting up, yawning and stretching, he pulled on his discarded jeans and wandered barefoot into the kitchen, where Val was fixing dinner. (Val was the cook; David was the eater.) For a minute, he watched as Val prepared the meal.

Val was naked and completely unselfconscious in his nakedness. His dancer's body seemed to move like he heard music in his head. He moved from the refrigerator to the stove to the counter.

"Hey, sexy."

"Hey, yourself."

David crossed the room and kissed Val. David loved him some Val. Love was the only thing that would have allowed him to do the things they did together.

He had so much to make up to Val. Mulling this over, he grabbed the milk from the refrigerator and was about to drink from the carton when Val, mumbling in French, took it from him, poured him a glass and put the carton back in the refrigerator. Leaning against the imported marble countertop, David drank his milk and continued to watch his lover.

"Smells good in here."

Val had been very busy while David slept. There was a casserole dish filled with bubbling three-cheese lasagna on the stove, and crusty French bread on the counter. The small table in the kitchen was set with good china, silver, wine glasses and a bottle of Merlot, all the trappings normally reserved for the large, oversized dining table in the next room.

"Welcome home."

David put down the empty milk glass, crossed to Val and kissed him again.

"You taste like milk."

"You taste like me."

"I really missed you, man."

"Me too."

They hugged then hugged again, tighter. Finally, they were getting the time together that they needed. Earlier, they had been too busy loving to talk. Just happy to be together, they sat and enjoyed their meal.

Once they had filled their bellies, they found themselves in the living room. They lay entwined on the couch as lovers do after their love play. Val's feet were in David's lap as David massaged them tenderly. Val, still naked, yawned and stretched, luxuriating in the feel of David's hands on his body.

"Tell me about your trip."

"What do you want to know?" David replied.

"Everything."

As David began telling Val about his tour, editing, of course, his escapade with Patti, the phone started to ring. They had been ignoring it all evening. But now, after their hunger for each other had been satisfied, it was time to allow for the intrusion of the outside world.

On the second ring, Val picked up the telephone. "Hello?"

"Oh, I'm sorry. I must have the wrong number," the Southern voice on the other end of the phone said.

"No problem. *Ciao.*" Val hung up and turned his attention back to David, only to be interrupted again by the ringing phone. Again Val answered. "Hello?"

"Oh, I'm sorry. I keep dialing the wrong number." It was the same person who just called. There was something familiar about the quality of her voice, something touching about the hesitancy she expressed in disturbing him. Southerners were bred to be polite.

"What number are you trying to dial?" Val listened as the number she recited was his own. "That's this number," Val responded, confused.

"Is Davey-Gene there?"

" 'Davey-Gene'?"

David eased the phone from Val's hand. Only one

person called him Davey-Gene. "Patti?" David said, placing the phone to his ear.

"Who was that?"

"Patti? Is something wrong?"

"Good God, no."

Patti hadn't called David in years. It was odd hearing her voice over the phone. *Damn*, David thought. *Damn. Damn. Damn.*

DAVID

When I got off the phone with Patti, I felt Val's eyes on me. "Looks like we're about to have a houseguest," I stated weakly, knowing that he had probably already figured that out from my side of the conversation.

"Yes, it looks like we are."

He got up from the couch and went into the kitchen. I followed him. He quickly washed and put away the dishes.

"Val, about Patti . . ." I began, the lie forming on the tip of my tongue. *I had my face buried between her legs!*

"What about Patti?"

The guilt I felt behind my duplicity was eating at me. If I touched him, my fingertips would surely burn his skin. "Would you rather I put her up in a hotel?"

"Of course, not. We have more than enough room. And besides, I want to meet Patti. I've heard so much about her. I feel like I know her." Val talked as he wandered upstairs to our bedroom.

I, with my deceitful self, followed him, watching his ass move as he took the stairs two at a time.

At our bed, he got beneath the covers and patted

the space next to him. I shucked my pants and crawled in. We kissed and cuddled. It was at that moment that my dick, with a mind of its own, decided to get hard. *Damn it. Not now!*

I had written in *Down Went Jonah* that all gay men weren't limp-wristed caricatures of women. All gay men weren't "faggots." All gay men didn't think with their dicks. All *men* did. Since I was thinking with mine and not with my head, I said the words I wish I could take back now.

"We can't do this when she's here."

"What are you talking about?" He was caressing me beneath the covers.

"I've known Patti all my life. I don't think she'll understand."

His hand had stopped fondling my dick. "Understand what?" He was being deliberately obtuse.

"I'm not ready to share this side of my life with Patti," I said, reaching for him.

He moved away. "Why?"

"Because."

"Because why?" He was going to make me say it.

"Because she doesn't know."

"No one knows, David."

Val and I had a very visible life, mainly because of Val. I didn't know when we had fallen into the act of playing it straight in public, but we had. There was no unmanly hugging or touching, and certainly no kissing. To the world, we were the chocolate Ben Affleck and Matt Damon, best friends from college who'd made it big. The world expected to see us together: Lakers' games, charity events, movie premiers and the like. But the world didn't expect to see us naked together. That was reserved for our bedroom.

"They might suspect, but they don't know," Val said.

"I don't want her to know. I don't want her to suspect."

"Why the hell not?"

"It's private."

"Are you telling me you want to put me in the closet like a dirty little secret?"

When he put it like that, it sounded terrible. Val and I had been husband and husband for nearly twelve years without the ceremony or ritual. We had crossed bridges and made personal commitments that only love would have allowed, and I was asking him to put that all away for a visit from a girl he thought was part of my past. How could I do that? *Because I'd had my face between her legs!*

Val sighed. "How long is she going to be here?"

"A week, maybe ten days."

"So, for a week to ten days, you want to play it straight?"

I faced him. "Yes."

"This is very important to you?"

"Yes."

Val thought momentarily before replying, "Okay." It was that simple, his acquisition and deferment to my wishes.

"Thank you."

"No problem." Val got up from the bed, grabbed his paisley robe and disappeared out the door.

Confused, I got up and followed him down the hall to the bedroom farthest away from ours. "Val?" I called, puzzled.

"Yes, David?" he answered as he was turning back the covers of the full-sized bed. *Our* bed was a California king.

"What are you doing?"

"I'm getting ready for bed."

"You're sleeping in here?"

We always slept together. It registered in the back of my mind that he had put on his robe. Val hardly ever wore the robe when we were alone. And this room, like I said, was farthest away from the room we shared. It was a nice room, decorated in paisley prints and antique furniture. It looked very much like a room Val would have chosen if we did not share a room.

"Isn't this what you want?" he asked. He got into the bed and reached to turn out the lamp on the nightstand. The room was cast into darkness.

"Are we fighting?"

"No."

"We're fighting." I turned on the light from the switch on the wall. Val was sitting up in the bed.

"Will you please try to understand?" I began.

"I understand perfectly well." He was angry. There was fire in his eyes and stiffness in his shoulders. When Val was mad, his accent was very pronounced. He was suddenly very "Hugh Grant" British.

"Can we talk about this?" I pleaded.

"What is the point in talking about this?"

"I don't want you to be mad at me."

"Well, I think it's a little late for that."

"Will you try to understand?"

"No," Val said firmly.

"Why?"

"We are not adolescents, David. We don't have to pretend for anyone or please anyone other than ourselves. I go along with your crap in public because I know it is something you feel you have to do. But here in our house? You ask this of me?" He hissed and clapped, casting the room into darkness again.

"Val, please."

"I'm too mad at you to talk to you."

"Don't go to bed mad," I said. I was standing in the dark, afraid to turn on the light again because I thought he would be able to see my face and glean from it the lies I was trying to hide.

"Get out of my room."

"*Your* room?"

"My goddamn room. I picked out the furniture. I chose the color scheme. I picked this room. It's *my* room."

"You're being silly."

"I'm being silly? I'm being silly?" Val exploded in a rapid series of French expletives.

I couldn't follow every word—my French sucked—but I did get *asshole* and *son-of-a-bitch* from his melee. Those words were in English. "Will you speak English, please?" I was getting a headache.

"Okay, in English—fuck you." Val got up from the bed.

Again I followed him down the hallway as he disappeared into our bedroom.

"What are you doing?" I asked as I watched helplessly while Val slipped into a pair of jeans and grabbed a sweater. It was my sweater, a blue cotton number I usually wore to the beach. "Where are you going? Can we talk about this?"

Ignoring me, Val pushed past me and was out the door and down the stairs. When I heard the front door slam, I knew that he was gone.

All of this happened the night before his huge benefit concert. I didn't see him at all the next day.

Contrite and wanting desperately to be forgiven, I ordered a dozen red roses for his dressing room. On the card I wrote: *We never know the things we say are stupid until after we say them.* I signed it *D.E.,* for David Eugene.

I dressed in my tuxedo and arrived at the Beverly Chandler Pavilion alone. As with all such events, the media was there en masse as well as stars and star watchers. Determined to put the best face forward, I walked into the Pavilion virtually ignored. Writers were not in as much demand as movie stars. I took my place center row, center aisle, and center seat, to await Val's appearance.

VAL

I had never met Patti. I had heard about her, of course. It was impossible to know David without recognizing her influence between the pages of his work. From his description, I knew she was pretty. *Tall, ample, healthy, earthy, breasts, hips, long, long legs, brown eyes, full lips, all woman. She could give an erection to a corpse,* David had written in *Cake Walk.* This was my competition. They had been separated for more years than I could count, yet he was so concerned about what she thought about our relationship that he was willing to start hiding—as if we had something to lose if she knew about the goings-on in our house and our bedroom. *It's none of her goddamned business!* I was so resentful of her and the power she had over him I could easily hate her without knowing her. She made me leery. I was so mad at David I could scream. I was mad at myself for acting like such a fag. *I am not the girl!*

These thoughts kept going through my head as I took my mark backstage. Dressed in a piece of cloth that left little to the imagination and with stark make-up and feathers in my hair, I looked the part I was ready to dance—the savage. As the curtains rose, the music, written by my father, started with great fan-fare. I detached myself from my thoughts of David and Patti and enveloped myself in the skin of my character then burst onto the stage in a haze of light, music and dance. David and I would talk later.

CHAPTER SIX

This was the after-party of all after-parties, rivaled only by the post-Oscar after-parties. The room was alive with laughter, food, drink and people. David found himself trapped in a conversation with an up-and-coming young starlet who was making it obvious that she would appreciate any influence he could exert over the producers and directors of *Cake Walk,* the movie.

David could see Andre at the baby grand piano. Val's father held up well with age. Like his wife, he kept in good physical shape. Years of dancing had seen to that. White-haired, blue eyes, full-lipped, he was still a striking man. His son had his bearing. He was accompanying the band with their rendition of "Sweet Georgia Brown."

Lola was across the room, an entourage of attendants dancing at her every command. Obviously, David could not expect a rescue from either one of them. As politely as he could, his early Southern upbringing not allowing him to be rude, he tried to excuse himself from the starlet's company when he saw Val, Kim and The Troupe arrive en masse.

Although they had removed their costumes and makeup, they still knew how to make an entrance. A hush fell over the crowd.

Standing at the piano, Andre raised his glass in toast. "The king is dead. Long live the king!" Andre shouted.

Lola curtsied low to Kim. With those two simple clichés, the torch had been passed. A roar went up through the crowd, flashes exploded as pictures were taken. The band broke into "Hail, Hail, the Gang's All Here."

David felt a rush of pride when Val received kudos and accolades. From his position in the room, he could see Val clearly. Val sported a non-traditional tuxedo. The jacket was orange, the shirt was a silk floral print with orange, yellow and blue highlights, and the pants were black. The colors were vibrant against his skin. He looked good.

While David had been meeting with his agent to discuss *David's Story,* Val had been busy removing all his things from their room and putting them in *his* room. David realized that Val did this at his request, yet it had torn at his heart to walk into their room and not see Val's paisley robe on the hook in the closet or Val's neat arrangement of clothes next to his. He had only been gone for a couple of hours. Apparently that was all the time Val needed to make it seem as if all they shared was the house, not the bed. Not a life.

David finally managed to extract himself from the young lady, whose name was Wanda or Wendy or Lisa or something, and made his way through the crowd to Val's side. "Hi," he said.

"Hi, yourself," Val replied.

"You were very good."

"I'm always good."

"You're not going to make this easy, are you?"

A waiter passed by, and Val extracted two glasses of champagne, one of which he gave to David.

"No, I'm not," Val said, taking a sip from his glass.

"I'm sorry, Val."

"How sorry are you?"

"Very."

"It's going to cost you."

"What?"

"I haven't decided yet." With that, Val walked away from David to join Heathcliff and Sampson in the crowd around Lola.

David wanted to follow him. They were talking. That was good. They were even flirting. That was better. But they weren't touching. That was bad. Downing his champagne, David went after Val. "Are you going to spend all night avoiding me?" David took Val by the elbow.

"I'm talking to you, aren't I?" Val responded. They smiled as someone snapped a picture.

"I want to be with you," David said sincerely. The room was loud.

"Be careful, David. Someone might hear."

"I don't care."

"Really? Did you move my things back to our room?" Val challenged.

David was trying to pick his words carefully. Val took his silence to mean that David hadn't moved his things. He hadn't.

"Just what I thought."

David took Val by the arm and led him away from

their clique into a corner where they could have as much privacy as possible in a room full of people.

"Why did you move your things out of the room in the first place?"

"Because you wanted me to."

"That's all it took—my wanting you to?"

"Yes."

"But you're mad at me?"

"Furious."

"I'll never understand you, Valentine."

"But I understand you perfectly. I will go along with this charade because this is what *you* want, but I don't like it."

With that, Val again excused himself from David to join Kim on the dance floor. Dressed in a red sequined short, short dress with her hair in a free-flowing mass around her pretty face, she was the epitome of youth and vibrancy. Watching them together, it was apparent that for as long as their careers consisted of dance, they should dance as a team. Even in the non-choreographed, free-flowing movements, Val and Kim were magnificent together.

"They look very good together," David heard someone say.

The voice at his side was not immediately recognizable to David. He turned to see who was addressing him with such familiarity. It was Wayne Carey. He and Wayne had met briefly some years ago when a major network had considered a TV pilot based on *The Drake Chronicles*. It had never materialized because the network was adamant about having Wayne Carey in the lead role. David wanted another not-so-well-known actor at the time, Isaiah Washington. As a black man who wrote about black people, it never ceased to amaze him that white people inevitably ignored his characters' descriptions and painted them white.

"Hello," David said.

"Hi," Wayne replied.

Hollywood was a small town. Even if the two of them hadn't met years ago, it was impossible for them not to know each other. Considering their respective public images, it was likely that an observer would know that it was Val, not Kim, who was responsible for their respective erections.

After the song ended, Val and Kim separated. Val turned in the direction in which he'd left David. He saw David. He also saw Wayne.

Shit, Val thought. There they stood, the man Val wanted and the man who wanted Val. David and Wayne, both of them, grinned like two fools as they looked at him. One had broken his heart, and one's heart he could break. Somehow, he had forgotten to tell David about Wayne. Maybe it was because he had enjoyed the flirting. Who knew? He had to be careful how he played this. They were, after all, in a room full of people.

David and Wayne were similar in build, but as different as night and day in temperament and personality. David's sexuality whispered to Val, beckoning to him with subtlety. Wayne's desire was a blatant, tangible thing that stood between them.

What David and Val did was make love. What Wayne wanted from Val was fucking. There was a difference, and Val knew this. He didn't need fucking. He had that covered. With two pairs of eyes piercing him, David's and Wayne's, Val walked toward them, smiling the smile of an entertainer.

WAYNE

He was coming my way. He was so fucking hot. I'd had this thing for him for longer than I wanted to admit. I wasn't going to boil a rabbit or follow him around or anything like that—I was infatuated, not crazy—but when I saw him at Heathcliff's, it had changed my whole perspective. Until then, I thought he was straight. But in my world, there are actors more deserving of Tony awards, Oscars or Emmys for their off-screen roles than for the ones they were known for. I knew this because I was one of them— straight-acting, heterosexual in appearance, a lady's man, but queer as a three-dollar bill. I liked boys. Men. I had known since I was six years old. Even then I knew I couldn't share my secret with anyone, and I certainly couldn't act funny or different in any way. It was an awfully heavy burden to bear at six.

When I turned thirteen, I was a pitcher for my little league team. Randy Greenbaum was also on that team. He was fifteen. Well, without going into detail, Randy taught me about all the fun two boys could have together as long as no one else knew. From Randy I learned discretion and the art of playing it straight. He's married now with three children.

By the time I was eighteen, I was on the West Coast, a theater major at UCLA. I went on an audition for an All-American boy type for a dog food commercial. The rest, as they say, is Hollywood history. Even though I was currently one of America's reigning heartthrobs, I knew it would come crashing down around my head if I ever got "outed." So, I was in the closet, but the closet I occupied was spacious. There were places I could go where I didn't have to be seen with the latest Wayne Carey conquest, usually blond, buxom and beautiful. There were places where I was allowed to be me. There were safe places, fun places, and discreet places. Those were the places I wanted to go with Val. He knew I was after his ass. It was making me hard, this game of cat and mouse we were playing in this room full of people. I was digging it.

CHAPTER SEVEN

Val made his way over to Wayne and David and struck up a general conversation with Wayne. David was totally oblivious to the fact that Wayne was after Val. Totally. He was so preoccupied with trying to figure out what to say to Val so that he could leave comfortably and without guilt, he missed the subtleties of body language that were passing beneath his nose and before his face. He was too busy trying to cover his ass. Oh, what a tangled web we weave when we lie. What a pain in the ass it was for David to have practiced infidelity.

After only a couple of minutes, Wanda or Wendy or Lisa or something intruded into their conversation, initially interested in stealing David's attention, but making it perfectly obvious that she found both Wayne and Val to be bigger fish. This gave David the perfect opportunity to excuse himself from the conversation. It was time to go get Patti at the airport.

David congratulated Val on a wonderful performance, told Wayne that it was nice seeing him again then exited the party.

"Want to get out of here and get a drink somewhere?" Wayne asked Val, once they had managed to ditch the young starlet by introducing her to a prominent director.

"You just won't give up, will you?" Val said.

"I told you I was very persistent."

"Wayne . . ." Val sighed. "You're just going to make me say it, aren't you?"

"Say what?"

"You're not my type."

"I'm an actor. I can be any type."

"Okay, Wayne. I like my men like I like my coffee."

"How's that?"

"Black."

"I can do black."

"You're crazy," Val said with a laugh.

"No, just infatuated."

Despite his better judgment, Val found himself warming up to Wayne. "I don't want to hurt your feelings."

"Have a drink with me."

"No."

"Okay." Wayne changed tactics. "Go to bed with me so that I can get you out of my system."

"I have a friend, Wayne."

"We haven't called them *friends* in a long time, Val."

Val took a sip of his drink. Would it be so bad to tell Wayne? Obviously Wayne knew how to be discreet.

"Ok, I have a lover." He said it out loud and nothing happened.

"Your lover doesn't seem to spend a lot of time with you."

"We live together."

"Okay already. At least you can tell me who this guy is."

"Hollywood is a small town, Wayne; I'm surprised you don't know."

"There's a lot I don't know. Hell, there's a lot *you* don't know," Wayne said. When Val didn't respond, he continued. "I'm sitting on pins and needles. Who is this mystery man?"

"He just left."

"Tell me."

"He was just here. We were just talking, the three of us." Val continued to sip his drink and watched with amusement the play of emotions wash across Wayne's face—shock, disbelief, amazement.

"David Lincoln?"

"The one and only."

"Well."

"Well."

"Well," Wayne said again.

"He does black better than you do." Val couldn't resist laughing.

"You two have the world fooled."

"We aren't trying to fool the world."

"Well, you had me fooled."

"Didn't try to fool you."

"Are you always this obtuse?"

"Yes."

"You're giving me a hard-on."

"Damn it, Wayne!"

He had been approached by men before. It was a hazard of his profession. Usually, a friendly smile and a pleasant refusal left them confused, thinking that they had been misled in their assessment of his sexuality. But Val couldn't push Wayne off because Wayne knew the score. He had heard with his own ears and seen with his own eyes. So, in being honest with Wayne, Val had opened himself up to being wooed and pursued.

"You like it," Wayne said with a twinkle in his eye and a smile in his voice. "You dig me digging you." Before Val could say anything, Wayne walked off. When he was halfway across the room, he turned to see if Val was watching him. He was.

WAYNE

Shit. I caught him looking.

VAL

Shit. He caught me looking.

CHAPTER EIGHT

Patti arrived at LAX a big-eyed tourist. She was looking for movie stars, expecting fame and fortune to slap her in the face. In anticipation of seeing David and being discovered, she had dressed to impress. She wore a pair of form-fitting jeans, a leopard print blouse and a pair of boots with a toe so pointed that she could put out an eye. Her toes were killing her, but she looked good! She had her hair re-done and wore her braids in a fancy upsweep. Admiring eyes were on her. She didn't care because she knew she looked good, hip, chic, en vogue.

By the time David showed up, late, she had already collected her luggage and been propositioned four times. One man had even given her his business card.

"My goodness, Davey-Gene. Will you look at you?" Patti said. David hadn't had time to go home and change his tuxedo. He was late, which had really pissed Patti off. She didn't care about the traffic; she didn't wait on men. But standing there, David looked like a tall glass of water on a hot summer day, and she forgot to stay mad.

"And look at you," David replied, embracing her. "Let's get out of here." After gathering her luggage, they headed for his car.

This old-ass car, Patti thought as they approached David's 1965 classic Mustang. Classic or not, it didn't mean a thing to Patti. She wanted to see a Porsche or a Ferrari or some kind of "star" car, not some car as old as she was. Hell, she drove an Escalade, and she hadn't been interviewed by Oprah-fucking-Winfrey! So, she got an attitude. Patti really didn't like cheap men. She figured, *Why have money if you're not going to spend it?* But once they pulled up to David's house, her thoughts changed.

Goddamn! Patti thought as her mouth dropped open. To her, the house looked just like something out of a magazine, all white and angular. That's when she knew that Davey-Gene wasn't cheap, and from that moment on, she had to have David. Confidence assured her that she would have him and that no other woman could put out the torch that had blazed between them for so many years. No other woman. He didn't have a ring on his finger, and if there was some woman in the wings, she'd put that bitch's eyes out.

The hardest thing for David wasn't picking Patti up from the airport, but taking her back to his house. Their house. The house he shared with Val. By allowing Patti to enter into their domain, he was essentially allowing her into his life, his skin, and his world. She had been in those places before, but then they were kids. There was no expanse of miles or education or wants and desires to separate Davey-Gene and

Patticake. There had only been a few thin layers of clothing. Now, as adults who had been dealt two totally different hands of cards, the question arose as to whether it was time to show their hands to each other.

Ever since David knew Patti was coming, he had been trying to figure out how to tell her that they were not going to be sleeping together. What happened in Dallas wasn't going to be repeated in L.A. because the price was too high. Luckily for David, he didn't have to do that.

"Look, Davey-Gene . . ." Patti began as they sat on the couch and drank a white wine nightcap.

She was the most sexual being David knew. All she had to do was stretch her legs and yawn, and he felt himself rubbing against his zipper. It was a purely physical reaction to her. It meant nothing. It was a sexual thing.

"What?" David said.

"I think we should take it slow." She was looking into her wine glass, running her finger around the rim. It was such a sexy, sexy gesture. "I mean, you know we haven't seen each other in so long. I think we should get to know each other again."

David could have kissed her.

"You know?" she continued hopefully.

"I know."

She sighed, relieved. "I thought you were going to explode."

"Why would I do that?"

"I mean, I fly all the way up here. You had to leave your big Hollywood party." She shrugged and her breasts jiggled. She wasn't conscious of the gesture. "The least I'd expect if I were a guy was a blowjob."

David almost choked on his wine.

"Gotcha." She smiled. David laughed. They were friends. No passes made and none caught.

David showed her to the guest room.

I played Davey-Gene like a goddamn fiddle, Patti thought to herself as she flopped down on the bed that was deemed hers for the next week or so.

As soon as she had seen that house, she knew she and David couldn't fuck. Hell, if she had given him some pussy, she'd be like every other bitch that came through that door. And in her mind, she wasn't no regular bitch. Man, with all that going for him, her Davey-Gene had to be wading kneedeep in pussy. Pussy to the left. Pussy to the right. Pussy on top. Pussy on bottom. She felt that she had to do something that made her so different from all the rest of that pussy that he'd be able to distinguish hers from theirs. That's why she couldn't sleep with David.

"Shit," Patti said as she lay back on the bed. He was so fine, and she was so wet. But she was not going to give in and be like everybody else. By the time David got into her pussy, he'd be salivating like a dog, and she'd have him where she wanted him.

CHAPTER NINE

David had mentioned Patti to Val, but he had somehow neglected to mention Val to Patti. They met in the kitchen the morning after her arrival, with no help from David. Patti had arisen with the intention of preparing a down-home country breakfast—hotcakes, bacon, eggs, grits, and coffee for David. For her and David. The way David liked it. The way to a man's bed might be through his dick, but the way to his heart was through his stomach. Patti was a good cook. She had learned from the best, David's Nanna.

When she stepped into the kitchen intent on fixing David the kind of breakfast she was sure he only got when he went to Denny's or IHOP, she found breakfast already prepared, and standing before her was the person who prepared it. Her eyes briefly locked with Val's.

She's pretty, Val thought, *with an earthly beauty like that of a young Rachel Welch dipped in chocolate.* There was an inherent sexuality about Patti that spoke to everything male in Val. On a purely physical level, he responded and was grateful to be able to hide his growing erection in the folds of his robe. It was a sexual response to her femaleness. Val's dick didn't care that her nails were too long for good taste. His dick didn't care that she must have used two cans of hairspray to make sure that her perfectly braided, upswept beehive didn't fall. His dick didn't care that she had on four pairs of earrings. All his dick cared about was that she was a siren. She was wanton. She was desirable. She held the promise of ecstasy between her legs. She was the kind of girl over whom guys would start bar fights and wars were waged. Helen of Troy had nothing on Patti of the Projects. *Damn.*

Patti nearly jumped out of her clothes when she saw Val. Talk about a pretty piece of caramel candy. And that was saying a lot because she liked her men black, blue and damn near purple. That's not saying she wouldn't fuck a yellow man or a red man, but as the saying goes, the blacker the berry, the sweeter the juice. She knew that for a fact. But there stood a pretty brown man decked out in silk like a Christmas present, and all she could think of doing was unwrapping him layer by layer. She didn't know what he did or who he was, but it didn't matter.

"Hi," Val said. He was putting oranges through the juicer. "You must be Patricia, David's friend. I'm Val, David's housemate." He held out his hand, and she shook it.

"Patti," she corrected him. "I like Patti."

David had never mentioned a housemate. True, he said he didn't have a girl. Patti had taken that for "man talk" to mean he had a lot of women. Most men did.

"Oh, okay. Sorry we didn't get to meet last night. I got in really late." He took the pitcher of freshly squeezed juice into the sunroom.

Patti had no choice but to follow him. She hadn't been prepared for Val. She had never met anyone like him, someone she couldn't immediately categorize by class, culture, or ethnicity. She didn't know there was anyone else in the house and had dressed for David. Clad in an overly large T-shirt with a great deal of leg and thigh showing, she looked irresistible. Val seemed not to notice, which irritated her.

He had arranged the table into a picture-perfect setting. There was fruit, croissants, an assortment of jams and the freshly squeezed juice. There wasn't any coffee or any meat.

Patti frowned. "I guess I better go wake Davey-Gene," she said.

"Please," Val gestured to a chair, "don't bother. David is very predictable. By the time you pour yourself a glass of juice, he'll be joining us."

Patti sat and poured a glass of juice. Val was right.

When David walked into the kitchen and saw Val and Patti sitting at the table like it was something they did all the time, his heart stopped for a second. His lover and his first love, the whole thing was too modern and "too Californian" for him to be completely comfortable with it. "Morning," he mumbled, sitting down.

"Morning," Val and Patti chorused.

David knew that Val was still mad at him. He knew because he knew Val. But looking at the duo, it was impossible to tell.

"I see you two have met."

"Val—what's that short for?" Patti asked.

"Valentine," Val and David said in unison.

"Valentine? Is that foreign?"

"No. It's Valentine, like St. Valentine's Day. I was born on February fourteenth. My mother thought it was cute and very romantic. My father let her get away with it." This was the canned explanation Val always gave; usually it got a mild chuckle.

Patti nibbled on her croissant. "Where are you from?"

"New York," Val answered.

"Come on, now. People from New York don't talk like you do," she snickered.

"I was born in New York; I was raised in London."

"Oh. Are you the person that answered the phone when I called?"

"That's me."

Val was answering Patti's questions as an adult would those of an inquisitive child.

David sat there on pins and needles, hoping that neither one would say anything to get the other up in arms. *Fuck!* David thought. *What a way to start a morning.*

All in all, the morning meal turned out to be uneventful. Val found the entire situation too amusing for words. Patti had been torn between David's sexuality and Val's sensuality. David was almost sick, but no toes were stepped on, and no feelings were hurt.

"If you gentlemen will excuse me . . ." Patti said when she finished her meal. She got up from the table, yawned and stretched. The thin cotton of her T-shirt stretched across her breasts. Her nipples were erect. She had the largest nipples Val had ever seen. The gesture on her part had been deliberate. She was proud of her nipples, but neither man knew of her ulterior motive. ". . . I need to put some clothes on." Aware that both men were too polite to openly stare at her breasts, she sashayed from the room with a secret smile on her lips. *Men.*

Alone with David, Val immediately began clearing away the breakfast dishes. "She's very pretty, David," Val started, trying to ease the tension in the room and stay the awkwardness they both felt.

"I don't know if *pretty* is the word I'd use," David replied.

"Okay." Val smiled. "She's hot."

"I think you're hotter." David got up from the table and went to Val. He stood close as if to kiss him.

But Val stopped him. "Don't start anything we can't finish, David."

"You're not still mad at me?" David ran his hand over Val's pecs.

"Yes, I am."

"Liar." David's lips grazed Val's ear.

"You're very bold this morning."

"She's taking a shower."

"I'm still mad at you."

"But your dick's hard."

"How do you know my dick's not hard because of Patti?" That statement made David pause. Seeing the look on David's face, Val relented and said, "David, David, David. I'm still angry and I'll get angry every time I sleep in one room and you sleep in another. I'll get angry every time we have to whisper in our house. I'll even be angry every time I can't reach over and touch you when I want to. But until that incredibly hot number upstairs heads back to the South, I'll pretend to not be angry."

"Okay. I can live with that." David reached for Val, intent on sharing a romantic kiss before it was time to separate and pretend to just be housemates.

"But pretending does not give you liberties." With

that statement, Val extracted himself from David's grasp and turned back to cleaning.

Though Val feigned indifference to David's touch, David knew better. His knowledge made him happy. He and Val were back on track. Humming, he went upstairs to dress.

CHAPTER TEN

At fifty-eight, Andre had limitations that he didn't have at twenty-eight. In his home studio devoid of audience and secure in his privacy, he danced like the fifty-eight-year-old man he was. The dance he performed, "Blessed Love," was one of his favorites. It was the first ballet he had choreographed, long before establishing The Troupe.

It was an extremely difficult dance that required strength, endurance and dexterity. He moved through the room, commanding the space. His body was one with the music. His movements were fluid. Only the trained eye would notice that the great rivers of sweat that poured off his body were from overexertion.

From his position in the doorway, Val watched his father with a mixture of admiration, awe and sadness. Val had a trained eye. The ballet was difficult. Andre's timing was off. He was taking his father's place as spokesperson for the company that Andre had established so many years ago. It was the natural order of things. The old regime steps down and the new one steps up.

Straining and sweating, Andre glided across the studio floor. When he came to a stopping point, his eyes met Val's in the mirror. He didn't say a word. He didn't have to. Val understood. Slipping off his Nikes and joining Andre in the middle of the dance, they were a picturesque duo. Side by side, step by step, they moved together in harmony with the music.

"Arch your back," Andre instructed. "Raise your head."

Val did as he was told.

Andre watched him in the mirror.

Val performed "Blessed Love" the way it should have been performed. The two Pardeaux men performed with skill and grace. By the time the song ended, they had culminated their dance.

Winded and breathing heavily, Andre accepted the glass of carrot juice Val got for him from the mini-refrigerator in the corner.

"When you arch your back and raise your head, it extends the line of your body," Andre said.

Val accepted the criticism benevolently. His father had, after all, choreographed that dance and knew how it should be done. Affectionately, he massaged his father's shoulders.

"You aren't even winded," Andre observed. "Oh, to be young again." He sighed.

"To be as good as you are."

"To be as good as I was." Andre downed his juice.

"How can you drink that stuff?"

"It's good."

Val made a face in the mirror. "Where's Lola?"

"I left your mother in bed. It's Sunday. She won't get up until well after noon."

"Who won't get up until well after noon?" Dressed in a calf-length silken robe, a copy of *Cake Walk* under her arm and a cup of cocoa in her hand, Lola entered the room and crossed to her husband. "Hello, love." As she did every morning, she kissed him and whispered, "I love you," in his ear.

Valentine had grown up in a house filled with this type of love, around two people who expressed their love openly and honestly. He was used to it and expected it for himself. That was why he was having such a hard time with David's recent choices.

"I love you too," Andre said as he hugged her to him. If Val had not been there, they would have made early morning love on the floor of the dance studio with the Neville brothers singing in the background. But Val was there, and decorum dictated they could caress but not copulate openly. That would be rude.

Sometimes as a child, Val had wondered if there was room in their world for him.

"And I love you, too, son of mine," Lola said, extending her hand to Val. The three of them hugged. "So, what did I interrupt?"

"Nothing but a little male bonding," Andre said.

Lola laughed. "My two men. Would you two like to join me for breakfast?" she asked as she ushered them toward the kitchen. The house they shared in Bel Air was very large, but there were no servants. There were only servants in their house in London. The servants there were kept out of tradition instead of necessity.

When Lola married Andre, she had married into a lot of tradition. It was the tradition that came with having old money. And though she had not been born of his family traditions, she quickly learned to adapt to them, break them or create new ones to suit her needs. She found this easy to do with money.

They had a lot of money. The Troupe was and had always been very successful, but before there had been that success, there had been Andre's money. When Andre's parents died, Andre had gotten it all. Lola made it quite clear that she was capable of managing a taxing career and whichever household they were occupying at the time. There was a house in Paris, a house in London, the apartment in New York and a farmhouse in Martha's Vineyard. There were servants that they continued to pay and never utilized. There were cars, a plane and a lot of money. A lot of money. A lot of money. A lot of money. The Pardeaux family owned a very successful vineyard in the South of France.

"What do you want for breakfast, Valentine?" she asked as Val watched her maneuver in the kitchen.

"It's after noon," he replied.

"So?" Lola was preparing fruit-filled crepes.

"Nothing for me."

"Where is David?" Andre asked as he set the table.

"We have a houseguest. She and David are at Magic Mountain or Disneyland or someplace." Val tried to sound nonchalant, but Andre could hear the tone of discontent in his voice.

"She?" Andre asked, accepting a crepe-filled plate from Lola.

"She," Val confirmed.

"Who is this she?" Lola asked through a mouthful of fruit.

Val reached for her copy of *Cake Walk*. After flipping through the pages, he found a rather descriptive passage and began to read. "She swallowed the whole of me as if she had been born to it. Her lips, her tongue caressed me, engulfed me, making me lose myself in ecstasy."

Val closed the book. "She." He sighed.

"Well," said Lola.

"Well," said Andre.

"Well," said Val, who had memorized the passage.

"That's quite a houseguest," said Lola.

As he visited with them, Val watched and admired, as he always did, how his parents anticipated each other's wants and desires. Before Andre could ask to see *Cake Walk,* Lola passed the book to him.

Andre flipped through the pages then re-read the paragraph on Patti. "David is very clever," Andre said, closing the book.

Val's parents had always loved and supported him. They had always communicated with him. He had never gone through that awkward adolescent stage during which he made their lives hell. The only time there had been tension in their relationship was when they asked Val about his relationship with David.

Val had been visiting with them then like now. He had his own key. He let himself in as he had always done. It was raining that day, a cold day for Los Angeles. Val was wearing one of David's sweaters. He always liked David's sweaters. They smelled like him, a mixture of Aramis and a strong, clean, manly smell.

When Val entered his parents' house, he heard no music. That was strange to him. There was always music in his parents' house, background noise that ranged in genre and style. The house was very quiet.

Val called, but there was no answer. To Val, that too was strange.

Val and David always had dinner with his parents

on every other Sunday. On that particular day, David wasn't able to make it. He was speaking on mystery writing at UCLA. *The Drake Chronicles* was very popular then. Val planned on taking him a plate. David always said, when Val went to visit his parents, "Bring me a plate." Val's Southern-born David loved Lola's cooking and took every opportunity to sample it.

On that day, Val found his parents in the kitchen. The first thing he noticed was that Lola had been crying. His mother never cried! His father looked pained. There was no food on the stove, no odors of a meal being cooked. That was not like his parents' house.

"What's wrong?" Val asked.

Both Lola and Andre looked up at Val as if surprised to see him.

"Kevin died," Andre said.

Kevin was younger than Heathcliff, either forty-three or forty-four. (He was Heathcliff's lover before Sampson.) They were together for years. Their "divorce" had been surprising, but they had both moved on. Seeing Heathcliff with Sampson almost made Val forget Kevin. Val hadn't seen Kevin in years. Occasionally Val would get a postcard from the far corners of the world. Kevin, Lola and Andre had kept in touch.

"How? When?" Val asked, shocked.

"AIDS," Andre said.

Lola burst into tears.

Val stood in the kitchen, not knowing what to do. He didn't know that Kevin and his mother were such good friends.

His father crooned to his mother in French in soothing tones.

Lola looked up at Val. "Are you sleeping with him?" It was the only time she just came out and asked him about his relationship with David. This wasn't the way Val wanted to tell her.

"Lolan!" Andre said sharply.

"I want to know," Lola said.

"Lolan, this is not the way to ask."

All the air had been knocked from Val. He knew that eventually he would have to say something. He just didn't want it to be this way.

Yes, David and I are sleeping together, Val thought, wondering if that was the best way to say it. Just say it. He and David had been dancing around their attraction to each other for so very long and had just gotten used to it. It was still too new and too personal to share, even with his parents, his wonderful, accepting, loving parents. It had taken David and Val almost a year to get past their eventful shower scene. For one year and six days after the event, they had just been housemates. Then David was shot. The thought of losing David was too much.

"Well . . . are you?" she demanded, snapping Val from his reverie.

"Yes," Val said. What else could he say?

Lola burst into fresh tears. Val's heart was about to break. Never in a million years did he expect this response.

"Don't cry, Mamie," Val said to Lola, suddenly feeling like a six-year-old boy seeking his mother's approval.

"People are dying, Valentine, dying, and you say, 'Don't cry,'" Lola said.

"Son," his father started, "have you been to the doctor? Has David been?" It was painful for them to ask him those questions.

"We are very careful, Paupee. Very," Val assured him.

"Kevin was careful too," Lola jumped in.

"Mamie, listen to me." Val took her hand into his. "David and I are very careful. Very safe."

"Have there been others?" she asked.

"Lolan, must you—" She silenced Andre with a look.

"I have to know," she said, turning her attention back to Val.

"No, Mamie. There have been no others. David is my one. My only. David is my Andre." Val knew the confession he was making to his parents.

"Before David, there have always been women?" she asked hopefully.

"Yes," Val answered.

"And you were careful then?" This had come from Andre, his father who had always preached sexual responsibility even before it had become popular.

"Yes," Val assured them.

They both let out a sigh of relief.

"Good. Good," Lola said, drying her eyes. "Now, what do you want to eat? I can always put something in the microwave."

"Why don't we go out?" Andre said.

They went out.

That was nearly two years ago. The question of Val's sexuality had never come up again. His parents, who liked David, did not treat him any differently once they officially knew that he was sleeping with their son.

"I always did like David's books," Andre said as he put *Cake Walk* aside.

Lola squeezed Val's shoulder affectionately. "Let's do something to take your mind off your houseguest."

She went and grabbed the Scrabble board from the cupboard. Val groaned. She always beat him and Andre at Scrabble. She cheated. They let her.

CHAPTER ELEVEN

By the time Val left his parents' house, it was late. They had gossiped, eaten, drank and played Scrabble. Val drank nearly half a bottle of wine and was very mellow. When he pulled his 450SL convertible into the garage, he noticed David's Mustang. They had never fallen into the trend of so many celebrities and filled their garage with fast, sporty collectibles. There were only two of them, and two cars were enough. They tended to spend their money on other things: art, travel and each other. Not knowing what to expect, Val entered through the kitchen to the sound of blues by Clarence Carter playing throughout the house.

The kitchen was a mess. There was a burnt pot on the stove, dirty dishes in one sink and a box that held greasy chicken on the counter. Frowning, Val walked into the living room.

David was stretched out on the couch, his head in Patti's lap. An empty four-pack of wine coolers and empty bottles from a Heineken six-pack were scattered across the coffee table. David's dominoes and a scratch pad that he and Patti had used to keep score were on the floor. It was obvious that Patti and David had had a good time.

"Is the party just beginning or ending?" Val queried, stepping over a stray bottle and sitting opposite David and Patti in a paisley chair he had imported from his parents' home in London. It was an antique that had been in his family for ages. It created a striking contrast to the overly large white slipcovered sofa and loveseat that occupied the room.

"Well, baby, since you just got here, I guess it's about to start," Patti purred. Her accent was beautiful, rich and full. It was unlike David's, which had lost some of its drawl since he'd been out of the South.

Val wanted to reach down and pick up the clutter but restrained himself because he didn't want to appear anal retentive.

"Thank God you got here, Val. She's about to wear me out," David said with a sigh, sitting up.

"I haven't even started on you yet," she replied as she stood and stretched. "I didn't come to Los Angeles to turn in at eight o'clock. I want to party. Let's go to a club."

David groaned.

"You'll have to excuse him. Sometimes he acts like an old man." Val apologized for David as he got up from the chair and extended his hand to him. "Get up, old man." David was only five months older than Val.

David took Val's hand and pulled himself up from the couch. Patti had turned from them and bent to pick up her shoes, so she didn't see the subtle interplay between the lovers as one's hand caressed the other. She wasn't looking for it, so didn't see the eye contact that was as intimate as a caress.

"Come on, Davey-Gene. I want you to show me this town," she said, heading up the stairs to the guest room.

Once she had disappeared, David looked over Val's shoulders to make sure that he couldn't see her. Satisfied that she was nowhere in sight, he pulled Val to him. "Let me kiss you." He planted a kiss on Val's ear. When Val didn't resist, he kissed him full on the lips.

At first it was a tentative kiss to test the waters, but as their lips touched, the fires of passion were ignited. They were two people who spent a great deal of time touching freely, and this was the first time they had been able to be intimate since the strain of the earlier rift. Without any more hesitation, they kissed passionately.

"God, I've missed you," David whispered against Val's lips.

"I've missed you too." Val kissed David deeply. It was so easy to get wrapped up in each other and forget that Patti was only one floor away. It was so very easy.

David reached behind Val and cupped his ass.

"David, David, David," Val moaned. "Let's not start what we can't finish." It was exciting, becoming intimate with Patti just upstairs.

"We can finish it."

"Yeah, right." Val tried to detangle himself from David.

"We can finish it," David insisted, dropping to his knees in front of Val.

"What the hell are you doing?" Val said anxiously, looking over his shoulder.

"You know." David caressed Val through his pants.

"Jesus." Val looked again to make sure that Patti was not there.

"You are drunk."

"Don't worry." David unzipped Val's jeans.

"I'm still mad at you," Val insisted.

"You're not that mad." David squeezed Val's hardening penis for emphasis as he eased him out of his pants.

"Yes, I am," Val insisted.

"Well, consider this an apology." David swallowed Val.

"Christ," Val moaned.

It had been so long since David did this for him. It felt good. It felt damn good. It felt like coming home. Val was home. He put his hands behind David's head and held on for dear life as David worked him expertly with his tongue. Thank God he could hear the shower running. That meant Patti was in the shower and not on her way down the stairs.

When he thought he couldn't take it anymore David stopped.

"What's wrong?"

"The water stopped."

David got up from his knees and Val zipped his pants just as Patti rounded the corner. She was dressed in a short robe that wasn't held together with the belt. They could see the curve of her breast and the flat plain of her stomach.

"Aren't you two going to get ready?"

"Sure," David assured her.

"Good. I want to use all my good-smelling soap." She disappeared back up the stairs.

David shot a glance at Val.

"I guess we better get ready."

"Yeah, I guess we better."

Without another word, the two men headed to their respective rooms. Val didn't really have to make a choice as to what to wear. His closet was very organized. His clothes were interchangeable. He only bought what he liked and only wore what looked good on him, which was usually anything. He preferred trendy casual designer clothes that clung to the lines of his body.

Hurrying, he grabbed a pair of slacks, white linen, lined, tailored; a shirt, mustard-colored raw silk; and traded his Nikes for a pair of Italian leather sandals. These things were the first things he grabbed; therefore, they were what he donned. Val had washed his hair that morning and decided to wear it loose and unbound. Content with his look, he ran downstairs.

The first thing he saw was ass; leather-encased, heartshaped, precious ass. Patti was bending over, adjusting the ankle strap on her three-inch "come-fuck-me" heels. She had on a form-fitting, red leather sheath and ultra sheer hose with a seam in the back. She had done something to her hair so that curly tendrils framed her face. Her eye shadow was stark, her lipstick fuchsia like her nails. She had circular hoops in her ears ranging in size from a penny to a silver dollar, alternating between fuchsia and red. Val counted eight earrings total.

Damn, Val thought, shaking his head. *If she had a brain, she'd be deadly.*

David joined them shortly. As he looked from Val's understated elegance to Patti's flamboyant fashions, he couldn't help wondering about the choices he had made in his life. There had been decisions that had landed him where he was now, with Val, instead of in South Dallas with Patti. He knew that if he were ever given the opportunity to redo or relive his life, there was little he would change. Everything he had done and everything he had experienced had made him who he was, and he wouldn't be David had he made different choices. He had loved Patti like a lover once. He would always love her, but he was in love with Val. There was a difference.

Patti felt more than privileged at the moment. She knew girls who'd kill to be seen with two men who looked as good as Davey-Gene and Valentine. But they weren't there and she was. She had Val on her left, looking just like he stepped out of *GQ* magazine, and David on her right in a pair of well-tailored slacks of fine cotton and a shirt that fit too nice not to be expensive. When they got to wherever it was where they were going, Patti knew she'd turn heads because she had them both with her. It made her feel good, important and desirable. She was getting wet just thinking about how envious her girlfriends would be when she told them about it.

Val's car, unlike David's, was a two-seater. There was never an issue over who drove or who paid because they took turns. But when Patti saw Val's vintage 450SL, she made it clear that she would much rather be seen in it. In order to accommodate everyone, Patti sat in David's lap while Val drove. By the time they arrived at Josepha's, the place was packed. Val handed his keys over to the valet while Patti gave the young man explicit instructions to be careful with the car. It was old, but it was still a Mercedes.

WAYNE

I saw them when they came in: David, Val and some girl who was a hot number. Her dress was too short, her nails too long, her hairstyle too extreme and her earrings too abundant. She walked that thin line between slut, whore, wanton and ladylike. If it were not for Val's understated elegance and David's virile masculinity, which managed to draw some of the attention away from her hemline and that ass, I'm sure she would have been mistaken for a lady of the evening. Oh, the duplicity of our society. Alone, my two friends' companion would have been taken for a whore. With the two of them, for all the crowd knew, she could be a model or a dancer on the rise.

From my perch at the bar, I watched them sit, and I couldn't help wondering which one of them was using her as a camouflage to cover their relationship. I knew the ploy. I had done it myself, exerting my masculinity for the public.

I liked watching people. It was what I did as an actor. I chose the best bits of their habits and traits to use in my characterizations, and now, watching the three of them at their table devoid of white people, I wonder if what one of my earliest lovers, Marc, said about black people was true—there is one face that they show to white people, and one face that they show to each other. Of course, Marc wouldn't have thought of Val as black. He would have been like the Thandie Newton, Mariah Carey, Paula Abdul kind of black, where you couldn't tell just how black they were, but knew there was a drop of black blood present.

Marc was such a bigot, with antiquated ideas and tremendous pomposity. We all made mistakes. Marc was mine. He had had a pretty face, old money and solid, Hollywood connections. I had let him seduce me. And when reality hit, I couldn't stand Marc anymore. But by the time I was through with Marc, I didn't need Marc. I was established in my career.

I watched as Val absently ran his hand through his

hair. It was an unconscious gesture on his part. I had seen him do it a hundred times. But tonight, it just got to me. Did he know what he did to me? What kind of effect he had on me? He was so different from me. He was so different from all the men who had previously been in my life. My dick was getting hard watching him eat.

PATTI

I couldn't believe it. I couldn't fucking believe it. David suggested coming to this place, Josepha's, like it was Burger King. Only it wasn't like Burger King. This place was all the best places of the world wrapped up together. It was a restaurant, it was a bar, it was a club. People were eating, talking and dancing all around us. We were part of everything and apart from everything where we were sitting.

It felt good to be in this room with all these stars. Yes, I said stars. There were movie stars, real movie stars, everywhere! And these stars were talking to David and Val just like they were stars too. Oh yeah, Davey-Gene was going to get fucked this night. And fucked good. I wasn't going back to the post office when I could go to places like this every night. Hell, no!

VAL

I saw Wayne Carey after we had been seated. I pretended not to see him. In acknowledging his presence, I'd be letting myself in for just one more complication, and I had my hands full with one major complication in the form of a buxom Texan who was all sugar, spice and smiles for clicking cameras while she was alternating between feeling up David and fondling me beneath the tablecloth.

The first time her hand brushed my thigh, I disregarded it as accidental. The next time I moved my chair over a little. The third time, I looked up at her and realized it was intentional. I don't know what happened to bring about this sudden change in her demeanor, this desire of hers to play me against David, but I didn't like it. I had not flirted with her. I had not led her on in any way. And here she was, groping me under the table. There was a time when she would have been a definite maybe for me. But not now. No way. No how. I was getting an erection. Shit!

CHAPTER TWELVE

As tactfully as possible, Val removed Patti's probing hand from his groin. He had done it quickly, forcefully, tactfully, but had not been able to halt the stirring between his legs from her experienced fingers, or hide his reaction from her knowing eye as she smiled a purely feminine smile of triumph.

She had ordered French fries and drowned them in ketchup and salt. "Come on, Davey-Gene," she said, licking ketchup from her fingers, "let's dance."

"Val's a much better dancer." David tried to decline.

"I'll dance with him too. Don't worry." Patti winked at Val as she took David's hand and led him to the dance floor. Val looked after them.

"What an ass," Wayne said as he took the seat David had vacated.

"Yes, she does have a nice ass," Val said, reaching for his drink, cursing himself because he had been so wrapped up in David and Patti that he had not noticed Wayne's approach.

"I meant yours," Wayne corrected him.

"How are you doing, Wayne?"

"Much better since I've seen you."

"Wayne, please, can we have a conversation without the come-on lines?"

"Okay."

"It was that easy?"

"I'll do whatever you want."

"Are you always like this?"

"I told you I was persistent. Can I buy you a drink?"

"Yes." Val sighed. He really did like Wayne.

"Yes?"

"Yes. Buy me a drink."

"What do you want?"

"Wine.

"A glass of wine? No Scotch?"

"I prefer wine."

"How are things with you and David?" Wayne asked as he signaled the waiter.

"Never better."

"Who's the lady?"

Val wanted to turn to look over his shoulder at Patti and David, but restrained himself. "Her name is Patricia. She's an old friend of David's."

"I'd like a bottle of Beaujolais, 1961," Wayne told the waiter. "I see," he said when they were alone again. The way he said it made Val want to turn and look at the couple on the dance floor, but he refused to take the bait. The music was slow and sultry. He knew what he'd see if he looked at David and Patti. Patrick Swayze and Jennifer Grey would have nothing on them. David was so obtuse he probably didn't realize he was being seduced in a crowded room to the sounds of Jill Scott.

"She's visiting from Dallas," Val said.

"I shot a movie in Texas once. It was a western,"

Wayne said as the waiter came back to their table with the expensive vino.

"What are you working on now that your show is on hiatus?"

"Nothing." Wayne poured Val a glass of wine. "Drink up."

"Are you trying to get me drunk?"

"Can I?"

"Wayne, I'm not going to sleep with you. Nothing will make me sleep with you."

"What if he sleeps with her?"

Val laughed and said, "I know David like I know the back of my hand."

"And?"

"And if he sleeps with her, I'll sleep with you," Val wagered.

"Here they come. And, Val, his dick's hard."

The only reason Val did not kick Wayne under the table was because upon their approach, he stood and pulled out Patti's chair. Old world manners were well ingrained in him.

"I'm in your seat," Wayne said to David as he started to stand.

"It's okay," David said as he pulled a recently vacated chair over from another table. "Wayne, I'd like you to meet a good friend of mine, Patricia Bolden. Patti, this is—"

"I know who this is." Patti cut David off as she extended her hand and pumped furiously when Wayne took it. "You're Wayne Carey. I love your movies, and your TV show is fantabulous."

"It's nice meeting you, Patricia," Wayne said.

"Call me Patti."

"Patti," he obliged.

"How are you doing, Wayne?" David asked.

"My agent got me a copy of the *Cake Walk* screen-play today," Wayne responded.

"What do you think?" David asked.

"You're damn talented, David."

"So are you, Wayne." David returned the compliment.

"Can't add a part for me?"

"Not unless you can play an ordinary black man named Sam."

"Damn, David. I don't know if I can play ordinary."

They laughed. Ice broken.

"Well, while you two boys stroke each other, I'm going to dance," Patti said. "Come on, Valentine." Patti was used to men doing what she wanted them to do. She had no doubt that Val would follow her to the dance floor. She didn't take his hand as she had David's. She merely walked toward the floor confident that he would follow her. He did.

For Val, this whole thing with Wayne was getting way out of hand. If Wayne had not seen him at Heath-cliff's, he never would have approached him. Val's mere presence there had given Wayne the encouragement to try to woo him, flirt with him and try to win him from David. As he mulled over these thoughts, he was sidestepping Patti's blatant seduction attempt. With all that was going on, it was enough to drive a man crazy. Val's life was complicated enough without the two of them, Wayne and Patti, trying to fuck him.

"You're a good dancer," Patti said as she and Val danced.

"Yeah, I'm a good dancer," he responded.

She didn't mention grabbing his dick under the table, and neither did Val. But before the night was over, Miss Bolden was going to realize that Val did not intend to fall under the hypnotic spell she cast with swaying hips and wet tongue.

While Patti and Val danced, David and Wayne sat at the table alone. David felt as though he had been seeing a lot of Wayne Carey lately. Everywhere he went, Wayne was either popping up or his name was being tossed in David's direction.

"So, what are you doing while you're on hiatus?" David asked.

Wayne had been hearing that a lot lately. "Reading scripts, eating and sleeping."

"What brings you to Josepha's?"

"The chicken wings."

"Yeah, they have good chicken wings."

David and Wayne weren't doing well with the small talk. David had the impression that Wayne was a little uncomfortable. Unfortunately, he could not locate the source of Wayne's discomfort. Val was much better at small talk than David was. David sat there wishing that the song would end so he and Patti would come back to the table.

Wayne sat at the table feeling like such a shit. David was basically a nice guy, a good Joe, and there was Wayne, checking out his lover and playing flirting games when David wasn't looking. Wayne felt like he should be on the up and up and tell him where he stood, but then again, he didn't want to end up on the eleven o' clock news as a casualty. He didn't want to provoke David. He had the feeling that if David were goaded, he could do serious damage to Wayne's million-dollar smile.

I'm such a shit, Wayne thought as he turned his attention to Patti and Val on the dance floor, before David attempted to strike up more small talk.

For as long as Patti had tits and ass, she'd had

men. She knew what made them tick, what made them hard, and what made them soft. She knew them better than she knew herself. She could have kicked her own ass for not noticing what became blatantly obvious when they went back to the table.

Both David and Wayne stood up for her. She liked that, but instead of looking at Patti, Wayne Carey was looking at Val. It was the way he was looking at him that let her know. She knew "that" look. It was the look a man gave a woman when he wanted her. Wayne was giving Val that look.

Wayne Carey was a faggot, a cock-sucking faggot! Patti felt like she had been hit in the head by a brick. Wayne Carey was one of the few white boys who filled her masturbatory fantasies, and he was looking at Val like he wanted to swallow him.

Patti looked at David. He had no idea what was going on. David and Wayne had been wrapped up in a discussion about the social responsibility of celebrity role models. Some shit that David was hot about. Patti looked at Val and realized that Val knew that Wayne was after his ass. Val looked at Patti, and she realized that he knew that she knew that Wayne was after his ass.

Val saw the dawning of knowledge behind Patti's eyes and wondered how she would try to use that knowledge to her advantage. *Shit*, Val thought. Everything was complicated. The longer they stayed at Josepha's, the harder it was for Val not to resent having to take part in this charade.

CHAPTER THIRTEEN

It was 3:00 A.M. by the time the trio said their good-byes to Wayne outside of Josepha's. Wayne drove away in a black Jeep Cherokee and once again destroyed another fantasy Patti had fabricated about one of her favorite movie stars. She had been in Los Angeles less than two full days, and already she had learned that things weren't as she expected them to be. *Wayne Carey is a fucking faggot.* His gayness seemed to have no effect whatsoever on either Val or David. That concerned her. The men she was accustomed to—loud, boisterous, fun-loving men, virile, masculine and sexually competent—hated faggots. They could not stand to be in the same room with them, and the thought of one of them coming on to them would be more than they could handle. The men she knew would have flown across the table and planted a punch right in the middle of that face and damn the consequences. From the way Val was acting, it was as if he had men coming on to him all the time. What kind of man could tolerate that? For the rest of the night, she had watched Val for telltale signs of effeminacy. There were none, but she had to be sure.

On the ride home from Josepha's, David realized that this was going to be the longest week he'd ever lived. In addition to not being able to be with Val like he wanted to, he had Patti fucking with him, and he did mean fucking with him. Patti was every man's sexual fantasy, a real live *Playboy* centerfold, leaving little to the imagination about the width and breadth of her sexuality. It was a sexuality David had experienced firsthand. When he was a young man just discovering sexual pleasure, there was Patti. She was all he could handle. He had loved everything about her, but that was when he had been a young man. Now, as an adult, he found her super-sexual, baby-doll come-on unnerving. All she inspired in him was an erection. It was easy to make a man hard. What is a dick but a muscle that enjoys stimulation? It was harder keeping his attention when he was soft.

David was beginning to wish that he had not seen Patti when he was in Dallas. He was beginning to think it was better keeping her a pleasant memory than an unpleasant tangible being with dull conversation and a shapely butt that squirmed on his lap in an effort to get comfortable on the drive home. The Patticake of Davey-Gene's memories was nothing like the lap full of Patti that David had to deal with during her visit. How was he going to convince Patti that D. E. Lincoln, noted author, was not the same Davey-Gene she had grown up with? How was he going to convince her that they should not resume their sexual relationship, not because she was a woman, but because she wasn't Val?

CHAPTER FOURTEEN

Val waited until Patti was asleep before he left his room to join David in the study. They had not pre-arranged a meeting; he just knew David would be at his desk writing. He was. Dressed in a pair of sweatpants, David sat at his computer. There was a half bottle of Scotch sitting on the desk by him. Johnny Walker Red, a gift from Heathcliff. In the dim lighting, he looked sexy and desirable.

The projects were big, multi-colored buildings, surrounded by a sea of broken glass and covered in graffiti. Everybody I knew started out in the projects. But nobody stayed in the projects. Nobody stayed but Mr. Hill. I don't know if he had a first name. He had been Mr. Hill all my life. He was her uncle.

Val crossed the room and stood behind David. He massaged David's shoulders as he read what David had written. Val reached across David and poured him a drink. He wasn't going to interrupt David's writing. He just wanted to be with David without Patti. David accepted the drink gratefully, but when

Val turned to leave, David took his hand and caressed it.

"Aren't you working?" Val whispered.

"No. Not anymore," David said as he kissed Val's hand then saved what he had written and flipped off his computer. "Lock the door."

"I did."

"Good." David pulled Val onto his lap. It was easy for Val to straddle David because there were no arms on his desk chair.

"Let's put her on the plane back to Dallas."

"I could never do that." David ran his hands up Val's thighs, feeling the muscles and sinew beneath his fingers.

"You're such a wimp, David."

"Yes. That's why you love me."

"That's only part of why I love you." Val stroked David's nipples into tiny pinpoints of ecstasy. David stood, carrying Val with him to the futon.

"Not here," Val managed to say between kisses.

"Right. It's too uncomfortable." For a moment, David stood with Val in the center of the room. He was sure that later they'd laugh, remembering the picture they created, David standing, supporting Val, his long legs wrapped around David's waist.

"There's always the floor," David suggested hopefully.

"No."

"You're not making this easy."

"I know. I'm making it hard."

"Where do you want to do this?"

"In our bed."

David froze. "Come on, Val. The bedroom's too close. She'll hear us."

"No, you come on. This is *our* house. Who cares if she hears?"

"But, Val . . ."

"What are you so afraid of, David?"

"You're getting heavy." David shifted his weight so he could support Val easier.

"Don't change the subject."

"Val."

"She's annoying, infuriating and incredibly ignorant."

"She's funny, crazy and a real character."

"She has bad taste."

"She has a great ass."

"Have you been looking at her ass?"

"Haven't you?"

"Put me down."

"No."

"I'm not going to make love to you in this room, on the floor."

David chose not to mention to Val that they had made love in that room before. Actually, they had christened every room in the house. "I don't want to make love."

"What?"

"I want to fuck," David growled low in his throat. Val threw back his head and laughed. He couldn't stay mad at David. David kissed his neck then silenced his laughter with a kiss on the mouth.

"Put me down."

David put Val down. For a moment, the two of them stood looking at each other. It was obvious that they wanted each other. Unlike women, men could not hide sexual desire. It was also obvious that on this issue, where to make love, they were divided.

"David," Val began in exasperation.

"Val," David responded, equally exasperated. But Val saw through David's feigned exasperation to the real emotion, fear. It had taken David a lot longer than Val to accept their relationship, to acknowledge that what they had was more than a fling. And maybe he had only been able to do this because there was no one David had to answer to. His friends on the force had been long forgotten, like the dead skin a snake leaves behind when it grows. When David left the police force, he had left those people like wrinkled skin against a rock. Only Patti had known him before he had known himself, and Patti had not been a part of his life again until recently. So, when he was making his decision to enter into a relationship with Val, there had been no one to please but Val and himself. Now, with Patti and her approval, disapproval or acceptance of his new lifestyle hanging on this visit, it was very stressful for him and it scared him. Scared him silly. Realizing this, Val chose to give in and not push his point just yet.

"David."

"Val."

"Shit. I can't believe I'm doing this," Val said as he slipped his hands into his boxers and pulled them off. He stood before his lover, a caramel-colored Apollo, finely muscled and semierect.

"God, I want you," David said, stepping out of his sweats.

Val allowed his eyes to travel over David's body. "I can see that."

"Come here."

Val stepped toward David. "I've wanted to do this all night." He kissed David deeply. They were so hungry for each other, so eager to give each other pleasure. Val ran his hands over David's body, caressing his pecs and weighing the heaviness of his penis in his hands. David was the only man Val had ever been with, but David wasn't the only man Val had seen naked. As a man who shared locker rooms, dressing rooms and showers at the health club, he had seen other men. He had realized with chagrin that the only myth about black men that was actually true was that black men were well endowed. The myth was that it was a myth.

Val liked the feel of David's penis, the strength of it, the feeling of being filled to capacity. In the beginning, it had only been easy for him to accept David when David was being gentle. With time, he was able to accept David no matter what mood he was in, like now, when David wanted to fuck. That meant it was rough, hard, sweaty. Athletic sex.

Val lay on his back, his legs up over David's shoulders while David pumped into him. This was Val's favorite position. He could see his lover's face while they joined.

Val's dick was hard. He grasped it and stroked it in rhythm to David's thrust.

"You like that? Huh?" David asked.

"Yes," Val moaned. "God, yes."

"I like it too." David kissed him then shifted his body so that Val was on top while they made love. There were advantages to making love to an athlete. There were advantages to being physically fit and able to shift easily into different positions that heightened sexual pleasures. David had rolled onto his back without breaking their union. Placing his hands on Val's hips, he maneuvered his lover's body. Val's penis slid back and forth against the muscles of David's stomach.

"Move with me, baby. Move with me," David said.

"I'm about to come," Val replied.

"Want me to stop?" David teased.

"Hell no." A thin layer of perspiration covered their bodies. Their skin was shiny with it.

"Good, because I'm coming."

"Me too." David came deep inside Val right after Val exploded against David's chest. Much later, sated, content, they parted and went to their separate rooms.

CHAPTER FIFTEEN

It was not uncommon for David to awaken to the gentle pleasure of his lover's touch, a kiss, a caress or even gentle sucking on his toes. So, it was with mixed emotions that he awakened with his penis buried deep in a sucking mouth. It felt good, this warm, persistent sucking, but their bedroom was too close to their guest's room for his comfort. He knew that Val was annoyed with him for insisting on the "housemate only" relationship for Patti's benefit. He knew Val was trying to prove that if they could fuck in the study and get blown in the living room, then why couldn't they make early morning love in their bedroom? He pondered this as he began to come.

"Jesus, Davey-Gene. You should have warned me! You know I hate that stuff in my mouth," Patti screamed, jumping from the bed.

Goddamn it! It was too late. David was coming. He couldn't stop. The sheets, the headboard and his chest were covered with it. David sat up. He was in a daze. It was Patti. It was Patti, not Val. He had been dreaming of Val and coming for Patti. Embarrassed, he eased himself back into his sweatpants and got up from the bed. The sheets were soiled. So was he. He didn't know he could come so much. Patti was in his bathroom brushing her teeth. Was she using his toothbrush too? His head was spinning. This was too much.

"You know I don't like that stuff. It's nasty," Patti was mumbling as she brushed her teeth.

David was about to scream. This was not what he wanted to happen. He began to strip the sheets off the bed so he could hide his indiscretion from Val, who chose that moment to stick his head in the door to announce breakfast.

David didn't know if he had guilt written across his forehead or if Patti's tirade about swallowing come could be deciphered through a mouth full of toothpaste. But as David looked into a set of condemning hazel eyes, he realized that his standing there with a come-splattered sheet in his hand and a half-naked Patti in his bathroom would take a lot of explaining.

"Good morning, Val," David said.

Val looked at the sheet. "Good morning."

Thank God for all that English breeding. They were not about to get into a screaming match or even a fistfight, but things were about to get pretty tense.

Val wasn't too pleased about having to sneak around in his own house. That in itself made him very angry. But to walk in unannounced into *their* bedroom and see them, David standing there looking guilty as hell and Patti, scantily clad in a polyester camisole and tap pants, angered him beyond words. No, he did not think David was simply making the bed or she was simply brushing her teeth. Val did not know if David could so readily bed her after having had him. It was not that it was physically impossible, but morally, spiritually, it would be a slap in the face to Val if David had slept with her. Val and David had more than sex. They had a life together. Val was becoming more and more angry with David.

Patti finished brushing her teeth. "Morning, Val," she said, strutting out of the bathroom. She took the sheet from David and began to make the bed with fresh linen.

Val wanted to be alone with David. He wanted to hear David assure him that though his eyes had seen one thing, the picture they revealed was not what he thought it was. In the years since David and Val had been together, they had never been unfaithful to each other. Val wanted to make sure that was still the case. It didn't bother him that Patti was a woman. It bothered Val that Patti was not him.

Val looked at David and David looked at Val. Patti was busy making the bed and didn't see the look.

"I made breakfast. I'll be in my studio," Val said. "I'm expecting Kim. Let her in, will you." He didn't wait on David's reply. He had to get away from his eyes, those guilt-filled brown eyes.

CHAPTER SIXTEEN

Patti finished making the bed and turned to David, who was sitting on the chaise lounge by the big bay window.

"Who's Kim?" she asked.

"Look, Patti, we've got to talk," David replied, ignoring her question.

"What do you want to talk about, lover?" Patti crossed the room and stood before David.

"Patti, I've got to talk to you."

Patti eased David back on the chaise and straddled his lean hips. "Did I surprise you?"

"Yes. You surprised me."

"I was just so horny when I woke up. Oh, Davey-Gene, thank you for letting me come out here."

"Patti," David began.

"Let's make love." She reached down and grasped his penis.

"No."

"No? What's the matter?" She stroked his penis lightly. "Your motor's running just fine."

"Patti." David removed her hand from his penis. "Oh, Patti."

"What?"

"Look. We can't just pick up where we left off all those years ago. I've changed. You've changed. We are different people. You said it yourself."

"So, what are you saying, Davey? Don't I turn you on?"

"Patti, you could give a dead man a hard-on," he said gently.

"Is there another woman?" She asked the question as if, had there been another woman, it would hurt her feelings.

"No," David said honestly. "There is not another woman."

"Then what's the problem?"

This was the perfect opportunity for him to tell her about Val. Instead he said, "Patti, we haven't seen each other in nearly seven years." The fact that he took the coward's way out sickened him.

"We just saw each other in Dallas," she reminded him as she kissed his ear.

"Those were different circumstances. Patti, Patricia, Patticake. Let's just be friends, okay?"

Did he just say that? Patti thought. *Let's be friends?* Could a man and a woman have the history they had and still be just friends?

"We are friends, Davey-Gene." She was practically purring.

"Yes, we're friends. But I want us to be friends without benefits."

"What?"

"No more sex, Patti. No more sex between us unless I initiate it."

"Oh, this is a man thing, right?"

Why was it so hard for her to realize that his response to her was merely a sexual one? And sex for sex's sake was something he hadn't been able to enter into lightly since he and Val had become lovers. Sex for sex's sake was very uncool in the new millennium. He almost laughed over that, thinking that when his hormones had gotten out of control in Dallas, he hadn't been moralizing. He only seemed to moralize when he wasn't the one in control of his sperm.

"Okay, Davey."

That son-of-a-bitch, Patti's thoughts continued. *He waited until after he came before he started that no more sex shit. Just like a man. Gets his rocks off and to hell with me. Well, fuck Davey-Gene. He isn't the only fish in the sea.* And Patti knew what bait to use to hook her a whale.

"If that's the way you want it," she said to David, "then we won't have sex unless you want to." With that statement, Patti removed herself first from David's lap then his room.

David immediately started toward the dance studio so that he could talk to Val. The doorbell rang before he made it. He knew it was Kim. It suddenly dawned on him that in all the time that he and Val had lived together, Kim had rarely been to the house. He had been to Kim's condominium and had seen her at Lola's and of course Heathcliffs, but rarely had she been here. Never before had he thought it odd, until now.

He had to let her in so that she and Val could practice. But if he let her in, that meant he and Val wouldn't be able to talk. *Shit*. David opened the door and let her in.

"Hey."

"Hey."

On the drive over to Val's house, Kim had a sudden

insight. She could count the number of times she had been invited to the house. It had never seemed odd until now. She pondered on that as David led her to the dance studio. She could sense his mood and kept her small talk to a minimum.

When she opened the door to the studio, she walked in on Val, who was drenched. Barefoot, his dance shoes discarded against the wall, he kicked, jumped and exerted a lot of energy. He was in a sweating mood. His expression was thunderous, the music loud, pulsating and continuous. He acknowledged her presence with a nod but didn't stop dancing.

Kim shed her layer of outer clothing and began to warm up against the bar. She was very traditional in her choice of dance attire, pink or white tights and black leotard. She was the product of twelve years of formal ballet and tap training. She couldn't do the loud, boisterous colors of her colleagues or begin to dance immediately just because she felt like it. She had to warm up first, loosen her muscles and ease into the steps as decorum dictated. She was a fabulous dancer, but cautious in her endeavor to be the best. She could not risk leg strain, charley horses or shin splints. So, as Val exorcised the demons that plagued him, Kim began her ritual against the bar.

Meanwhile, David figured working might kill some time and take his mind off of things until he and Val could finally get down to business. He was typing at his desk when Patti entered the room. He had written well over fourteen chapters on *David's Story*, but was not near a stopping point, so he continued to write. David was used to Val checking on him while he wrote. He was used to Val massaging his shoulders and reading quietly behind him. He was used to Val pouring him a drink or handing him a sandwich then leaving him alone. He was not used to Patti. Patti had taken it into her head that if sex with her were to be initiated by David, then she would damn sure make him want to initiate it. Dressed in a bikini that was little more than strings, she chatted constantly while he typed. David couldn't decide if the concentration problem he was having was due to her incessant chatter or her scantily clad figure.

The aqua-colored material managed to cover only her nipples and a small patch over her neatly trimmed pubis. Her body was supple and flawless. Her bikini was impractical. She might as well have been naked. The effect she was having on his body made him wonder if men really did think with their dicks.

Ever since her arrival, his dick had been behaving, with no assistance from him, as if it had an identity of its own. His dick led, he followed. Sometimes it pointed toward Patti. Sometimes it pointed toward Val. When it was hard, he had no control. It was like it was his master and he was its willing follower. It had become too hard for him to concentrate on *David's Story*. He saved what he had written and turned toward Patti.

"I'm not being a very good host, am I?" he said.

"You're doing fine." She smiled.

"Usually when we have guests, Val plans an itinerary and schedules everything, you know, and I just go along with it."

"How long have you and Val been living together?"

"We were roommates in college. We've been living together ever since."

"Whose house is this?"

"I never really thought about it."

"What kind of answer is that?"

"Well, Val found the house. I was in New York promoting my book, *Down Went Jonah*. He called me and said he'd found this really neat house—no, he didn't say really neat." David did a very good imitation of Val's cultured English accent. "A great house, David. The perfect house." He laughed over that. "I told him to buy it." He shrugged. "He did."

"So, it's Val's house?" Patti said.

David never really worried about money; how much of it was Val's, how much of it was his. That's what accountants were for. He vaguely remembered Val joking that the house was an anniversary gift. So, maybe the house was his. It didn't really matter.

"It's both of ours," David said.

"It can't be both your house." Patti giggled.

"Why not?"

"Because you're not married. And that's another thing. What if you wanted to get married, what would you do then?"

"I guess it never really crossed my mind."

"A lot of things never crossed your mind. It doesn't look right, two grown men living together like ain't nothing wrong with it."

He wanted to say, "There's nothing wrong with it." Instead, he said, "It's a big house."

"So?"

She took a seat across from him. "You need to start thinking about how things look. You famous now and everything."

Appearance and how things looked were things he didn't want to discuss, so he decided not to pursue this train of conversation with her. *Coward.*

"I see you're dressed for the pool."

Just mentioning the pool excited her. The only swimming she had ever done had been in the pools found at city parks. She had always dreamed of owning a house with a pool. "Want to go swimming with me?"

What David really wanted to do was write, but his Southern upbringing by an elderly grandmother demanded that he saw to the comfort and need of his guest. Other than taking her to Six Flags, Magic Mountain and coming in her mouth, he had been a bad host. "Let me change into my trunks."

"Where's Val?"

"He's in the studio with Kim."

"There's a music studio here?"

"No, it's a dance studio. She's his dance partner."

"What are you talking about?" It had never occurred to David that Patti did not know who Val was or what he did for a living. Val and The Troupe were to modern dance what Baryshnikov was to ballet. Anybody who had a television should recognize him and usually did.

"Val is a professional dancer."

"Really?"

David looked over his shoulder at her to see if her disbelief was real. It was. "He dances for a living."

"Like the girls in the videos on BET?" Patti asked seriously.

David laughed. He was sure Val would have something to say about that comparison. "Well, he's a dancer. They are dancers. So, I guess you could say that."

While Patti waited for him, he changed into swimwear in the bathroom. His newfound prudishness was a little unbelievable to her.

"Ready?" he asked when he came out of the bathroom.

"I've been ready." Patti noted his attire with chagrin. His body was too nice for him to hide it in those cheap, twenty-dollar K-Mart cut-offs. "You know, Davey, you need somebody to pick out your clothes." She took his hand as they headed toward the large outdoor pool.

"I hate to admit it, but I've heard that before. Val usually picks out my clothes," David responded.

"Val does a lot for you."

"Val likes to shop and spend money. I like to write."

"Is that all you like to do?"

"I like to swim too." David dove into the pool. Patti refused to dive in because she did not want to mess up her hair, but she gingerly took a seat on the second step allowing the warm water to settle under her neck.

"Why is the water so warm?"

"Is it too hot?"

"No, it feels great."

"Val keeps it heated. After a workout, he usually swims a few laps. The warm water is better for his muscles."

David realized he was babbling. He knew that it was because when he and Patti weren't talking, they were fucking. He couldn't do that to her again. He couldn't do that to Val again. He couldn't do that to himself again. Fucking Patti again would be more than a physical release; it would be an emotional commitment he could not invest in. He knew now that it was not re-establishing his contact with her that was wrong, but the way in which he allowed their newly re-established relationship to develop.

When he had given her the "Let's be friends" speech, he should have been giving her the "Val and I are more than housemates" speech. He never considered himself a coward like those men who put on one face in public, going as far as to include a wife and children in their charade. He did not hide his desire behind a woman's companionship, using her femininity as a shield against prying eyes and waggling tongues. The photos taken of him at society functions were with Val, Lola, Andre, Kim, Sampson or Heathcliff. He did not hide. He had never hidden, never, until Patti showed up. It angered him. It upset him. It confused him. It made him uncomfortable. Maybe he wasn't as brave as he thought he was.

CHAPTER SEVENTEEN

"Time out," Kim called to Val as she abruptly stopped dancing.

"What do you mean, 'time out'?" Val asked.

"No more. You can kill yourself, but I'm not ready to commit suicide." She and Val had been dancing for almost two hours. Kim's auburn tresses hung in limp strands, having worked themselves free of her braid. Her leotard and tights were so wet that they were transparent. "I'm tired, tired, tired." She leaned against the mirror.

"You're tired?" Val asked as he watched Kim slide to the floor for emphasis. Val had stopped dancing too. He bent from the waist, breathing heavily.

"You're tired too," Kim said.

"I'm never tired," he answered.

"Yes, you are."

"Okay," Val relented. "I'm tired." He sat down on the floor. Kim massaged her aching feet.

"Want to talk about it?"

"Talk about what?"

"What's eating you?"

"Nothing's eating me."

"Yeah, right."

"You really know me, don't you?" Val said as he stretched out on the floor.

"Yeah, I really know you." Kim crawled over to him and, straddling him, began to massage his shoulders.

"Um," he murmured. "That feels good."

"I know."

"Bet you are going to want me to do you too."

"Most definitely." She kneaded his muscles expertly.

"I love it." Val sighed.

"Val?"

"Hum?"

"Whenever you want to talk about it, I'll listen," Kim said sincerely.

Val didn't say anything. Kim began to run her hand expertly down the sides of his ribs. Even though she was sitting on his back, most of her weight rested on her knees. She was getting a little tired in this position. As if sensing her predicament, Val said, "You're not heavy. Sit on me if you want." She did.

"Kim."

"Yes, Val?"

"I lied. You're heavy. Get up."

"I am not heavy," she said, popping him upside his head playfully.

"You're huge. You must be putting on weight."

"You ass." She popped him again.

"You better lay off the ice cream sundaes." She was about to pop him again when he caught her off guard. He turned his body quickly and shifted his weight so that he was on top of her. "Say uncle."

"No." She giggled. "Not until you tell me I'm not fat."

He began to tickle her.

"Damn it, Val. Stop," she squealed through gales of laughter.

"Not until you apologize for popping me."

"I won't apologize until you say I'm not fat."

"Okay. You're not fat. You're corpulent."

"Stop it, Val!"

He was still tickling her.

"You're going to make me pee my pants."

"I've never seen a fat lady take a piss."

"Valentine, you son-of-a-bitch." She was laughing so hard tears were streaming down her face.

"Say it."

"Okay. Okay. I'm fat," Kim said in surrender.

"I told you so." Val stopped tickling her.

"Get up. I've got to pee."

Val rolled off her. She jumped up and ran to the bathroom.

"You're not fat, Kim," he called after her. He expected a smart retort. When there was none, he assumed she didn't hear him and grabbed himself a bottle of orange juice from the miniature refrigerator that was stocked for such occasions.

"Val?" Kim's voice was hesitant and somewhat embarrassed.

"What?"

"Bring me my dance bag, will you?"

"You're not fat, Kim," he said again as he handed her the bag through the door.

"I know I'm not fat."

"Are you okay in there? You didn't fall in, did you?"

"No. You made me pee my pants."

Val laughed so hard that tears started to run down

his face. God, he loved Kim. She was one of his best friends. When he heard the shower start, he decided he'd better do something to appease her. If he didn't appease her, she was going to retaliate for his making her wet her pants. He decided the best defense was to attack her weaknesses, so by the time she came out of the bathroom, he had gathered his defenses. Laid out on the table in the breakfast nook was an assortment of chocolate delights: Godiva chocolates, a pint of chocolate chocolate chip Häagen-Dazs ice cream, double chocolate chip macadamia nut cookies that he had brought from Lola's, and a frozen white chocolate almond cheesecake from the Cheesecake Factory that he kept in the freezer for special occasions.

By the time he had arranged everything, Kim was finished with her shower. She had even washed her hair. It fell in damp ringlets around her shoulders. Her dance attire had been replaced by a light cotton sundress. She was barefoot and her skin virtually glowed with radiance. Her eyes were blazing fire, her nipples hard. She was ready for battle. He smiled at her and indicated the table before she could fly into him. She looked at the table, then at him.

"Oh, Val. Dirty pool. I can't eat all this, but I'll damn well try," she said as she got a fork and dove into the white chocolate cheesecake.

Val watched Kim while she ate. She had often said going on a chocolate binge was better than having sex. He always laughed at that until he had the opportunity to observe her as he was doing now. She got a glazed look in her eyes that indicated she was experiencing great pleasure. Sounds of delight, as she discovered a half-hidden chocolate morsel beneath a more obvious chocolate treat, emanated from her mouth as she ate a cookie then licked her fingers. He was pretty sure that the seductive manipulation of her lips and mouth as they surrounded a chocolate éclair were not aimed at him, but merely expressions of her delight.

In the beginning, Val and Kim had a warm relationship based on respect for each other's talents. Eventually, it became the deep friendship that they now shared. He knew that at one time she had harbored the silly schoolgirl crush that students get for teachers. But since she dated, he assumed she had gotten over it.

Smiling at her as she indulged in her sinful pleasure, he took a seat opposite her.

"What are you smiling at?" Kim asked through a mouthful of ice cream.

"You." There was a smudge of chocolate on her cheek.

"Why?" She licked her fingers.

"You're precious." Val leaned over to kiss her on the nose like a brother would a sister, but as fate would have it, she moved her head. Their lips touched then parted. Soon, they were kissing as if kissing was something they always did.

It could have ended there, but it didn't. Giving in to the kiss, Kim got up from the table and straddled Val's lap. She managed to do this without breaking their connection. It had been a long time since Val had kissed a woman when it wasn't a part of a routine or performance, a long time since he had kissed anyone other than David. Although his mind kept telling him "No," his body told him "Yes." His reaction was purely physical. He grew hard as her nipples pressed into his bare chest. Her long legs wrapped themselves around his waist and the chair. He ran his hands up her supple thighs, beneath the thin cotton of her sundress, all the while not breaking the kiss, the wonderful, sweet kiss. When his hand touched the delicate lace of her thong, he had a reality check. This was Kim. This was Kim! Although he was going through the motions because it felt good, he could not do it to her. So, gently, oh so gently, he stopped the kiss. Gently, oh so gently, he slid the sundress back down her thighs. She looked at him in a daze, her mouth parted in a little "oh" of surprise.

"What's wrong?"

"Kim, sweet Kim."

Gently, oh so gently, he eased the movement of her most delicate parts against his hard parts and took her hands in his.

"You are a beautiful girl." He kissed her hands.

"Are you rejecting me, Val?" She tried to make a joke out of it. He wasn't laughing.

"If things were different . . ." He picked her up and sat her on the table in the only spot where there was no chocolate.

"If things were different what?"

Gently, oh so gently, he said, "I have someone, Kim."

When she heard the words, Kim felt as if the wind had been sucked from her lungs. She never expected him to lie to her. There was no way he could have someone and she not know it. They spent too much time together for her not to know. The lie hurt more than the rejection.

"I didn't expect you to lie to me, Val."

She got off the table and was about to leave the room when he stopped her with a hand on her arm.

"Kim," he began, wishing he had started this a different way. Of all people, maybe he should have told her about him and David. "I would never lie to you. Never."

It was just beginning to dawn on him that she liked him more than he realized. Kim stopped mid-stride and turned to look deeply into his hazel eyes. She had never known him to lie. He was telling the truth. Her mind raced, trying to see how there could be someone and she didn't know. Had she been so obtuse that she missed all the telltale signs? It was at that moment that David came in from the pool. Kim looked from Val to David and from David to Val. Her thoughts were doing laps in her head. She was just making a connection that she didn't want to when Patti entered from the pool. Seeing this new girl . . . there really was a girl she didn't know about! Kim's mind went into overdrive. He had been telling the truth. And despite herself, she loved him more. So many men would have taken advantage of her, open, willing and wet. He was a gentleman. Val was a gentleman and Kim was a lady. So, Kim smoothed her dress and gathered her composure.

Well, Patti thought, knowing they had walked in on something.

Well, David thought, wondering what the hell they had walked into.

Well, Val thought, *I too have crossed the line into lies and duplicity*, because he knew without a word being said that Kim thought Patti was Val's mystery girl. *Damn it.*

CHAPTER EIGHTEEN

This was the first time Kim had seen Patti, and the first time Patti had seen Kim. The two eyed each other, sizing each other up the way women do. The men watched the interaction, totally unaware that anything other than an introduction was going on. They were unaware of the subtle intricacies of probing that women did in order to determine if they were or were not going to be a threat to each other.

Patti quickly put Kim in the category of women that she didn't find "black enough." Her hair was too good. Her features were too thin and straight. But her ass, that ass said "nigger," natural nigger. She looked like she had just been fucked and fucked real good. What the hell had they missed while they had been out at the pool? Kim's face was flushed. Through the thin cotton of Kim's sundress, Patti noticed that her nipples were still hard. She had a good body, a little skinny, but firm. She could have gotten away with a much tighter, shorter skirt. She was barefoot. Val had on a pair of blue jeans. They were so old and ragged, his knees had worn through and half his ass was hanging out. Patti never could understand rich people. Here Val sat with all that money and walked around in raggedy pants. It was just like David driving that old-ass car. It didn't make any sense.

"Hi." Kim eventually spoke. She had to get out of there.

"Hello," Patti said.

"Patricia Bolden, Patti, I'd like you to meet Kimberly Dubois, Kim," Val said, his hosting skills kicking in late.

"It looks like you two are coming down off a marijuana high and have a serious case of the munchies," Patti said, indicating the chocolate-laden table.

"Oh, no. It's nothing like that," Kim was quick to reassure her. She was on her best behavior. She had to be. She had just been all over Val while his woman was in the pool. She wasn't that girl. She didn't do things like that! *How could I not know?*

"I mean, all this chocolate," Patti said, selecting a Godiva morsel and popping it into her mouth. "This is good." She got another piece.

"Isn't it?" Kim chimed in. To her credit, she acted as if nothing had just happened. *How could I not know about this woman?*

"What's this?" Patti asked, examining a cookie.

"Chocolate macadamia nut cookies," Kim informed her.

"My God," Patti said, taking a bite as she sat down at the table. "This is great."

"Try this," Kim said, spooning up a bite-sized serving of the white chocolate almond cheesecake. Patti eyed it skeptically then swallowed it. Her eyes rolled into the back of her head and she sighed with contentment.

"Isn't it great?" Kim smiled nervously. She was hiding her discomfort so well. Her acting teacher would be proud of her.

"Yes," Patti answered.

The men watched as the two women began to devour the chocolate. David looked at Val. "I don't think they need us, do you?" he said.

"It doesn't look like it," Val replied.

"I'm going to change clothes."

"Yeah, me too." Val started to walk off then stopped to look at Kim. "You going to be all right?"

"Sure." Kim laughed nervously.

"What do you think I'm going to do to her?" Patti called after them as she dove into the ice cream.

"Nothing," Val said quickly. Too quickly. "Nothing."

With that, the two men left the room. Kim looked to Patti, who was enjoying the chocolate feast, and did the only thing she could do. She sat and joined in. If there was one thing Kim was, she was a lady. So, the two women had found a common bond in the sharing of chocolate confections. The men were temporarily forgotten.

CHAPTER NINETEEN

"What do you mean, you kissed her?"
"What don't you understand?"

The two men stood whispering in their bedroom. The women were downstairs and out of earshot.

"How did you accidentally kiss Kim?"

Again Val explained what happened. When he was through, David took a deep breath then let it out. He knew that Val thought he had been unfaithful, but all Val had been was Val. He had stopped it before it went any further. That's what a real man would do. Val was a real man.

"It's okay, Val. It's okay."

And it was. How could he fault Val for accidentally kissing a beautiful girl when he had committed adultery? Val's indiscretion, a sharing of intimacy between friends, was in no way as heinous as David's act, his crime. The only person to be hurt was Kim. Val would have to fix that later. But David's act was a crime. David was the hypocrite with the dirty little secret. He looked at Val, his Val, his love, his lover, and all he wanted was to forget everything. He wanted to forget Patti because their joining had been such a mistake, a very big mistake. He wanted to forget Kim. Beautiful, naïve Kim, who was so much in love with Val that David ached for her. He wanted to just start over. But this wasn't a novel in which he could delete a whole paragraph or page or chapter if it didn't fit. This was his life. There was no backspace. You only get once change to live it.

I want to finish David's Story, David thought; *I need to purge my soul.* Val looked so forlorn that David's heart hurt. He reached for his lover and hugged him tightly.

"I want you so bad I can taste you," David spoke, thinking that sex would make everything better.

"I want you too," Val said.

"What are we going to do?"

David tried to steer Val toward the bed, but Val resisted. He knew that sex wouldn't make it better. Sex was a Band-Aid. They needed a tourniquet.

"I'm tired of this game, David. People are getting hurt."

"You can fix it with Kim."

"It's not about Kim. It is about us. We are grown men. This is our house."

"Can we not fight right now?" David could see where this was getting ready to go, and he was trying to cut it off before it got started.

"It depends."

"On what?"

"What you've been doing." They were still standing in the middle of the bedroom. Now they were facing each other. Throughout the entire conversation, they stood no more than two feet apart. The women were an entire floor away, and they still whispered, afraid to be heard.

"What do you mean, what have *I* been doing?" David heard his own voice. He heard the defensiveness and tried to neutralize his tone. In less than a minute, he had gone from comforting Val to being defensive about his own indiscretion.

"Have you fucked her?" There, Val said it. The questions he had been thinking was finally out in the open.

"Of course I've fucked her," David answered.

"You son-of-a-bitch." Val said the words slowly, succinctly and with emphasis. He turned on his heels and started from the room. If he stayed, he would have punched David.

David caught him at the door. He pinned Val with his body. Val was not a small man. He was lean, finely muscled and in good physical shape. It would not be easy to pin him unless he wanted to be pinned or unless you were a man like David who was three and a half inches taller and almost thirty pounds heavier.

"She's my ex-girlfriend—of course I've fucked her. Hey. Hey," David breathed in Val's ear. He had Val pressed against the bedroom door.

In all honesty, Val wasn't putting up much of a fight.

Slowly, David began stroking Val's shoulders and flanks, trying to calm his anger. "Listen to me, Val. I said I *fucked* her . . . past tense. What Patti and I *had* isn't what you and I *have*."

"It's the way you look at each other. The way you act together. It's driving me crazy," Val confessed.

"You're jealous," David teased, throwing up a smoke-screen.

"I'm not jealous."

"You're jealous."

"I'm not."

"Okay." David kissed Val on the neck. "Whatever you say, baby."

He slapped Val's flank and let him go. He had to. If he kept holding him, they would be naked in minutes, using sex as a distraction. Sex was where they still connected, and they had neither the luxury of time nor privacy.

Meanwhile, Patti and Kim continued devouring the chocolates, none the wiser of the goings on of the men. They had their own thing going on. Kim was checking out Patti and Patti was checking out Kim. Patti had sized her up in seconds; she had Kim's number. The girl had it bad for Val. It was so obvious that you'd have to be blind to miss it.

Kim thought Patti was a shark. Patti wasn't the kind of girl she would ever have picked for Val. She had an overblown sensuality that attracted men and intimidated women. Kim could see that. Maybe the old adage, opposites attract, was true in this case.

Patti was not the kind of girl men had platonic relationships with. So they were having sex. Kim wasn't as naïve as some people believed or as unsophisticated as others hoped. Val had never hidden his and David's relationship from Kim, however, he had never shown her into his bedroom either, so she had always had her suspicions. In Kim's opinion, both Val and David were too virile, too sexual and too sensual not to be sexually active. She knew they were not leading chaste, celibate lifestyles. She had often wondered if, in times of sexual need and desire, had they turned to each other? But she didn't know for sure. And despite her suspicions, she had nurtured a silly, silly crush that was evolving into full-fledged infatuation. If she had any pride at all, she'd leave and get on with her life. But she had spent too much time lusting after Val to give up just because his little bed partner was visiting. Kim decided to wait her out. When he was done with Patti, he would come to her. She knew it. So, she decided to befriend the enemy. It was the only way she could keep an eye on her.

By the time David and Val rejoined the women, Patti and Kim were chatting like old friends. They had cleaned up the aftermath of their chocolate devastation and were talking in hushed whispers. When the men entered the kitchen, the women looked at them, giggled like teenagers, and abruptly stopped talking. David looked at Val. Val looked at David.

"What's going on?" David asked.

"Wouldn't you like to know?" Patti laughed. He smiled at that. When she laughed, it made her look younger. It made her look like the Patticake he had grown up with instead of the Patti he had become reacquainted with. He liked the Patticake of his young adulthood memories. Patti was too much of a strain on his continence. Patti kept him in a constant state of arousal and clouded his judgment.

CHAPTER TWENTY

Later that evening, it was with mixed emotions that David saw his houseguest and his lover to the front door. On one hand, he was happy that Val was making an effort to get to know Patti and see in her what he had always seen. On the other hand, he was afraid that without his supervision, Patti might let something slip about the times David had allowed himself to think with his penis instead of his head. David knew that he hadn't been exactly honest with Val. He had hidden behind semantics when answering Val's query about the extent of his new involvement with Patti. He felt uncomfortable about that. He was a master of language. His skill with words could be classified as a lethal weapon, like the hands of a boxer. He had maneuvered around Val's direct inquiry, sidestepping the jabs and punches of emotion like a young Muhammad Ali. He had used his talent to land a ghost punch. It was in David's nature to protect what was his, so he had gone against the grain and hit below the belt with a lie.

Val, too, was having mixed emotions. He wasn't an actor. He was a dancer. He didn't know how long he could play this without a slip of the tongue. It was just too damn hard. The truth would set them all free. When he had walked Kim to her car, promising to call her so that they could talk, he wanted nothing more than to just spend the evening with her, repairing the damage of their earlier kiss. But that wasn't going to happen. Not this night. Kim kissed his cheek, got into her convertible BMW and drove away. Val felt sad. He wanted to simply end the charade that was growing by the minute.

"What time should I expect you back?" David asked as they stood in the doorway.

"I figured we'd get something to eat after the game, so we'll be late."

"I can't believe I'm going to a Lakers game," Patti said.

"Not *a* Lakers game, *the* Lakers game," David corrected. "The Lakers are playing the Bulls."

Patti still couldn't believe David had given her his ticket. She knew how much he liked basketball. At least that hadn't changed. But he was on some deadline or other and she didn't want to miss the game just because he couldn't go. She didn't mind going with Val at all. Not at all!

"I hope you guys enjoy yourselves," David said.

"It's the Lakers and the Bulls," Patti quipped. "Of course we will."

She was so excited she was about to wet her pants. She was going to be sitting mid-court with people like John Singleton and Jack Nicholson. She wanted David to go so that she could be seen on his arm, but if he didn't go, she'd still be there.

David eased them closer to the door so that he could get back to his writing. They took the hint and left him to his work. Once they were gone, David padded up the stairs to his study. Being alone would give him the perfect opportunity to purge his demons with a written confession. He was well into *David's Story*. The more he wrote, the more convinced he became that *David's Story* was going to be a feather in his cap. When he was writing, he even allowed himself to fantasize about the Pulitzer. He knew that if anything he had ever written would be considered, it would be this story. It was that big.

As she and Val sat making small talk in the pre-game traffic on their way to the Staples Center, Patti thought about how things were working with her and David. It wasn't exactly going as planned, but she was on her way to a Lakers game. She couldn't do that in Dallas, Texas.

Hollywood was a city of beautiful people, broken dreams and powerful cliques. At any given time, at any given function, there could be some of the most beautiful, most powerful people in the world. Here is where the super chic and super rich came to play. Anybody who was anybody could be seen at a Lakers game. Patti was so busy looking at everybody, she didn't realize she had tripped until Val caught her.

"Hey, are you okay?" Val asked Patti.

"Sure. Sure. Look, Val, there's Denzel Washington!" Patti exclaimed.

"Yeah. That's him all right." Her enthusiasm was refreshing and her excitement endearing. She hadn't been in Hollywood long enough to be cynical of the glitz and glitter. "Come on. Our seats are over there," Val said. As unobtrusively as possible, he took her arm and began to lead her toward their seats.

Everybody knew Val. No one knew Patti. Tongues wagged and speculation arose as to her identity. A few people even wondered as to David's whereabouts. He and Val were such a constant at Lakers games, his absence was noticeable.

CHAPTER TWENTY-ONE

The chapter he was writing was so personal that David had to stop in the middle of it and catch his breath. He knew that the characters he had created were just that, characters. They were not real, consisting of flesh and blood, but their traits, their personalities, their experiences were derived from the reality that was his and Val's life.

If there was one thing that police officers universally abhorred, it was a call to respond to an incident of domestic violence. Micah was no different. He would rather work traffic duty than show up at someone's house trying to split up a fight. People were unpredictable, true, but throw in the dynamics of family and home territory, and there was no telling what you'd get. There had been numerous incidents of family members who had called the police in the first place then ended up turning on the police officers who had come to rescue them.

When this particular call had come, Rick, Micah's partner, swore under his breath and Micah sighed. It was 5:39 P.M. and his shift was over at 6:00 P.M.

"Maybe we can pretend we didn't hear it," Rick said.

"Want me to drive?" Micah asked. Rick had been driving all day.

"Naw. I'll drive." Rick and his wife, Maria, were expecting their first child. Rick was moonlighting as a security guard five hours a night to come up with some extra money. Nevertheless, he insisted on splitting the driving and sharing the load.

"Okay." Micah stretched out his long frame as much as possible in the cramped quarters of the patrol car. *"Well, step on it, will you?"*

"All right, already." It had been only when the announcement came over the radio that the domestic dispute was at the residence of one Sean Michael Calloway that both officers let out a sigh of relief.

Sean Michael Calloway and his family of eccentrics were almost like the station mascots. Domestic violence usually meant that Sean Michael, the seventy-three-year-old patriarch of a fourteen-person clan, had probably gotten drunk again and was hanging from the bedroom window of their two-story house, shooting at his daughter's cats with a B.B. gun. Sean Michael hated cats. His middle child, April, had nineteen of the hairy buggers at last count. His oldest daughter, June, had called the animal shelter to pick up the little devils, but May, his tenth child, got tired of seeing April pout and mope about it, and bailed them out of kitty prison.

The first time Micah and Rick had ever responded to a call at the Sean Michael Calloway residence, Gomez, the ten-year-old, had baked cookies for them while they broke up a fight between Hoss and Shivago. The Calloway household was good for at least two calls a week, a dozen cookies and a lot of laughs. Micah and Rick couldn't wait until they got there.

At one time, the Calloway house had been a church.

There were still stained glass windows downstairs and several pews in what was now the living room. When Micah and Rick arrived at 1114 Mockingbird, the Calloway house was in an uproar. It did appear that Sean Michael was upset. It seemed that not one, but four of the nineteen cats had given birth within thirty minutes of each other. So now, instead of nineteen cats, there were nineteen cats and thirty-five kittens. That made a total of fifty-four furry felines. Angered beyond endurance, Mr. Calloway had begun killing cats. Six were disposed of with his trusty antique six-shooter. He dropped four out of the second story window. They made broken, bloody spots upon impact. By the time he turned to dispose of the remaining cats, his daughter, April, had turned on him with a butcher knife. She only meant to stop him, to show him the error of his ways. Enraged, he took her by the throat, and in a drunken stupor, snapped her neck like it was nothing more than brittle spaghetti. Whether it was the sound of her neck popping or the meowing cats, no one would know what pushed him over the edge. All they knew is that funny Sean Michael Calloway had barricaded himself into his second story bedroom with the body of his seventeen-year-old daughter, April.

David broke into a sweat as he created the scene that would make his character, Micah, stop being a cop. As he reread it, he saw the underlying macabre humor in the imaginary world of the Calloways. In actuality, when David was shot, there was nothing funny about it. There was no bloody battlefield littered with the bodies of slaughtered cats. In reality, Timothy Joseph McMahon, father of twelve, six boys and six girls with two sets of twins, had not snapped in one day like the imaginary Sean Michael Calloway. It had taken the real life character of Timothy Joseph

McMahon exactly four months, twelve days, eighteen hours and approximately ten minutes to sexually molest, physically abuse and slowly starve to death ten of his twelve children and then feast on their corpses. The reality of the McMahon case, which fascinated and repelled America, is what changed David's life forever.

He remembered that day as if it were yesterday. For three months after breaking the case, David dreamed, and in essence, relived walking into a cramped studio apartment with his partner, Larry, to discover piles of bones picked clean of sinew, tissue and flesh. Two gaunt children with eyes as big as saucers were chained to the radiator. They were too thin, too weak, too mortified by the horrors their young eyes had seen to move, let alone issue a warning to David as he bent to unchain them.

"What the hell—?" had been the only words Larry was able to utter before his head exploded from the impact of three bullets fired in rapid succession. It happened so fast. One minute David was kneeling to unchain the children, and the next he was falling against the wall with particles of his partner's gray matter on his clothing. He screamed and got off one shot before Timothy Joseph McMahon shot him twice and fled. David looked down at himself, covered in pieces of flesh from Larry's exploded head and oozing blood from a wound in his upper shoulder, and got dizzy. He looked at the two children, who had not moved, blinked or yelled, and he looked again at himself. He would not, could not, die in that cramped efficiency apartment with those children's eyes on him.

Later, he was told that he had crawled out to the street, radioed for help and called Val to tell him he would be late for dinner. He didn't remember that. What he remembered was waking in a hospital room filled with flowers and cops. Val was noticeably absent. As David looked up from his hospital bed, his policeman buddies informed him that Timothy Joseph McMahon had died not a block from his crime from loss of blood from the wound that David had inflicted.

David paused in his writing as he planned what he was going to say. Sometimes reality was too intense for fiction. David indulged in poetic license to make it more palatable for human consumption.

Micah and Rick arrived at the Calloway house as they always did. Were it not for the bloody cat carcasses and the screaming Calloway clan, they would not have known that this time would be any different from the others. No sooner than Micah stepped from the car was he thrown back against the open door with the force of a bullet that caught him beneath his breastbone, only centimeters away from his heart.

When Micah awakened, he was in the intensive care ward of Mercy General. His room was filled with flowers and cops. Rick was waving a copy of the daily paper at him with the recap of the Calloway story. Micah wasn't interested in any of that. All he was interested in was Aaron. As he looked up from his hospital bed into Aaron's expressive dark eyes, it was as if the rest of the world ceased to exist.

"Hi," Aaron spoke.

"Hi," he heard Micah reply. Micah's voice cracked from nonuse.

"Don't you ever, ever scare me like that again," Aaron stressed.

"Trust me. I didn't try to scare you."

"Well, you did."

"I'm sorry."

"God, if I had lost you . . ." Micah reached for Aaron's hands and squeezed.

"But you didn't."

"No, I didn't." Then Aaron leaned over close enough to kiss Micah. Micah held his breath, looking at Aaron. He had never felt this way before, especially about Aaron.

"Wait until I get you home," Aaron whispered. And surprising himself, Micah realized he couldn't wait to get home.

Yes, David thought as he typed, this was going to be big.

Two weeks later, after Micah had been released from the hospital, he found himself in an interesting situation. They were in Micah's room. He didn't know how they had gotten there. He wasn't conscious of having led or having followed Aaron. He was aware that the window was cracked to allow in a breeze. There was a whisper of cool air across his skin. The calico curtains, a house-warming gift from Aaron's mother, moved slightly against the breeze. Each time they parted, a sliver of moonlight peeked into the darkened room. But it wasn't really that dark. He could see Aaron's body, hard, firm, smooth, aroused. They were nearly the same height. Not even an inch separated the tops of their heads when they stood side by side or facing each other, like now. Micah liked that. As a tall man, Micah had spent a great deal of his time looking down at his conquest. To be standing face-to-face and eye-to-eye put them on equal standing. No cat and mouse games, no conqueror and conquered. Equals.

Somebody had to make the first move. Somebody had to

*claim responsibility for altering the course of their lives.
And it would be altered. Even if this, the first time, were the
only time, their lives would be different because they would
have reached out and grabbed hold of temptation. And in
embracing desire once, even once, denying it in the future
would be too much of a burden to bear. Self-denial, absti-
nence, restraint would be like self-inflicted tortures instead
of character builders.*

"What's the matter?" Aaron asked.

"Nothing," Micah responded.

"Are we going to do this or what?"

"Do you want to do this?" Micah asked. There was a
croak in his throat.

"Yes," was Aaron's reply. With hands trembling, with
anxiety and passion, Aaron reached out and touched Micah.
Micah was hard, elongated, throbbing and ready for Aaron's
touch.

"It feels funny," Aaron mused.

"How?"

"It's like touching myself." The words came from Aaron's
mouth with wonder. Of course Aaron had touched a penis
before. There was no question of that. But to touch another
penis this intimately, to examine it for length, texture and
width was, until that moment, beyond Aaron's grasp.

"Not so hard." Micah placed a hand over Aaron's to
guide the pressure and strokes.

"Sorry." Aaron smiled. Micah loved Aaron's smile, the
quirkiness of it, the spontaneity, the way it touched Aaron's
eyes. "How should I do it?"

"Do it the way you like it done." It was so simple saying
it like that. Quid pro quo. "If you keep doing it, I won't be
able to stand it."

"I like doing this to you. I like the way you feel."

Micah reached out and touched Aaron's face. It was a
soft touch. A gentle caress. Then, dark eyes gazing into darker

ones, Micah kissed Aaron. At first there was the slightest bit of resistance.

"Hey," Micah crooned. "Hey," he coaxed. "Let me, baby. Open your mouth." And Aaron relented. Aaron relented because he liked it. He liked it because it was Micah. There had been no other man but Micah. There would be no other man but Micah. Micah was his alpha and omega, and he had almost lost him.

Again, David paused in his writing. He had written sexual scenes before. His writing was often described as provocative, erotic, and titillating. It was not difficult for him to paint a picture of a love act that was so finely choreographed it looked as if the participants were two parts of a whole. The beast with two backs. He did this effortlessly, though he had never written about two men. He had no problem with his characters in bed. That was easy. Sexuality could be written in universal terms, even if the characters were men. *His* problem came when he tried to make the transition from the bedroom to the conversation his characters were going to have about why Micah had to stop being a cop. The imaginary conversation they would have would be nothing like the stark reality that faced David upon his awakening in the hospital.

David woke in a hospital room of flowers, fellow policemen and copies of the newspaper highlighting his heroics. Val had been noticeably absent. For nine days, David lay in his room expecting Val to walk in any minute. When there was still no Val on the thirteenth day, the day he was to be discharged, David had given up. He took the customary ride in the wheelchair from his room to the discharge desk, to the front door, and lastly to the awaiting taxi that would take him home.

The first thing he saw upon exiting the hospital was Val, standing with an armful of flowers and a bouquet of helium-filled balloons. At first David was so happy to see Val that he wanted to shout with joy. Then he became angry. It had been thirteen days, thirteen goddamn days. Thirteen days with no word from Val. And now he stood grinning like a fool, trying to get David's attention. David wasn't having it. He ignored Val and went to his taxi. Val intercepted him, paid the cab driver and sent him on his way. Silently, David ignored Val's peace offerings and got into Val's convertible. Val accepted David's silence and tied the balloons to the door handle, placed the flowers in the back seat, then took his seat next to David. They rode in silence until they got home. Once there, David got out of the car and raced up to the front door. Val followed silently behind him.

Once inside, David absolutely refused to be in Val's presence and went straight to his room. He had lain in that hospital room for thirteen days without a word from Val. If he stayed in his presence, they were going to fight. He did not want to fight. He was too tired. He lay down on his bed, and within minutes, fell off to sleep. He would deal with Val when he woke up.

A few hours later, David woke up to the feeling that he was being watched. He was. Val sat in a rocker by his bed. David looked up at Val. For a moment their eyes met; angry dark eyes and sad hazel ones.

"Thirteen days, Val. Thirteen goddamn days," David hissed, not able to contain himself. Val said nothing. "I did not see you for thirteen fucking days."

Val got up from the chair and climbed into bed with David. David didn't move. "Not a word. Not a sound. I thought something had happened to you."

Val reached for David. At first David resisted, then he allowed himself to be pulled into Val's embrace because there was nothing sexual in it. It was simply the embrace of one friend for another. Ever since the eventful day when they had acknowledged their shared sexual attraction, they had both put a reign on their hormones and walked around each other gingerly. It hadn't been an easy task to acknowledge that with virtually no provocation they could easily begin making love.

"Thirteen days," David stressed again.

"I know," Val said.

"Why?"

"You know."

"I don't know." Their bodies fit so well together. Back to chest, groin to butt, thigh to thigh, like two interlocking puzzle pieces.

"Yes, you do." Absently, Val began stroking David's back, calming him, quieting him as he would a skittish colt.

"No, I don't, you son-of-a-bitch."

"Are you calling my mother a dog?"

David laughed, which was what Val wanted. When David realized this, he elbowed Val in the chest. "Don't try to make me laugh."

"Okay."

David could feel Val's breath on his ear and he liked it. Despite himself, he liked it. In the thirteen days that he had lain in the hospital, he'd done a lot of thinking. He had made his decision early in life to be a policeman. As a child, policemen appeared to be larger than life, giants, all powerful and omnipotent in their strength. He was fortunate in that the policemen he had encountered as a child had not been the purveyors of atrocities and corruption that he later worked with.

When David became a policeman, he became privy to a world filled with an ugliness he had never imagined, both on and off the force. Usually he could deal with it. The brutality, the racism and the corruption angered him, but it didn't jade him. He was a part of it but apart from it. He felt he could remain clean. He felt he could make a difference. But the Timothy Joseph McMahon incident had been more than he was willing to handle. Just having been in the room where it happened made him feel dirty. Not only had Timothy Joseph McMahon physically abused his children, he had sexually abused them. Not only had he starved them, he had eaten them. Each atrocity was more heinous than the last. It was horrendous. It was sickening. It was more than anyone should have been forced to endure. That the victims were children upset David beyond tolerance. The fact that he nearly lost his life in protecting theirs was also sobering.

For thirteen days, he wondered how what he had seen would influence his life. He hadn't been able to sleep without seeing that filthy, cramped, little room. He hadn't been able to think without wondering to what extent the two surviving children would be damaged both physically and mentally. Sometimes, he thought he would go crazy. But, of course, he did not. He chose another way to exorcise his demons.

On the additional paper provided to recap his statement for the record, he had written what happened. As he wrote, the dawning of an idea was born. When David was a child and read stories he didn't like, he recreated in his mind the ending the way he wished it had happened. If he could rewrite the scene in the McMahon house, he could get over it. The idea sounded simplistic, but as he started writing, stories began to form. They made him feel better.

He wished he were able to discuss his new calling with Val, but Val wasn't available. For thirteen days, Val treated him with silence. David hadn't realized just how much he had come to depend on his talks with Val to cleanse his system of the poison he encountered on his job. Without Val to talk to, he resorted to writing.

David's pen became his voice and his paper his audience. The thirteen days passed rapidly. He felt better. He became stronger. His self-induced therapy worked. As he had re-read what he had created, he toyed with the idea of sending his stories to a publisher. All this happened without Val to share his decision.

"I couldn't come see you in the hospital, David," Val confessed.

"Why?" Davis asked.

"Because I think I've fallen in love with you."

David thought about how he and Val had been together since their freshman year in college. When Val made this confession, they had been in their apartment almost a year. In actuality, they had been together longer than some people stayed married. "Because I love you," Val continued, "the thought of seeing you lying in a hospital bed with tubes in your nose and holes in your body was more than I could handle."

David listened quietly. He knew that he and Val had been more than friends for some time. He and

Val were as close as two people could be. At that point in their lives, they had done everything but commit the physical act of lovers. Thirteen days was a lot of time to think, and in that time, David realized that his feelings for Val were stronger than he wanted to admit. Sometimes just thinking about Val would give him such a hard-on that he'd have to touch himself to relieve the tension. He had these feelings ever since their infamous shower scene. And now, he lay in his bed as one would with a lover, hearing lover's words.

"I didn't have tubes in my nose," David said.

"Did you hear what I said? The thought of seeing you in that hospital bed was too much for me because I love your black ass."

"Yes, my ass is black." They laughed at that. Then Val turned David toward him. David turned willingly.

Soon they began acting like lovers in earnest. David gave his resignation, and with Val looking over his shoulder, he committed to paper *The Case of the Crazy Maniac,* his first book in *The Drake Chronicles.* In his story, no children died. So had been born David the author, and so had died David the cop.

David flipped off his computer. The story of Micah and Aaron would have to wait until after he got something to eat. He had been writing non-stop for several hours. Since he had not participated in the chocolate feast, he was famished. Yawning and stretching, he walked downstairs to the kitchen.

CHAPTER TWENTY-TWO

Wayne Carey hadn't jerked off in a while because he hadn't had the desire. Then it hit him out of the blue like a ton of bricks. He was so horny it was almost painful. So, while Heathcliff and Sampson watched an old movie, Lola and Andre made love, Val and Patti watched a Lakers game, Kim drowned her sorrows in a eucalyptus-scented bath David wrote, and Wayne Carey jerked off. He didn't have a problem with jerking off. Actually, he had a ritual he usually performed. First, he chose something mellow to place on his CD player, like David Sanborn or Harry Connick, Jr. Next, he poured himself a glass of wine then lowered the lights, which were on a dimmer, to set the mood. Lastly, he took off his clothes. Sometimes he did a strip tease in front of his bedroom mirror, exciting himself by watching his own undulating reflection.

When he knew that he was going to indulge in an act of self-love, he donned flowing silks or brisk cottons because they felt the best against his skin. But he hadn't planned on it today. It happened by accident. One moment he was going through his mail, gas bill, light bill, Sparklet's water bill, and *People* magazine. He loved *People* magazine. Tossing the bills aside— that's what accountants were for anyway—he glanced at the cover, preparing to scan the index for the first story he would read. On the cover was Valentine Michael Pardeaux. He turned to the cover story, intrigued. There he was, Val, dressed in flesh-colored tights, leaning against the dance bar. The caption read: *This dancer is all beef cake.* Desire hit him hard. The next thing he knew, he was unbuttoning his jeans and removing his dick. He pulled, stroked and manipulated himself until he came.

Afterwards, somewhat contrite, he threw the soiled magazine in the trashcan and got into the shower. It had been a long time since he had masturbated over a fantasy figure in a magazine. His obsession with Valentine was getting ridiculous. He needed to do something to keep his mind off Val. Slipping into a pair of linen slacks and a silken shirt, he grabbed his car keys and headed for his sleek Jaguar. He hadn't been out in a while. His notoriety and desire for discretion made his cruising options limited. But he did have options, and this night he chose to exercise them. Safe sex with a nameless, faceless stranger would work better than no sex to ease the hunger in his loins.

Marco's was a discreet, private club where men of distinction went to meet other men with discriminating taste. Located in the Valley on three acres of choice real estate, it posed under the guise of a private, members only resort. Membership was offered by invitation only to the most discriminating clientele. Discretion and privacy were guaranteed via the nature of the club. The annual membership fee was $75,000.

Wayne had been a member for two years. One of the benefits of a $75,000 membership was twenty-four-hour access to the ranch house, dance floors, bars, Jacuzzis and club facilities. There was entertainment, exotic male dancers and female impersonators who rotated between stages. There were also several fantasy rooms complete with disease-free males whose only purpose was to fulfill sexual fantasies. Members were free to partake of the pleasures of the gentlemen or each other, depending on their mood and mutual agreement.

After Wayne checked in at the front desk, where he had reserved two nights, he wandered toward one of the basement stages. Accepting a glass of merlot from the circulating, scantily clad, muscle-bound waiter, he selected a seat by the stage. He knew that his desire to watch the exotic dancer stemmed from his desire to be with Val. The man on the stage was a lithe, sensuous beauty. He moved gracefully with the music. He looked good, but he wasn't Wayne's type. He was too effeminate, too thin, and too dainty to maintain Wayne's interest. Wayne Carey was a man who liked men. If he wanted a man who looked like a woman, he would have gotten a woman. Women had never been his sexual preference.

Sitting back in his seat, he continued to watch the show and survey the room. Soon, another dancer took the stage in the place of the first. Another thing Marco's offered was variety. There were different body shapes and sizes. There was someone for everyone. It was a virtual smorgasbord.

It was a little after midnight and the room was packed. Wayne saw people he knew, if not personally, by reputation. There was a senator, a prominent attorney and a fellow thespian. Unlike Val, Wayne exuded no surprise over the caliber or number of people who led double lives, one private and one public. He was one of those people.

As Wayne continued to drink his wine, he scanned the room. He knew he wanted someone that reminded him in some way of Val. His obsession wouldn't be fulfilled until he had actually played out his fantasy. There was no one in the room like Val. No one had his perfectly proportioned body or fantastic, flowing, off-black mane with auburn highlights. No one had his funny way of talking, with speech filled with zany New York colloquialisms, Texas twang and cultured British inflections. Val was an individual, a sexy, exotic, dark beauty.

Before Val, Wayne had never really thought much about black people. He knew some black people. Everybody did. There was a black secretary, Risa, who worked on his show. She was an attractive girl, polite, hardworking and congenial. She graduated from UCLA and had just begun her career in the business. There was a black man who delivered his cleaning. There was a black woman who was a checker at his favorite market. The black people he was acquainted with were decorations on the fringes of the tapestry that made up his life. He had no black friends. Risa was the only black person he had an extended conversation with. It wasn't that he avoided black people or deliberately sought them out, it was simply that the whole concept of blackness had held no interest for him until he became infatuated with Valentine. And until Valentine mentioned Wayne's whiteness, Wayne hadn't really thought of Valentine's blackness. In Wayne's mind, Val was just Val, erotic, exotic, desirable and talented.

David, on the other hand, was definitely black.

Whenever Wayne thought of him, he thought of David's blackness, David's intensity, David's dick that stood between him and Val. The myth that black men possessed monster penises and unlimited virility had been haunting Wayne ever since he decided that he wanted Val. To get Val, he had to eliminate David and his black man's dick. When he thought of eliminating him, he didn't mean killing him. His obsession with Val hadn't turned him into a homicidal maniac. He just needed to figure out a way to either get David away from Val or Val away from David long enough for him, Wayne, to get Val, to see if what he felt for him was more than a passing infatuation.

"Hello."

"Hi," Wayne said as he turned to the voice at his side and was faced with the bluest eyes he'd ever seen.

The man was blond, athletic, good-looking, and masculine. He was a surfer type who played volleyball on the beach. The man was dressed in a silken toga, the sign of an escort. Under normal circumstances, Wayne could find him very attractive. But this wasn't a normal circumstance. He wanted a man like Val. He wanted a black man. Then it dawned on him. In his two years as a member of Marco's, he had never noticed a black member. He assumed there was a black escort simply because there seemed to be escorts of every shape, size and disposition. Color had to also be a factor.

"Are you finding everything to your liking, sir?" the man asked.

Out of the corner of his eye, Wayne noticed that the young exotic dancer on the stage was stepping down and another was taking his place. "Everything is fine," Wayne answered.

"My name is Apollo. Feel free to call on me if you need anything."

The invitation was there in Apollo's eyes and body language. Wayne chose to ignore it. He wasn't craving the chicken breast tonight. He needed something filling like legs and thighs—dark meat. When he realized this, he went back to his room. It was time to order room service.

Wayne was very specific in the order he placed. If he could not have Val, he could at least have as close to Val as possible. It was his fantasy. After he hung up the phone, he became as nervous as a virgin on his first date. He had never participated in a fantasy at Marco's. He was unaware of the proper protocol. What was he to do? Should he get undressed? Should he let his escort undress him? He settled on a happy compromise. He pulled his shirt from his pants, removed his shoes, socks, belt, tie and rolled up his sleeves. He poured himself a glass of wine.

There was a quiet knock on his bedroom door. He swallowed the wine in a gulp.

"Come in," Wayne called.

He heard his door open then close. With drink in hand, he turned to face his escort. The man was magnificent. He was tall, six foot two, an inch taller than Val. He was heavier, too, more muscular and dark like David. His head was covered in a multitude of intricate, shoulder length braids. He was masculine, athletic, sexy and available. He was just what Wayne had requested. And, he was black. Very, very black, and Wayne had never been with a black man.

"Hi," Wayne said.

"Hi," the black man said. There was no accent. Well, Marco's staff wasn't perfect.

"What's your name?" Wayne asked.

"What do you want it to be?"

"No, seriously, what should I call you?"

The escort paused as if debating whether to tell the truth. "My name is Lance."

"You are kidding, right?"

"No, it's really Lance. Tell me about your fantasy."

"Didn't they tell you?" Wayne began nervously.

"No, Wayne, I was just told that there was a very sexy man in room 212."

"A very nervous man is what they should have said."

"There's no need to be nervous."

"Well . . ." Wayne began again. He was at a loss for words, which wasn't like him, but his nervousness did not bother Lance.

"Do you like music?" Lance asked in an obvious attempt to break the ice.

"Sure."

Lance flipped on the compact disc player. The melodious sounds of Harry Connick, Jr. filled the room.

"How did you know?" Wayne asked with surprise.

"I'm psychic." At Wayne's skeptical look, he continued. "Seriously, I'm psychic."

Wayne laughed. The ice was breaking.

"So, why don't you tell me about yourself, Wayne?"

It didn't surprise Wayne that Lance knew his name. His television show was in its fourth year. During that four-year span, *Space Frontiersman* had always been in the top ten.

"What do you want to know?"

Lance held out his hand and took Wayne into his arms as they began to dance to the music. "What do you like in your men?"

As Wayne danced with Lance, he was vaguely

aware that Lance let him lead. He preferred to lead. He liked being in control. "I like a sense of humor, ambition, drive, talent."

"Admirable traits."

"A nice ass doesn't hurt either," Wayne finished.

"I have a nice ass," Lance said.

Wayne ran his hands over Lance's ass. "Yes, you have a nice ass." Wayne was warming up to Lance's wry humor.

"Want to see the rest of me?"

"Yes."

As if on a pre-arranged signal, the two stopped dancing. Wayne expected Lance to remove his clothes and stand before him naked. Instead, what he got was a very sexy strip tease. While Wayne sat in a plush, oversized chair, Lance changed the music from Harry Connick, Jr. to Prince. It was vintage Prince. The song was "Head." Wayne watched, mesmerized, as Lance removed his clothes to the pounding beat. He was a good dancer, but he wasn't Val. Nevertheless, Wayne was becoming easily entranced by his escort's moves.

Wayne focused his attention on Lance as he removed all his clothes save a navy blue G-string. He really was magnificent. His body was a study in perfection. In all fairness, he could not be compared to Val because there was no comparison. They had different body types, hues and accents. It was like comparing a linebacker to a tennis player, a brownie to a butter cookie, and an English gentleman to his American cousin.

Lance removed his G-string with much aplomb. Naked, he stood before Wayne. Wayne allowed his eyes to travel over Lance's body. From head to toe, Lance was perfect. There were no birthmarks or flaws in his chocolate flesh.

"Do you like what you see?" Lance asked.

Wayne did like what he saw. "Yes."

Lance covered the space that separated them with a few strides. Wayne looked up. He meant to look into Lance's face; instead, he was faced with Lance's dick.

"I like what I see too." Lance produced a condom magically, as if from the air. He handed it to Wayne.

"Will it fit?"

Lance laughed. "It'll fit."

In this age of safe sex, Wayne had become a master of condom application. He placed the condom on Lance's penis, which was hard, elongated, and monstrous in size.

"It fit." He stepped closer to Wayne. Wayne opened his mouth and accepted Lance easily. The condom was mintflavored. He would never be able to taste mint again without thinking of this room, this night or this man who was nothing like Val but acting as a substitute for Val.

In the back of his mind, Wayne wondered how did Lance really taste? Was there a different taste between black flesh and white? Was there an assault on the senses, a burst of exotic spices like cinnamon and curry? Through the mintflavored latex, Wayne could not tell. He was dying to know. He removed his mouth from Lance's flesh.

"God, don't stop now," Lance begged. Wayne moved his mouth over Lance's body to his flat belly. He licked his navel, the muscles of his stomach. Lance tasted good.

Lance entwined his hands in Wayne's hair. "I can't take much more of this." They were words every whore says to enhance the john's prowess.

"Yeah?" Wayne asked.

"Yeah."

"You don't have to lie."

"They don't pay me enough to lie." Lance pulled Wayne up from the chair. Wayne was still dressed. "Let me make you feel good too." With expert hands, Lance began to remove Wayne's clothes.

"I think I'm going to like this," Wayne speculated.

"You're going to love it."

Once Wayne was naked, Lance slipped a condom onto his semi-hard penis. The two of them stood facing each other. Even though Wayne had never had this fantasy, he had been in this situation, naked before a man he found exciting. He wasn't naïve enough to think that the chemistry between him and Lance was more than hormonal. He knew that once he achieved physical release, he and Lance would have nothing else to share. Lance was a whore. He was a john. There was a line that should not be crossed. But he would not think of that now. Wayne was suddenly enamored with black skin, the varying shades, degrees and taste of it. He was sure that once he indulged his flesh, he could get on with his pursuit of Valentine, his wooing of Valentine, his lust for Valentine.

"You're a million miles away," Lance said with a pout. Wayne was stretched out on the bed. Lance straddled his body and slowly sucked his toes into his mouth. Lance was a skilled lover, adept at soliciting the most climactic responses. There was none of the awkwardness that first time lovers experience. There were none of the uncomfortable angles or clumsy fumbling to make sure that body parts fit. As an escort, Lance was an expert. It was a blow to his ego that Wayne seemed to be able to separate his body from his mind while they made love. Normally, Lance didn't care how his johns felt, as long as he came. He always came. He came because the johns liked it and when the johns liked it, he got better tips.

LANCE

The braids were a compromise. I really wanted dreads. Unfortunately, in my line of work, I had to always look "respectable." I say that with tongue in cheek because working at Marco's, as well as anywhere else, it was the white people who determined what looked respectable. Dreads were just too radical, revolutionary and soulful for the décor.

I had been at Marco's three years, ever since I entered law school at the ripe age of twenty-three, two years later than most. Having been disowned by my parents when my father caught me in bed with the captain of the football team, I ended up having to support myself. I don't know what had upset my father, a staunch Republican dentist, more; the fact that I was gay or the fact that the man he caught me in bed with was black. My father, who was a dark-skinned man, had been very disappointed that I was born dark like him. He had married a light-skinned woman to prevent just that. I guess she never told him her parents were dark and her fair skin, light eyes and "good" hair were just a fluke. There were no other children after me.

"Now who is a million miles away?" Wayne asked with a chuckle.

I snapped myself out of my reverie and turned my attention to Wayne Carey's dick. "I'm not a million miles away. I'm right here."

With Wayne, I had steered away from slipping into

the skin of one of the two characters I was most requested to play at Marco's. It seemed I was always the big black savage raping little white virgins, or the jive-talking, extra-cool black stud. Rarely was I the intelligent, horny law student paying his way through college the easiest, least stressful way possible. I sensed early on that Wayne wanted me as close to authentic as possible, so I dropped the façade and was very much myself. He wanted the real me, and I was happy to oblige him.

I took an instant liking to him, the Wayne outside of his *Space Frontiersman* persona. He was cute and funny in a goofy kind of white boy way. Though I fucked and was fucked by white men at Marco's, I rarely dated white men. I had grown up a child of parents who were black in color only. I had my fill of white people and whiteness. I had to deal with them then, and now at work, so that I could live the life of comfort I had learned to appreciate. But on my own time, I reveled in my blackness. It had to be a rare white man to get my attention. I never dated men I met at Marco's. There had to be a line. I wish I had met Wayne outside the club so there wouldn't be that "thing" between us.

WAYNE

I liked his body. His maleness. His physique. His dick. Lance had a hard body like mine, like Val's. He had a dick like David's. I was sure; a black man's dick. As we got naked and performed the dance that lovers dance, I wondered if this is what Val saw in David. Yep, that was it. It had to be the dick, this monster dick, strong, virile and beautiful. It had to be bigger than everybody's. It was a study in perfection, a symbol to inspire worship. I worshipped it. I fell spell to it. If we had met under different circumstances, I could have fallen in love with it. Oh, the taste of it, salt, passion and sweat. The feel of it, hard, strong, and powerful, was magnificent. The perfect way our two bodies fit was glorious. As I rode him and thought of Val, I don't think I have ever come like that. Ever.

When I woke up, he was gone. But I could still taste him, mint, chocolate, licorice and salt. Under different circumstances I could really learn to like him. Under the same circumstances, I could learn to come and not think of Val. He was very good at what he did. Vaguely I wondered what he did when he was not at Marco's. He couldn't be a whore twenty-four hours of the day.

LANCE

After my time with Wayne, I knew I was going to be late to my Criminal Law class. Shit. It wasn't like I was prepared anyway. Double shit. I'd probably get called on. Triple shit. No way for the son of a dentist who had always been an overachiever to behave. When class was over, I knew I'd have to duck through the crowd of milling students and head across campus to my car. Wednesdays were always busy. Hadn't I learned not to play escort boy on Tuesday nights? I volunteered as a basketball coach two days a week, Wednesdays and Fridays, at the Jackie Robinson Community Youth Center in South Central L.A. One of the volunteers, a professional dancer named Kim, had gathered some of her dancer friends to put on a dance exhibition for the kids. I would be headed there after class.

CHAPTER TWENTY-THREE

Patti was drunk and almost too much for Val to handle. As he drove home, he reflected on the fact that he had made a few wrong decisions concerning their night of fun after the basketball game. Conscious of the fact that Patti was a tourist, he decided to stop in at The Conga Room. The crowd, celebrities and hype would impress her, and she would have favorable memories of her visit. As unobtrusively as possible, he pulled his hair into a ponytail and slipped into David's Ray Bans, which were in the glove compartment. Val took his notoriety in stride; however, he didn't want to overwhelm Patti with the crowd's reaction to him.

What he had planned was an uneventful, fun night. What he got was chaos. He was recognized in line before they made it inside. Rescue came in the shape of a silver Rolls Royce.

"Some people are such publicity hounds." He had recognized the voice before he turned to see Heathcliff leaning out the window. Sampson was driving.

Thank God. Val had gracefully extracted himself from the autograph-seeking crowd and escorted Patti into the car.

"We were passing by and we saw the crowd," Heathcliff said, tearing away from the curb.

"And we decided to go somewhere else," Sampson finished.

Patti's eyes glazed over at the sight of the Rolls.

"Who are you?" Heathcliff asked.

"Please forgive me, Patti. I seem to have forgotten my manners. These are dear friends of mine, Heathcliff and Sampson," Val said by way of introduction.

Patti was so busy looking at the car that Val doubted that she realized he had forgotten his manners.

"Hi," she responded.

"Hello, darling. Girl, you are working that outfit," Sampson said, obviously liking what he saw as he gave her the once-over from head to toe in the rearview mirror.

"Where are we headed?" Val queried, realizing he'd have to go back for his car.

"The Stud!" he replied.

Val rolled his eyes. "Well . . ." He hedged. He wasn't sure what Patti's reaction would be to such total abandon.

"What's the Stud?" Patti asked accepting a class of champagne. The Golden Stud was a posh nightclub made famous by its exotic acts, homosexual comedians and female impersonators. Its clientele was varied, from the rich and famous to the seedy side of Hollywood society.

"I can't explain. You've got to see it."

From that point on, the night had not gone as planned. Champagne flowed freely in the back seat of the Rolls. At the Stud, Val picked up the $100 cover fee for each of them without a second thought.

Once inside, Val watched the play of emotions that washed across Patti's face as she took in the surroundings. At one point, she even said of the female impersonators, "Damn, he looks better than I do." It hadn't been easy for her to loosen up and enjoy the show. She had not been able to appreciate the performances or the lively conversation of her companions. She felt threatened by the fact that the men looked more feminine, acted more ladylike and solicited more attention than she ever could in that room. Being ignored was something she wasn't used to. Her overblown sensuality and voluptuousness made her appear to be a caricature of the real thing instead of the colorful butterflies that occupied the stage. She felt inadequate, unappreciated and masculine.

Val thought she was going to burst a blood vessel, when Heathcliff leaned over and tongue-kissed Sampson during a performance of "Sisters in the Name of Love." It was one of their favorite songs.

Val excused himself to go to the bathroom. The bathrooms were simply labeled bathrooms. They were unisex. He urinated next to a woman—at least he thought it was a woman until she peed standing up. When he got back to the table, Patti was doing Jell-O shots. Val groaned. Jell-O shots tasted liked Kool-Aid and were 150 proof. There were nine empty shots on the table. Val watched worriedly as he drank his wine. By the time the Bette Midler impersonator took the stage, Patti was falling all over him, sloppy drunk. Heathcliff was so pickled that he removed one of his legs and was waving it over his head. When it was time to go, Sampson easily carried Patti, and Val tucked Heatheliff into a bundle and stuffed him into the Rolls.

On the way home, Val cursed his inability to foresee what too much alcohol would do to Patti. He drank, and yes, he had been drunk, but rarely did he drink to drunkenness in public. There were always too many cameras, too many people wanting to catch him in a compromising position. If he ever got drunk in public, he could easily see himself draped over David. He was not going to be seen on the front page of the *National Enquirer* sloppy drunk with a hard-on for David. Some things were private.

As he was pulling into the garage, a commercial for *Space Frontiersman* came on the radio. For a brief second, Val thought of Wayne. He really was an okay guy. Val would not mind embracing Wayne's quirkiness into the eccentrics who surrounded his circle of friends; however, the mere nature of their meeting prevented him from allowing himself to get too close to Wayne. He knew Wayne had a thing for him. He wasn't blind. But suddenly, his life had become too bogged down with pretend relationships, and he wasn't going to have him as a lover. He turned off the ignition and cut off the end of the commercial. If he had not heard the commercial, he would not have even thought of Wayne.

"Are we there yet?" Patti moaned.

"Yes, we're there," Val replied as he walked around to the passenger's side and gathered Patti into his arms. She wasn't much larger than Kim, but unlike Kim's slender size six athletic form, Patti's size eight curves were very uncooperative. She wanted to stand, while it would have been much easier if she would let him carry her. She wasn't in the mood for easy. She was in the mood for love.

"Oh," she purred, sliding herself sensually down Val's body.

"Now, now," he chastised her and batted her hands away from his crotch.

Val was trying to lock the door that led from the garage into the kitchen when she slid to the floor in a leather-clad puddle of giggles.

Deciding he had had enough, he picked her up in one smooth gesture, threw her over his shoulder like a bag of potatoes, and started for her bedroom.

"Oh, baby." She still managed to wiggle against him. "I've been watching you." She kicked off her remaining three-inch heel. She had lost her other pump somewhere between the car and the stairway.

"We're almost there, Patti." He spoke to her as if he were speaking to a child.

In her state of mind, she could only complete simple sentences. "You are such a pretty, pretty yellow thing." She was very drunk. Her Southern drawl was very pronounced. The words had come out like *yella thang*.

Southern blacks are so preoccupied with skin color, he thought as he carried her upstairs.

Why had they bought such a large house? There were only two of them. Val felt as though he would never make it to the guestroom. Where was David? David should be doing this.

Once he got Patti into the guestroom, he was tempted to dump her on the bed because she was annoying him so much. Instead, he laid her down gently. That is what a gentleman would do. For a moment, he debated whether to pull off her clothes or leave her in the tight dress.

"Do you think I'm pretty?" she asked while he

pulled off her pantyhose. She wasn't wearing underwear.

"Yes, you are very pretty." He could smell her. The rich, womanly smell emanating from between her legs beckoned him.

"You like?" she giggled, spreading her legs farther. She was the epitome of all that was sexual. Ignoring her drunken come-on, he began to remove her dress. The sheath peeled off her body like the outer skin off of a sausage.

"Let's fuck. I know you want to," she cooed, reaching for him. Even in her drunken state, her hands were skilled.

"Stop it, Patti." He pushed her hand away. Again she grabbed for him. It was when she grabbed his dick the second time that David walked in. He had been working out in the gym, so he had not heard them come in

"Well," David said, more than amazed by the picture he saw. Val removed Patti's groping hand from his crotch. "Well." Val slid Patti's naked form beneath the comforter and sheets. The two of them looked down at her as parents would a wayward child. She looked oddly out of place in the room that Val had decorated. It was a masculine room, straight lines and angles. There was no place for curves and fluff.

"Hey, guys, let's party." Patti giggled.

"She's drunk," David said, wiping sweat from his brow.

"Yes, yes, she is," Val said as he hung Patti's dress in the closet.

"Let's play," Patti said, throwing back the covers. "See." She rubbed her finger between her legs. "I'm sticky." She giggled hysterically. David gathered her blanket and covered her again. Val wanted to dunk her head in a bucket of water. Her outright debauchery was annoying.

Val turned to David, his patience gone. "You deal with this," he said. Without waiting for David's response, he left the two of them alone. As he walked down the stairs to the kitchen, he briefly entertained the idea of them together. Ever since her arrival, she had been giving off signals that she would be more than willing to indulge in the pleasures of the flesh. Even in her drunken state, when she would not remember the incident in the morning, she was hot and ready. Her pussy beckoned him. Her scent called him. He could resist her. He would resist her. But he wasn't David. He wasn't her childhood sweetheart who had shared in the loss of virginity and the finding of sexual desire and cravings. Sex was not the thing that lasting relationships were formed on, but sex was a powerful motivator and memory stimulator. It could make young people believe it was love. When those same young people got older, the conflicting emotions of rediscovery that became love could be hypnotizing and blinding. Val had left the two of them alone for more than one reason. True, she had gotten on his last nerve and drained him of all his patience, but he could not stand watch, guarding David's dick. David was a grown man capable of making his own choices.

Val would not allow himself to behave like a fishwife. Giving himself busy work, he made some hot chocolate. He was on his second cup by the time David made it downstairs. David had showered; it was obvious because he had removed his dirty sweats and put on a pair of cut-off denim shorts. Val gave himself a mental kick because his immediate thought was that David had erased all the evidence.

"She was wasted," David said, going to the stove to pour himself a cup of cocoa. He had smelled it as he came down the stairs. Val made cocoa the old-fashioned way. He didn't use the microwave. "This is good." David sat facing Val and put his bare feet in Val's lap.

Val pushed David's feet out of his lap. "What?"

"If I weren't here, would you fuck her?" Val asked.

"What?"

"You want her, don't you?"

"What's with you?"

"Its 3:00 A.M. Did you have to take a shower?"

"I had just finished working out."

"Oh." Val picked up David's feet and put them back in his lap.

David rubbed his feet over Val's crotch. "What's with you, man?"

Val smiled sheepishly. "I'm acting like a fishwife."

David laughed. "Something like that. Would you like to start this conversation over?"

"Yeah." Val watched as David got up from the table, poured his cocoa back into the pot, and left the room. He had just put his cocoa to his lips when David re-entered the kitchen.

"She's wasted," he said as if they had not had their previous conversation. He poured himself a cup of cocoa. "This is good." He sat down and put his feet in Val's lap. "How was your day?"

Val laughed and said, "You are crazy."

"Crazy about you. Thank you for taking care of Patti tonight. I managed to get a lot done here alone."

Val tweaked David's toe. "Tell me about your story."

David groaned. "Not yet."

"Not yet? Not yet?" Val managed to put enough indignation in his voice to make David laugh.

"I'll let you read it when I'm finished."

This was a first. Usually David kept Val abreast of his characters' exploits and developments. But he didn't push.

"Want some more cocoa?" David asked.

"Naw. I think I'm going to bed."

"Okay."

David got up to join him.

"Alone," Val said for emphasis.

"Okay." David watched Val walk up the stairs.

CHAPTER TWENTY-FOUR

Patti woke up with a taste in her mouth as if she had been sucking on cotton. Her head was pounding and her eyelashes were stuck together. She groaned all the way to the bathroom that she had to reach by crawling. When David found her, she was sprawled on her back in the doorway between her bedroom and the guest bathroom. She had found that this was the coolest spot in the house, and her skin was hot. Sometime in the night, she had pulled on some clothes. Her slip was pulled up over her head. David took one look at her and was tempted to back out of the room before she saw him. But it was too late.

"I hate you," she hissed.

"I'm sure. In the state you're in, you probably hate everybody," David replied.

"No, just men." She allowed him to help her up from the floor.

"I thought you liked men."

"They're all faggots." Her head was spinning and

she was turned away from him, so she did not see the look that washed across his face.

DAVID

I hadn't been called a faggot in a long time. And the person who had called me that was the one person I had learned to love more than life. I remember it like it was yesterday. I had just been released from the hospital. Val and I had finally taken the steps that began our journey together. We had made love, real love, with exchanges of kisses in which our tongues touched, our penises dueled and we explored each other's bodies as true lovers, venturing past the mutual masturbation stage that our initial fears and inhibitions had not allowed us to pass. In the tradition of my newfound bravery, I had taken the initiative in our lovemaking. I assumed a role I was comfortable with.

I was a man, a skilled lover, and a compassionate bed partner. I knew what to do to please my sexual partners. I surrounded it with my mouth, licking, sucking, and teasing it with my lips. I pulled on the head and caressed his thighs until I had him climaxing into my mouth. Even when he warned me that he was coming, I didn't stop. For the first time, the very first time, I admitted that Val was my lover, my love, and accepted his sperm as my lovers had done for me. I knew I had changed.

We lay as lovers do after the dance. He looked into my eyes and ran his hands lovingly over my head. He played with my hair and pulled on my ears. He had wanted to touch me. I had wanted to touch him. We kissed. We were lovers. We had knocked down barriers. Then he said, "Faggot."

But Val's endearment had been nothing like the curse Patti muttered. "Faggot" from her was a different reflection of her opinion of effeminate men, dickless men, unmasculine men; in other words, men who did not find her attractive. I was not a faggot.

"What are you talking about?" I responded to her comment as she made her way past me and lay down on the bed.

Val and I bought this bed in Scotland. We had been on a tour of an old Scottish castle. Val saw the bed and fell in love with it. It was a full-sized wrought iron bed with intricately carved decorations on the head and the foot posts. We had made love in this bed. Val loved this bed. It just wasn't large enough to accommodate both our frames on a continuous basis.

"Do you know where we went last night?" she demanded. She was holding her head in her hands. She had a hellacious headache.

"You went to the Stud," I said.

"Those people . . ." Patti shivered.

"What people?" I was toying with her, choosing again to hide behind semantics. Playing word games with Patti would not be difficult.

"Those faggots." Her disdain was obvious. The venom in her voice was almost painful to hear.

"Which ones?"

"Those faggots we rode with. They were kissing." She grimaced. "And that little one didn't have any legs. They made me sick looking at them."

I didn't know what to say to that.

"And Val," she started, raising her head on that statement. Her eyes were bloodshot. Her carefully coifed tresses had come unraveled and hung to her shoulders limply.

"What about Val?"

"It didn't phase him at all." She brushed her hair from her eyes. "I mean . . . he fit right in."

"It's entertainment, Patti."

"There's entertainment and there's entertainment. Christ, why is it so hot in here?" She pulled off the slip and threw it against the wall. The panties she wore were skimpy, red and transparent. She wore nothing else. She hadn't pulled off her slip to entice me, solicit me or seduce me. She had pulled off her slip because she was hot. I knew that. I hoped Val did. As fate would have it, my lover stood in the open doorway with the phone in his hand. I wondered how it looked to him, his lover and his lover's ex-lover sitting in another very compromising position.

"There he is," Patti said as she threw out her hand haphazardly indicating Val. "The fag lover." She fell back against the bed and pulled the sheet over her face. Patti's face was covered in her bed sheet, which was good because if she had seen Val, she would have run for cover.

"What did you call me?" His words were clipped. His accent was very pronounced.

"You heard me," was her muffled reply. I saw Val's eyes change color from the light hazel that was their usual hue to a sharp, piercing green. I knew it was the light that played off the hazel highlights and picked up the green tint that was so like his father's that made his eyes appear to change colors. Whereas Val had been fortunate to have inherited an equal distribution of traits from both his mother and his father, he had been unfortunate enough to inherit his mother's temper.

"Who is that on the phone?" I asked in an attempt to distract him before he laid into Patti. I was the master of semantics, skilled in "*word*-upmanship"; however, Val was capable of delivering some pretty devastating verbal blows himself. Patti would be no match for his sharp tongue and quick retorts. She would not understand his anger and would be shocked by the intensity of his attack. It would make her think *faggot*.

"Val," I said again. "Who's on the phone?"

The look he gave me let me know that I was in for it. Maybe I'd take him on a trip to Australia. We had been talking about Australia. "It's Lola. She wants to invite us to dinner," Val answered.

"What's she cooking?" I asked.

"Who is Lola?" Patti asked from beneath the sheet.

"Lola is Val's mother," I answered.

Patti groaned and turned on her side. The sheet fell away to reveal her partially clad figure. Both she and Val were as comfortable without clothes as they were with them. That was something else they had in common.

"Tell her we'd love to come by."

Val relayed my message to Lola. She must have said something funny because he broke into loud laughter.

Patti cringed and said, "Do you have to be so loud?"

"Sorry," Val called as he left the room. I heard him speaking in French as he headed down the hallway. Patti pulled the sheet from over her face. "What kind of talk is that?"

"French," I said.

"He speaks French?" It clearly annoyed her that Val was able to carry on a conversation that she could not be a part of.

"And Spanish, and Italian, some German and a little Japanese," I said proudly. Languages were easy for Val. I took pride in his accomplishments just as he did in mine. I had spent two Christmases at the Pardeaux château in France, making the language not so intimidating, but still not easy for me.

"What kind of nigger is he?" she asked.

Did she say that? Yes, she did. I heard her with my own ears. It should not have surprised me. I knew Patti. I knew her upbringing. I knew the language she was comfortable with because I too had spoken that language in my youth. But I was no longer a youth. With maturity and experience, I learned the power of words. There was strength in mastering language. There were mystical properties in dialogue. Knowing this, how could I allow her to continue to abuse the power of speech in her ignorance?

"You know, Patti . . ." I began, trying to be tactful in my observation of her faux pas.

"What?"

What was I going to say? Did I tell her I chose to be responsible with that word? I chose to be politically correct. I never, never, never used it in reference to an entire race of people, our race of people. As a black man in America, a dark-skinned black man, that word, the powerful, noxious word had labeled me, haunted me and almost stomped me. But I had outsmarted it. I had lived down the stereotype and refused to allow the brand to keep me from reaching my potential.

"What?" she repeated.

I chose my words carefully. "Val is a black man. Just like me."

"He is not like you."

"Val is a black man, just like me."

"Baby, please." She dismissed that idea as if it were ludicrous.

"What do you mean by that?"

She got up from the bed and began searching through the closet for something to wear. "I mean"— She held a pair of leather shorts against her body— "look at him. Ain't nothing black on that boy." She put the shorts back and selected a denim mini-skirt that was so short it bordered on the obscene. "He doesn't talk black." She chose a transparent fuchsia blouse and a fuchsia tube top to wear beneath it. "He doesn't act black, and he sure as hell don't look black."

"He's black," I assured her.

"If he's black, I'm white."

"He's black," I insisted.

"How does this look?" She held up her ensemble.

"We are having dinner with his mother," I said, hoping this would intimidate her into wearing something else. She did not have to know that Lola was unshakable. She did not have to know that Lola could care less about what she chose to wear and how it looked. She did not have to know that I was the one who wanted her to put on a good face and show her character and not her ass, no matter how delectable it was.

"Oh." She pouted and exchanged the mini-skirt and the transparent blouse for a pair of skintight jeans and an oversized shirt. "Much better?" she asked.

I nodded.

"What's Val's mother like?" she called over her shoulder as she disappeared into the bathroom. Her ass was perfect, the cheeks smooth, round and flawless.

"Black. His mother is black," I called after her, but she didn't hear me.

CHAPTER TWENTY-FIVE

Kim volunteered at the Jackie Robinson Youth Center in South Central L.A. two days a week. She had been doing this since September 11, 2001. She wanted to do something to help the kids, uplift their spirits and show them something positive. She taught three beginning dance classes: jazz, modern and tap. She even convinced Lola to donate three scholarships to the center.

Even with her busy schedule, she was able to give her kids two days a week, Tuesdays and Wednesdays. Thank God she was a dancer. She had the kind of schedule that let her do what she wanted to do when she wanted to do it. Kim always told herself that if she ever reached the level of financial independence that Lola and Andre had, she would do more special projects. She was big on special projects, community service, giving back, and had always been fortunate. Some people had not, like the kids at the center and Patti.

She got in the shower intent on keeping busy and

not thinking about Val. But try as she might, he was still foremost in her thoughts. As she stood under the constant beat of water, her nipples got hard thinking about their kiss. It felt good to rub the soap over her body, imagining that her hands were Val's hands. If she couldn't have him in person, she could have him in her mind. After indulging in a climactic sexual fantasy, she washed away the sweet-smelling bubbles from her bath gel, dried off and jumped into her dance clothes. She hadn't had to partake in one of Lola's rigorous workouts this morning and she was glad of it. Grabbing her dance bag, she rushed out the door. *Shit. I'm late.*

Val knew about the work Kim did at the youth center. He commended her because she was able to give it more time than he ever could. There were a great number of charities and good causes that made demands on him. Due to a hectic and vigorous rehearsal and performance schedule, he was only able to work on the two causes that were most important to him: homelessness and AIDS. There were so many worthy charities, he often wished he had more time, yet he realized that he couldn't be all things to all people. But he could be a good friend to Kim. Because he was a good friend, he'd be at the community center.

He was down the stairs and almost out the door when he decided to stop being such a shit and ask David and Patti if they would like to accompany him. Had Patti not been there, there would be no question that he would mention his outing to David. But Patti was there, and the thought of spending more time with her than was necessary was driving him crazy. Still, he was a child of generations of genteel breeding. His desire to make his guest feel welcome and enjoy her stay was as much a part of him as David's Southern accent. So, he swallowed his annoyance and approached the two of them as they ate beignets in the breakfast nook.

"What's up?" David asked as soon as Val stepped into the kitchen.

"Just heading out," Val said, taking a bite from the beignet on David's plate. He had made the pastries because David loved them and he wanted to do something nice for David. He had gotten up an hour earlier than normal to have them ready for David and Patti.

"You have on your 'I-don't-want-to-be -recognized' clothes," David observed. Val was dressed in a pair of well-worn faded 501s and a Kelly-green T-shirt. His hair was pulled back into a ponytail, and covering his head was a Malcolm X hat. He had on a pair of trendy, round Poindexter shades and his comfortable Nikes. He had replaced his diamond stud with a simple gold hoop. He kept on the cluster of bracelets he had picked up in Africa and usually wore, but replaced his Rolex with a Fossil watch. He looked like anyone else in L.A.

"I guess I do, don't I?" Val said in perfect "Valley dude."

"How'd he do that? How'd you do that?" Patti asked, amazed that he had dropped his accent so easily.

"Do what?" he asked her, particles of powdered sugar all around her mouth and on her fingers.

"If you can talk normal, why don't you do it all the time?" she inquired.

"Talk normal?" Val and David both asked incredulously. Maybe he would not ask them to come with him.

"Yeah," she said, licking her fingers. "This stuff is

good. What do you call this?" She did not seem to realize her remark was offensive.

"Beignets," Val said, recognizing her ignorance and choosing to ignore it.

"What do you mean about normal?" David asked, refusing to let her remark slide.

"What?" she asked as she took another bite.

David sighed, realizing she was not going to get it. "Where are you going?" he said, turning his attention to Val.

"I'm going over to the Jackie Robinson Youth Center," Val replied. His accent was back.

"Youth center?" Patti asked. She finished her beignet and started on David's.

"Kim's dancing," Val said.

"Yeah?" Patti said, interested. Only the mention of her new friend made her stop eating. "I'd like to see that," she said.

"Well, I think that can be arranged," David said as he cleared their plates away from the table. He was glad that he would be able to spend some more time with Val. During the two-week period when The Troupe was on hiatus before the vigorous fall rehearsal schedule began in preparation for a very busy performance season, he and Val usually took time to add a little romance to their relationship. During this time period they caught up on movies, went out to dinner, took romantic trips and basically dated. They hadn't been able to date while Patti had been in the house.

KIM

For my quick little demonstration, there would be no media coverage, news flashes or publicity hounds trying to get their faces on TV by being seen at the Jackie Robinson Youth Center. I did this out of the goodness of my heart, not for the publicity or to get my name in the paper. I did it because I liked it. I had the time. I had the commitment. I had the drive.

As I prepared for greatness—that's what Lola always said before a performance, "Prepare for greatness. Be the best."—I looked out on the scene of collected bodies. I saw the thirty-six students who made up my three classes. For some of these girls, there would be nothing but a lifetime of Welfare, which would begin with a teen pregnancy. For others, there would be low-paying, dead-end jobs. For a few, the lucky ones, there would be a way out. Nevertheless, I would dance for them all.

I saw the boys. We didn't have as many boys as we had girls at the center. It seemed that so many young boys found life more interesting on the street than confined within the protective walls of the community art center where they would have to learn to play basketball by rules instead of the swift, vicious code of the street. I saw our director, Lady Stacy, and the counseling staff, most of whom were volunteers like myself. Then I saw Val. My Val. He, David and Patti must have come in while I was getting ready.

Even though I knew he would be there, I still felt a little tug at my heart seeing Val. Despite yesterday, he was still a good friend and loyal supporter of my endeavors. I was, however, surprised to notice that he somehow managed to fit in with the crowd. I don't think anybody recognized him beneath the X hat and behind the glasses. In his garb, he looked almost like everyone else in the room. He smiled at me, and like a silly schoolgirl with her first crush, I smiled and waved back.

PATTI

Niggers, niggers and more niggers. Everywhere I looked there were niggers. None of those "play black people" I'd been seeing since I arrived in L.A. These people were the real thing. Jheri curls, big booties, expensive tennis shoes, crying babies and attitudes. Most everybody in the room had that "I know I'm bad, fuck you, impress me" attitude. I almost had to slap the shit out of this little slut when we walked in. She was so busy trying to get David's attention that she almost knocked me down. She had on shorts so tight that I could see the outline of her kit-kat in her pants. Damn thing was almost purring because every time she walked, the seam cut into her stuff. Slut! She couldn't have been no more than fifteen. Didn't she know Davey-Gene was a man, not one of those boys she'd been rubbing up against?

When we sat down, I snuggled real close to David and whispered in his ear. I made sure that bitch saw the tip of my tongue graze his ear. He was mine. Hands off, bitch! She might be a tempting little kitten, but I was a lioness ready to roar. Fuck meow—RRRROOOAARRRR!!!

DAVID

I had been black all my life and poor most of it. Once I became successful, I was free with my money. I gave to the United Negro College Fund, the Urban League and the NAACP. I made sure that when I spoke at literary functions on the college circuit, my agent contacted historically black colleges as well. I still supported the Police Athletic League and spent more time in the "hood" than Val ever did. Occasionally, I'd skip down to Venice Beach for a game of pick-up basketball. I knew where I came from. I knew where I was. I knew where I was going. Most of the kids I saw around me didn't even know my name. But as I looked into their eyes, saw their faces, glanced at their lives, I knew theirs. They were the Jamals, the Peanuts, the Shaniquas, Laquitas and Keishas I had known all my life. They were the characters who would inhabit the neighborhood of my next book, *Hoodsville*.

But I would not start on *Hoodsville* until I finished *David's* Story. I had come up with the idea for *Hoodsville* when we were driving down Crenshaw Boulevard. So many tourists came to L.A. and missed the section of the city *Hoodsville* would characterize. This was far from Hollywood Boulevard. There were no signs leading to Disneyland or Universal Studios, and movie stars belonged to another world. This was *Hoodsville*, South Central, the center of reality, the neighborhood of the oppressed. *Hoodsville* would be a commercial success, frank and realistic. The critics would say "D.E. Lincoln, a voice of his people. David Lincoln speaks in a loud, angry voice about the harsh realities of today's urban youth." I had heard it before. I would hear it again. But, of course, they would only say this after the hoopla over *David's Story* died down.

I worked on *David's Story* on the drive to South Central because Val drove. I was free to peck away on my laptop in the back seat. I typed forty words a minute with two fingers. If I ever learned to type with all my fingers, I'd be awesome.

Before we got out of the car I re-read what I had written:

"Oh, shit," Micah said with a voice that was half whisper and half moan.

"You like it?" Aaron asked.

"Yes," Micah managed between lips that were compressed in an effort to keep from moaning. It felt so good that he thought he was going to die.

"I like it too," Aaron said as he licked Micah's outer ear.

"Baby, baby, baby," Micah managed as he began to move beneath Aaron. His own dick was hard and pressed against the cool cotton of the sheet. He eased his hand under his body to adjust himself because he didn't want to come yet. Not yet. An electric bolt shot up his arm when he touched his dick. It felt so good. He had to force himself to stop. Uncontrollably, he began rocking, giving in to the feeling. The wondrous feeling of being filled had him about to dissolve into a mass of quivering, gelatinous flesh. If he had only known that it felt this good, this goddamn good, he never would have hesitated.

Above him, Aaron began a rhythmic motion that increased Micah's pleasure. He gritted his teeth to keep from crying out in ecstasy like a woman. He was a man. A man. And as a man, he came with his hand wrapped around his dick, bucking into the sheet beneath him as his lover, another man, raised himself and plunged deeply into his ass. But it wasn't over. Oh, no. He wasn't even really soft. Not yet. He allowed Aaron to maneuver his body up onto his knees.

"Hey, man," he panted. *"What are you doing?"* Micah asked.

But if he had waited, he would have known. Aaron answered his query with a kiss. Then another. Then another. His lover covered his ass with a multitude of sensuous kisses. And this, too, felt good. As Aaron kissed Micah's ass, he ran his hands over his flanks and back. This was a first for Micah. Usually he was the initiator, the aggressor. It excited him that this time someone was putting his pleasure above their own.

"Sweet Jesus," Micah moaned.

"Don't call on Jesus, baby. Call my name," Aaron said right before he slid his body beneath Micah and swallowed his still hard member.

"Aaron," Micah groaned as he fucked Aaron's face. Micah was a young man in the full prime of his life. He was full of wild oats and sperm but never, never had he come like that in the mouth of another man.

Yes, *David's Story* was very graphic, but I had a story to tell that could not be told with flowery words and sugarcoated phrases. Before we stepped out of the car, I stored the file I had written and put my computer under the front seat. I could not wait to get home with it. I would be completely comfortable only when I put it with the rest of what I had written.

As we took our seats and I saw the children who looked skeptically at Kim, I thought of how different my life might have been had I never discovered the magic inside my head. I would never have discovered that magic had it not been for Val. After I got shot, his inability to come see me in the hospital forced me to entertain myself, and in doing this, I discovered the power of my imagination and the ability I had to create wonderful stories with just a thought.

Patti pulled me from my reverie. I felt her warm, wet tongue as it grazed my ear. I felt her breast pressing insistently against my arm. Whenever we were in public, I recognized the signal for what it was. Patti was staking her claim. With a simple brush of the tip of her tongue and a subtle shifting of her hips, she was telling the other women in the room, "Hands off, he's mine."

I glanced nervously at Val, but Val hadn't seen anything. Val had his head turned away. He was looking at Kim.

LANCE

I knew who he was as soon as he walked in. The hat and glasses didn't do much to hide the aristocratic features, the regal bearing. Jeans and a T-shirt did not hide his perfect body. Then there was that walk, a dancer's walk, a slew-footed, even-keeled walk. I had been enjoying his performances for years. He was one of the few, the fortunate, blessed with real talent and an air for showmanship. He was also sexy as hell. But he wasn't my type. Neither was the chippy walking ahead of him. I knew she wasn't a dancer. It wasn't because she had too much ass or too much on top, but it was the way she carried herself. There was no discipline in her stride. Her hip movements were outrageous undulations. She was hot, hot, hot. Half of the men in the room and a great number of the boys almost got whiplash turning their heads to watch her ass as she passed by.

I was about to turn away from them when the girl said something to someone over her shoulder. Curious to see what type of women Valentine Michael Pardeaux surrounded himself with, I strained for a good look. Only it wasn't a woman.

It was a man. I knew who he was, too! David Lincoln! I felt my dick start to get hard. I was his biggest fan. I hadn't started reading his work until two years ago when I caught him speaking at UCLA at a conference on the Art of Writing. The title of his lecture had been "So You Want to Write a Novel."

After his speech, I bought a copy of his book,

Down Went Jonah, because I thought he was cute and his lecture was funny. When I got back to my apartment, I started reading. I remember that it was raining. By the time I put the book down, I had a raging hard-on and a case for a straight writer that sent me out in the pouring rain to purchase any and everything he had ever written.

I nurtured my infatuation with frequent re-reading of his work, and accepted my adoration for the crush that it was. The odds of my meeting him had been slim, even though I traveled in some pretty fast circles. Who would have thought that I'd run into him at a community youth center in South Central L.A.?

I shifted in my seat to ease the tension of my dick as it strained against my zipper. Much taller than I remembered, and fine, he had the body of an athlete, smoothly muscled, with fascinating skin the color of dark chocolate. All he had on was a pair of jeans and a T-shirt that read: A MIND IS A TERRIBLE THING TO WASTE. He looked very ordinary, very straight. I had read in *The Wall Street Journal* that he was paid a couple million plus for the paperback rights to *Cake Walk.* It seemed Kim had some pretty impressive friends.

CHAPTER TWENTY-SIX

After getting more accolades from the crowd than she expected, Kim was overjoyed. She had one last dance to perform when an idea hit her. She took a deep breath and addressed her audience.

"So, now you see what I do when I'm performing. But I don't do it alone. I'm just one person in a group of very talented dancers. One of them is in the audience now."

The audience started looking around.

"I'd like to introduce you to Valentine Michael Pardeaux, head choreographer of The Troupe."

Val definitely wasn't expecting that. *Now what am I supposed to do?* He felt a roomful of eyes turn in his direction.

David nudged him to stand up, so he stood. Only the counselors clapped. The kids looked at him with a mixture of hostility, curiosity and indifference.

One of the boys muttered, "Faggot," under his breath. Yes, this was going to be an experience to remember.

Val was a good sport about it. Kim knew he would be. They had not planned this, but Val went along just the same. Kim held out her hand and he quickly joined her on the dance floor. He wasn't dressed to dance, but when he stepped out onto the gym floor they were using as a dance stage, he assumed the personality of a dancer. He stepped out of his Nikes, removed his glasses and took off his hat.

There were gasps of surprise when he shook out his hair. There was even a muttered, "Punk," and one more "Faggot," But this came from the boys who didn't know that a man could be a dancer and still be a man. The girls, on the other hand, were developing crushes that rivaled Kim's own.

When Val joined her, he kissed her cheek and whispered so only she could hear, "I'm going to get you for this."

Kim smiled and kissed his cheek. "Let's do 'Lovely.' "

He nodded and took his position.

"Lovely" was a very uncomplicated ballet they taught to their beginning classes. Nevertheless, it was graceful and exciting. Kim was glad that she had decided to do this.

Patti had never heard of anyone being a professional dancer. When she was a kid and somebody asked her what she wanted to be when she grew up, she never said a dancer. She wanted to be a schoolteacher. She tried cosmetology school and didn't like that. She made it through one year of community college, but really didn't like it, and who cared if $Y+X=Z$? She went to fashion design school and met Leon, the mailman who delivered mail to the school. One day Leon told her that they were hiring at the post office. She filled out an application and took the test. She passed. The rest, as they say, is history.

All Patti ever wanted was a nice house, a sharp car, fine clothes and a man who waited on her hand and foot. If she found the right man, she might even have a baby or two. Patti never had dreams of being famous. She never saw herself as a prima ballerina or a movie star. Until she made this impulsive trip to visit Davey-Gene, she had experienced elation over her job at the post office. Anybody with sense knew she was bringing home the bucks. Until she came to California, she thought she was hot shit. But until she came to L.A., she had never ridden in a Rolls Royce. She had never gone to a club that had a $100 cover. She had never drunk Dom Perignon. Until she came to L.A., she had never been surrounded by greatness, and as she watched Val and Kim, she knew she was watching greatness. These were the people Davey-Gene surrounded himself with. Patti wondered how someone like her, someone with no talent and a boring job, looked to them. Patti watched Kim and Val dance, half paying attention to their moves as these thoughts filled her head.

She was good. He was better. They danced across the gymnasium floor as if it were the most elaborate of stages. Soon the children, who had taken a long time to be impressed, were impressed. They watched with fascination as Val raised Kim above his head then lowered her against his body. There were gasps as Kim bent over backwards, touched her hands to the floor and raised her leg in a perfect arch over Val's shoulder. He ran his hand up her extended leg and pulled her up along his body so that she was draped against him. As if she weighed no more than a feather, he leaped across the room with her over his shoulder. He heard the gasps. He saw the looks of admiration on the eyes of the students. He saw David,

David with a big grin and a thumbs-up sign, David who loved to watch him dance, David with the big heart and big checkbook. No doubt before they left the center, David would leave a nice check with the director. Val was sure there was someone out there who would have liked to speculate on which one of them had more money, he or David.

He never really thought about it. He never really tried to calculate it. He knew there was a lot of money. Every time David wrote another book there was more money. Val's finances, on the other hand, were a little more ambiguous. There was the money that was his salary. Then there was the money from his inheritance. There was just a lot of money.

When they finished dancing, there was a round of loud clapping and cheers. Val searched for David's eyes above the heads of the students. When he saw them, they smiled at each other.

Lance didn't clap when Val and Kim finished dancing. It wasn't because he didn't like what they had done. He was just busy. While everybody else was clapping, he was tying his shoelaces. They had come undone and he wanted to make sure that when he introduced himself to D.E. Lincoln, he didn't trip over his Nikes and land ass up at his feet. Lance wasn't like some of his friends. He didn't throw himself at straight guys. It was humiliating.

It was when Lance was looking up from his shoe-strings that he saw them standing next to each other. David was talking to the director of the center. Val had extracted himself from his admiring crowd of teenagers and taken a stand beside him.

As Lance watched unobserved, David reached up casually and placed his arm around Val's shoulder. He squeezed once then lowered his hand to his side.

There is a way that people who have been intimate behave. They communicate with each other in ways that exclude all others. They were doing it. Lance felt a flutter in his stomach and a tug at his groin that was the onset of excitement. Mentally, he kicked himself for not having seen what was plainly obvious. They were lovers.

Lance had never been one to sit back and allow things to just happen to him. When there was something he wanted, he went after it, and he wanted David. The realization that David and Val were more than friends had been all the encouragement Lance needed to introduce himself to David, the object of his desire and make it obvious he wanted to be more than a fan.

DAVID

I've always been observant. It's a trait that fortunately has endeared me to my friends but can be a rather annoying character flaw. I was watching a movie once and one of the characters was using the phone. He dialed only six digits and his party answered. I hadn't been able to watch the rest of the movie in peace. The fact that he had dialed six digits bugged me to no end. I doubt if anyone else noticed our hero had only dialed six digits. The movie had made a bundle.

So, of course I had noticed *him*. When we took our seats, I saw him looking in our direction. He had that look people got when they recognized Val and were working up the nerve to approach him for an autograph. So I wasn't surprised when he came over. I was just surprised when he addressed me instead.

"David Lincoln? Hi. I'm your biggest fan," he said.

That shocked me. I thought he wanted to be introduced to Val. He held out his hand and I took it. It is true that I had achieved a level of notoriety. But my fame was nothing like Val's. My fans did not approach me with autograph books and pen in hand unless it was at a book signing. I could go for weeks without anyone approaching me.

"Thank you. It's good to meet a fan," I said humbly.

"I really connected with the characters in *Down Went Jonah*. You captured the essence of awakening sexuality."

He was a good-looking guy, athletic, strong, and very intelligent. I could tell by the eyes. His comments made me think he really read *Down Went Jonah* and wasn't just trying to get next to me to get to Val.

"Thank you," I said again, flattered.

"I found it fascinating that you were able to contrast the concepts of institutionalized racism and learned prejudice."

"You really did read it." I laughed, sensing that he could take a joke.

"I've read all your stuff, even *The Drake Chronicles*."

"Don't remind me," I groaned. I had closed the door on that chapter of my life.

"They're great, aren't they? I read every one of them several times," Val quipped from over my shoulder.

"Val, I'd like you to meet . . ." I had to pause. I did not know my newfound friend's name.

"Lance," he interjected. "Lance Dennis." He accepted Val's hand eagerly.

"It's nice to meet you," Val said. "What's your favorite *Drake Chronicle*?" he asked Lance.

"*The Case of the Roguish Rogue*," he answered.

"*The Roguish Rogue?*" Val said. "You're kidding. It's my favorite too."

"It seems we've found a common ground," Lance said.

"What do you do here at the center?" Val asked him.

"I'm the basketball coach."

"What kind of team do you have?"

"I could say they were lousy, but I don't think that's strong enough."

Val laughed. As I watched the two of them talk, I was struck by the similarities they shared, although they didn't look anything alike. They didn't sound anything alike. I didn't even know Lance, but I had a feeling that if I got to know him, I'd find that he and Val shared more than an interest in basketball and a passion for my old books. There was just something there.

"We love basketball," I said, joining in on the conversation.

"I know. I've seen you at the Lakers game," Lance replied.

"You go to the games?" I asked.

"Season passes."

"We have season passes too."

"You have much better seats than I do."

"Maybe we should all go together sometime," I said.

"That would be cool."

"I hate to interrupt this little male bonding session, guys," Kim said as she took Val by the hand. "Let me borrow him for a few seconds. Okay?" She led Val away and I was left with Lance and Patti.

CHAPTER TWENTY-SEVEN

As David and Lance were talking, while Lance was trying to be charming and cute and intelligent, Lance realized that David had no idea he was flirting with him. This was a first for Lance. He was not used to flirting and being ignored. Men paid money for his attention and this guy, this straight-acting, good-looking guy, thought they were experiencing male bonding and developing a new friendship.

"What say we get a bite to eat? I'm famished," Val said as he and Kim rejoined them.

Kim seconded Val's suggestion. "Food sounds good."

"Well, it was nice meeting you all, but I've got to get to my boys. We have a game coming up Friday night," Lance started off.

"Lance?" He turned at David's request. "I was serious about the Lakers games. Gimme your number and I'll plug it into my cell."

Trying to contain his excitement, Lance exchanged numbers with David.

"Keep in touch, okay? It's not often that I run into someone who's read *all* my books."

As soon as David and Lance parted, Patti approached David and pinched him hard.

"What was that for?" David asked.

"Are you crazy?" Patti said.

Kim looked after Lance's retreating back and shook her head.

"I'm not crazy. Are you?" David rubbed his arm where Patti had pinched him.

"How can give that guy your number? You're just asking for trouble."

"What a waste." Kim shook her head.

"What are you two talking about?" Val asked, confused.

"He's a faggot," Patti said, pinching David again.

"Will you stop pinching me?" he said.

"He's very gay," Kim confirmed.

"Him?" Val asked.

"Yes, him," Kim stressed. "Men," she turned and said to Patti. "They are so dense." The four of them headed out to David's car.

DAVID

You could have knocked me over with a fucking feather. Faggot? Lance? No way. He was such a guy. I felt with him a kinship and camaraderie I hadn't felt since my days on the football team in college or on the force when I had been a cop.

In our brief conversation, there had been the beginning of a relationship founded on a common ground, which was an interest in basketball and a desire to get to know each other. There had been nothing sexual in our communication, so faggot was not what I expected. His sexual orientation, or mine for that matter, had not been an issue for me. I was surprised, however, that I wasn't able to see what was so plainly obvious to the women. Faggot. Faggot. Faggot. If he called, I was still going to the game with him. I didn't give a fuck.

VAL

Faggot? That word again, said with such vehemence. I hadn't really thought about Lance Dennis. He was just a guy, just a guy talking to David. So what? Was the fact that he was a man who loved men supposed to make me look at him differently? If I were a woman, would I have felt any differently if David had been talking to another attractive woman? Was I supposed to see red and get all pissed off? Because of Lance's sexual orientation, was I to assume he was doing more than having a conversation with David? Had he been flirting? Had David been flirting with him? P-L-E-A-S-E. The only man David had eyes for was me. I didn't care that David had a new friend. I had no fear of David developing new friendships. I was confident in our relationship. Our union could stand the introduction of new friends. It was the old friendships that made me antsy.

PATTI

Men were so damn stupid. What would it take? Did that man have to stick his tongue down David's throat before David would have known he was a fucking faggot?

KIM

If I weren't so wrapped up in Val, I'd be positively drooling over Lance. He was everything I looked for in a man: intelligent, kind, ambitious, smart and sexy with a dynamite body and out of sight ass. We had been working together at the center three weeks before we formally met. It was during our first conversation that I realized he was not interested in me, or people like me, at all. He did not announce his sexual preference or defer to another man in my presence, but the chemistry that existed between a man and a woman who were aware of each other sexually wasn't there. Any lust was one-sided and solely mine. What a shame. He would have been considered a good catch for some woman.

CHAPTER TWENTY-EIGHT

After leaving the community center, they had lunch at a little bistro downtown not too far from The Staples Center. Surprisingly, no one approached Val for an autograph. Occasionally there was a glance in his direction that held a hint of recognition, but they were allowed to eat in peace. After lunch, they went to the horse races at Hollywood Park. Val won $62. He lost $318. Kim broke even, and Patti lost $117 of David's money. David didn't play. He contended it was too easy to get hooked on the horses. By the time they made it back to their retreat in the Hollywood Hills, they barely had enough time to change before they were due at Lola's.

If Patti had been impressed with David's house, she was nearly rendered speechless by Lola's. Choosing to live in Bel Air so that they could be part of, but apart from, the Hollywood hype, the Pardeaux house was a traditional Bel Air mansion. The location alone guaranteed a measure of dazzle power. Flanked by rows of perfectly manicured trees and surrounded by a high tech security system, it was a star's home.

As Val punched in the security code that opened the gates to the mansion grounds, Patti looked down at her clothes with a smile. She was glad she had decided to wear something dressy. Her suede dress was more than appropriate. Val and David, on the other hand, didn't look that spectacular. They both wore jeans and shirts. Big deal.

"Are you sure you guys are dressed all right?" Patti asked worriedly.

"Sure," David reassured her. "We'd be lucky if Andre puts on shoes."

"Who is Andre?"

"My father," Val answered.

"Your father?" Patti asked Val incredulously.

"Yep." He glanced at her. In deference to Patti, he had gone out and rented a car. It was a Mercedes SUV. That seemed to appease her. She liked Mercedes.

"What's so shocking? Didn't you think I had a father?"

"Everybody has a father," Patti said defensively. Val's accent was starting to annoy her. "Just everybody's father is not at home."

David reached across the seat and tugged Val's ponytail. Patti saw the horseplay that went on between them. It annoyed her. Mother, father, fortune, fame, David—it seemed Val had it all.

Patti grew up in an environment in which the single parent household was commonplace. Usually the homes were female-headed, and sometimes no more than fifteen years separated the mother's age from that of her children. When David said they were having dinner with Val's mother, Patti's only frame of reference did not include his father. The jealousy she felt confused her. She found herself possessively holding David's hand. For the life of her, she couldn't figure out why. She and Val weren't rivals, but it suddenly seemed like they were in a war and she was losing the battle.

"Stop that," she hissed as they got out of the car. "You look like a couple of sissies."

Val shot a look to David. This would be the perfect time to address the issue. David looked away from Val's piercing gaze.

"We aren't sissies," he said, opening the double doors to the Pardeaux house.

Lola greeted them at the front door, cutting off any additional conversation based on Patti's heartless comment. She was dressed in a silken kimono. To the surprise of both Val and David, she had braided her hair. If it were possible, she was even more beautiful than usual.

"Lola. Your hair. It's great," Val exclaimed as he fingered an intricately woven tendril.

"I'm glad you approve," she said, kissing his cheek.

"If you weren't spoken for, I'd give Andre a run for his money," David added.

"You're so good for my ego, David. I love you." She kissed David's cheek as well. Patti thought she was one of the most beautifully exotic creatures she had ever seen. "You must be Patricia, David's friend from Dallas."

"Yes. Yes, I am," Patti stammered, suddenly conscious of her heavy Southern accent and lack of worldly sophistication. She felt that on some level she should have known who this woman was. It was obvious she was not ordinary. There was an air of sophistication, an aura of greatness about her. She was Val's mother. No wonder Val was such a pretty man.

"It smells good in here," Patti said. The odors emanating throughout the house were delightful.

"Yes, it does," David agreed.

"Thank you. Thank you, but it was no trouble. I love to cook. I'm always cooking something," Lola said as they walked toward the kitchen.

"And she's always testing it out on me," Andre called as he came down the stairs.

Val could tell from Patti's expression the moment she saw Andre that she didn't know. She really didn't know who his parents were. The look on her face was priceless and too genuine not to be real. Val did not gain comfort from Patti's unease. Actually, her unease made him uncomfortable.

Lola had not gone all out for her cozy little dinner party. Patti thought she had. The Cajun cuisine she prepared was an easy one for her. The oyster and shrimp fondue, broiled scallops, red beans and rice were comfortable, easy recipes she could whip up in her sleep. Only the main course of blackened catfish required a little extra work. She had to mix her spices just right so that they weren't overpowering.

Throughout dinner, Val felt as if had unknowingly played a joke on Patti. It hadn't been his intent to pull the wool over her eyes. His mother was black. Val was brown. His father was white. Val hadn't grown up a dark-skinned woman of the South. He didn't know how his multi-colored family would affect her.

Dinner wasn't the charming experience it usually was with Lola and Andre. David had never seen Patti so withdrawn. She seemed to be so careful of everything that she wasn't comfortable enough to be herself. David felt as if he should have said something to make her more comfortable. He just didn't know what he should have said.

PATTI

Nobody told me his daddy was *white*. Nobody told me they were *really* rich. Nobody told me that when we ate dinner we'd have more than one fork. Nobody told me anything. I got so mad that my attitude was hanging all out. Davey-Gene tried to make me laugh, but that didn't do any good. Val and his parents were something else. They were white, whiter and whitest, and I don't mean skin color. Lola was black as me, black as David, but they acted so white, *so white,* and they got along like friends. He called his mother Lola. He called his father Paupee. They all sounded so funny that I didn't know what anybody was saying. I had been black all my life. I had known white people all my life. You just couldn't get away with forgetting that they were white. As soon as you forget, they forget, and "nigger" coming from them just didn't sound the same as it did coming from us.

I had never seen a house like theirs. Each and every room looked like something out of a magazine. There was so much old furniture it had to be antique and expensive. The pictures on the wall were just like the ones you saw in museums. After dinner, we went to the library. There were books everywhere. All four walls had built-in bookcases like at the public library. It didn't surprise me to see pictures of Lola and Andre with all those famous people. I had figured out that they were famous too. But it did surprise me to see Davey-Gene and Val in some of the pictures. Before I came to L.A., I hadn't known. I really hadn't known that David wasn't my Davey-Gene anymore.

LOLA

I had known David for a long time. I had met no one from his life before Val. This girl was so different from David, so different from my son, that I didn't know what to make of her. She wasn't like Larry, David's partner on the police force, who for some time had been an important part of our lives. His violent death and David's subsequent injury had been the catalyst that transformed David into the literary genius he now was. I remember Heathcliff speculating that maybe David and Larry's relationship was more than a friendship, but each time I saw David, each time I saw my son, each time I saw them together, I knew that neither David nor Valentine were lovers of men. They were both a lover of one man. Val was David's lover. David was Val's lover. David's friend from Dallas did not fit into the picture.

VAL

Lola and Andre loved David. David loved them. This fact made me so happy I could shout. I don't think that I would have been able to choose between my parents and my lover. I loved them differently, but did not love one more than the other.

David looked up. Our eyes met. I smiled. So did he. Then my mother put her arm around my shoulder and kissed my cheek. We were all gathered around my father who sat at his piano playing songs from one of his early musicals. Who could ask for more? I loved these people. Thank God I never had to choose.

PATTI

This could have been my life. These could have been my friends. Davey-Gene could be looking at me the way Val's white daddy looked at his black mother. They were all gathered around the piano singing like the fucking Brady bunch. And what's so bad about it was that I wished I knew the songs. The longer I stayed, the more their closeness started to bother me. They had so much together it was like they were a couple.

As soon as I thought it, I dismissed it. They didn't act like lovers. They were just friends. Good friends. I wanted to be David's friend. If I had played my cards right, I'd be sitting next to him instead of that half-cast boy who was as graceful as a deer and as sleek as a cat. I made up my mind right then and there that I wanted to be part of this. I wanted fancy things, expensive parties, grand houses and a fine, rich man. Fuck friendship. I was gonna fuck Davey-Gene. I didn't come all the way to California to be no houseguest. I got up from the couch—it was leather and soft as skin—and joined them. I didn't know the words, but I could fake it.

CHAPTER TWENTY-NINE

By the time the trio pulled into the garage of their home, Patti had mapped out her plan to recapture David's affection. She was a pretty girl, sure of her sexuality and confident in her abilities to get a man. When she decided she wanted David, she went after him with guns loaded. The first thing she did was slip into the T-shirt she slept in then joined Val and David in front of the TV in the viewing room.

Though there were several televisions in the house, Patti had counted eight, she preferred the television room. The big screen plasma television fascinated Patti, and she was more than impressed with the collection of videotapes, DVDs, compact and laser discs. This room, like the rest of the house, had Val's decorating stamp on it. Colors were chosen to inspire comfort and aesthetic appeal. It was a friendly room, comforting and homey.

When Patti entered the room in her T-shirt, she was not surprised to see David dressed in sweats, slumped on the couch. She was, however, annoyed to see Val in a pair of boxers doing sit-ups on the floor. *Is he always here?* His belly was rock hard and finely muscled. *How many sit-ups can one man do?* Patti stepped over him and took a seat next to David on the couch.

"What are you watching?"

"*9½ Weeks.*"

"Cool." Life couldn't be better than if she had picked the movie from the extensive library herself.

PATTI

What man in his right mind could watch all this fucking and not get a hard-on? Shit, before the night was over, I'd have David eating out of my hand. Hell, I might even have David and Val fighting over me. Wouldn't that be interesting?

VAL

I glanced over at David, trying to judge his reaction to the movie. Patti was enjoying the infamous kitchen scene, so she didn't see him wink at me. He was so fucking sexy. All he had on was a pair of Adidas sweat pants. They were a rich royal purple, just a few shades different from his skin. Between him and the movie, I was getting a hard-on so painful that I didn't know what I was going to do. As unobtrusively as possible, I crossed my legs and wished Patti would leave.

The three of us sat there like robots programmed to respond to the demands of our hormones. We were all sexually excited. You could smell the sexual tension in the room. My dick was still hard and refused to get soft even when I thought of destroyed rain forests, massive oil spills, and the greenhouse effect. David moved from the couch to the floor and lay on his stomach to hide his erection. He was so transparent. If Patti weren't here, I'd be all over him. I'd show him what to do with a hard dick. But Patti was here.

I got up from the couch, yawned and stretched. It was a little after 1:00 A.M. "Okay, guys, I'm going to bed," I said. Somebody had to make the first move.

"You guys?" Patti mimicked me and rolled her eyes. "I still can't get over that accent."

"What accent?" I asked.

"Your accent."

"No accent here. Do you hear an accent, David?"

"I don't even hear you talking," David answered.

"You guys," she mimicked again. "Why is it sometimes you have it and sometimes you don't? Like earlier today?"

"I was just fooling around today," I said.

"So, people give you a hard time about it?"

"No. Only you."

"I like giving you a hard time."

"Why?"

"Because you seem so unshakable."

"I'm shakable."

"What shakes you up?" She was flirting openly with me.

I glanced at David. My lover had turned over onto his back. His dick wasn't hard anymore. He had managed to think of something to stifle his erection. I envied him, his peace of mind and his ability to control his libido. Whenever we were alone again, I'd ask him his secret.

"Right now, you shake me up."

"Good. That's what I was trying to do."

She was such a fucking tease. I was getting mad at myself because I was falling for her act and I wondered why. What was it about Patti that kept me in a state of arousal? All I could think of was that David had been more than adequate in his description of her in *Cake Walk*. She was wanton. She was a siren. She held the promise of rhapsody between her legs. She teased and toyed with both of us like a bored cat playing with a trapped mouse. I was tiring of the game.

" 'Night, all." I started for my room.

"Wait on me." David got up from the couch.

"Well, if you two are going, I am too." Patti got up to join us. I turned off everything and we headed to our separate rooms. I could tell that she was counting the seconds before one of us knocked on her bedroom door. Two hours later, she was probably pissed off because neither one of us had taken her up on her offer or snapped at the bait she left out.

CHAPTER THIRTY

By the time Lance rolled into Josepha's, he had had a very full day of class, basketball practice and two hours of study at the law library. He was too tired to cook, too hungry to sleep, too health-conscious for fast food and too wired up over meeting David Lincoln to go home. He selected a table in the back away from the crowd, ordered grilled chicken breast, a fresh green salad and iced tea. He pulled from his backpack a wellworn copy of *Cake Walk* and began to read.

The sex was awesome. Together they had gone places and done things that some only dream about. It had been a long time since he had been with anyone with his stamina, enthusiasm and skill. She made him come with soft, delicate, cat-like flicks of her tongue against the insides of his muscular thighs, and kept him as hard as Pennsylvania steel by sucking his big toe into her mouth.

Her well-rounded ass stared him in the face, pink slit glistening, moist and smiling at him as she faced away from him, feasting on his feet. He grabbed her waist, pulled

her back against his hard self and thrust into her from be-
hind as she maneuvered his entire set of toes into her mouth.
He came, spewing thick globs of seed into her as she contin-
ued to chew gently on his toes and lick his ankles.

Afterwards, he was still hard, ready and anxious for her.
She laughed softly as he molded her body into positions he
enjoyed as he took her again and again. After their marathon
of sex, they fell, glistening with sweat, into a lover's embrace.

He whispered, "I love you," into her ear and fell asleep.

When he awakened, she was gone. The only evidence of
their night together was the odor of sex, hot, heavy and lin-
gering against his skin and in the air. She had left like a
thief in the night, stealing his heart and capturing his soul
between her legs. He didn't even know her name. But he knew
who she was. She was woman. She was love. She was . . .

Lance was so wrapped up in *Cake Walk* that he hadn't
noticed Wayne Carey until he took a seat across from
him.

"Hi," Wayne spoke.

"Hi," Lance said, closing his book and looking at
Wayne.

This was very unusual. The clientele Lance had
was an exclusive one. Some of his clients had very
high profiles and would experience nothing short of
catastrophe if their relationship with Lance or their
membership in Marco's were ever exposed. Needless
to say, they had more to lose than gain if there were
ever a hint of scandal. So of course, on those occasions when Lance spotted or had been spotted by
members of the Marco's elite, they did not acknowledge each other except under the best circumstances.
There was an unwritten code of decorum that dictated that they remain discreet. Wayne seemed to be

unaware of the rules of the game. Sitting across from Lance, he was cool as a cucumber.

"Can I buy you a drink?" Wayne asked.

"No. I'm fine." Lance sipped his tea.

"Good book." Wayne indicated *Cake Walk*.

"Yeah. I like D. E. Lincoln."

"He's a nice guy," Wayne said in an off-handed way.

"Yeah," Lance responded, not sure of which direction the conversation was taking. "Look," Lance blurted.

"I had just about gotten you out of my mind when I looked up and there you were. I think you bewitched me."

"Maybe I did."

"Are you working tonight?"

"No."

"I see." Wayne took a sip from his champagne. "Would you like to have some fun tonight?"

Lance laughed. "I wasn't expecting to have any fun tonight."

"Oh." Wayne started to get up from the table.

"I meant," Lance started, halting Wayne as he got up from his chair, "I don't have any rubbers."

"I do."

"Okay." Lance got up from the table, leaving payment and a generous tip for the waitress. Wayne raised an eyebrow at the amount of money Lance set down. "We people in the service industry have a special affinity for each other," Lance explained.

"I see." Wayne smiled. "I'll follow you. Okay?"

"Okay." Lance left first.

Wayne went to the bathroom, urinated, washed his hands, waited five minutes, then met Lance at the corner. On the way to his house, he kept looking in

his rearview mirror to make sure Lance was following him. He was.

"I must be out of my mind," Lance muttered to
himself as he followed Wayne. He never did things
like this. Men he saw at Marco's were not men he'd
let into his personal life. But there was something
about Wayne Carey. His quirkiness and sexiness might
be just what Lance needed to tide him over until he
was able to deal with this thing for David Lincoln.
Wayne would be a pleasant pastime.

WAYNE

I decided that I had obviously lost my mind. I hadn't
picked up a guy in ages. It was a bad habit to get into,
and I couldn't afford the possible complications. But
this guy, Lance, I knew him. I had fucked him. I had
gotten under his skin, and he obviously had gotten
under mine. Ever since we had our tête-à-tête, Val
wasn't foremost in my thoughts.

"Nice place you have here," Lance said upon en-
tering my home.

When he said it, I felt like he meant it. He was sitting on the sofa. I poured us a couple of brandies
and was getting ready to serve him his drink when I
noticed he was flipping through my copy of *People*
magazine. I had run out to buy a new copy to replace
the one I had soiled. I don't know if it was because I
had so recently used it as fuel to ignite my masturbatory fantasies or because he hesitated over the layout
of The Troupe in which Val was prominently displayed,
that I felt a special kinship and affinity with him.

"Thanks," he said, taking the brandy and putting
the magazine back on the table.

"I know how to treat my guest," I said.

"And how is that?" He was looking at me over the rim of the brandy glass.

"Like this." I took his glass from him and kissed him. He tasted like seven-year-old brandy, mystery, and good times.

"Mmm." He leaned into the kiss.

"You taste good."

"You feel good." He stretched out onto the couch and pulled me with him like he was seducing me instead of me seducing him. He began to nibble at my chin and lick at my ears. It was pleasant. It was nice. It was hot. It was good sex. Great.

"Where do you keep the condoms?" he asked.

"In the bedroom."

"Don't you think you need to go get them before this gets serious?"

I got up off him and tripped over the coffee table as I raced to my bedroom. "Fuck!" I slipped on a sock and stubbed my toe as I tried to maneuver past the weights I had left on the floor. I should have put them back in my weight room this morning. I opened the drawer to my nightstand and stared at an address book and the screenplay to *Cake Walk*. There were no rubbers. "Shit."

"Problem?" I heard Lance say as I turned to see him standing in my doorway. He had unbuttoned his shirt. The blue-black of his skin gleamed against the white silk. His pecs were well defined. The muscles of his stomach were hard. His torso angled into a perfect *V*, which disappeared into the open button of his 501's. He was a study in muscular perfection, masculine pride.

"What would you say if I told you I lied?" I tried levity.

"I'd say you have the wrong guy." He was deadly serious.

"I was joking. I thought I had rubbers, but I don't."

"It's okay," he said with a shrug.

"Yeah?"

"But that doesn't mean I'm going to let you fuck me." He buttoned his pants and turned back into the living room. Like a dog sniffing at a bone, I followed him. He was sitting back on the couch, the *People* magazine opened in his lap. Standing in my bedroom doorway looking at him sitting my couch, I was struck with a feeling of déjà vu. He looked as if he had been sitting there all the time. He belonged here.

"So," I said, crossing to him.

"So." He again looked up from his magazine.

"What do you want to do?"

"You know, Wayne, I don't do this all the time."

"I know that." How did I know that?

"How do you know that?"

"I just know."

"I don't know what it is about you . . ." he began. He was looking into my eyes. His eyes were as dark as night.

I felt the stirring in my groin as my dick continued to rise against my jeans.

"We are not going to fuck, Wayne."

"I know."

"I'll leave if you want."

"No, no." I crossed to him and sat on the floor facing him.

"You want to talk, right?"

"Yeah," I said, shocked because that's just what I wanted to do.

"Okay, so talk." Again he closed the *People* magazine. I knew he wasn't going to pick it up again as I began to speak freely about myself.

LANCE

"Valentine Pardeaux?" His confession was startling. This was the first time I lay nearly naked in the arms of one man while he openly confessed his infatuation for another. Were it not for the fact that I was guilty of wishing he were someone else, I'd be offended. What was shocking is that the man of his dreams was probably doing what I was doing with him with the man of my dreams. It seemed that Tinseltown was a small town indeed.

We were lying on the floor in front of his fireplace. Some time during the night he had removed the pillows from the couch and placed them on the floor. After a lot of talk and a lot of wine, we had cuddled and kissed like teenagers. Because neither one of us had any rubbers, we weren't going to fuck. That was out of the question.

Beneath his jeans he had on red Calvin Klein briefs. Mine were green. Red and green were the colors of celebration and liberation. Maybe I'd teach him about Kwanzaa. I had my hand in his briefs. I cupped his balls and felt the weight of his penis. He was semi-erect. I loved it.

"So, I remind you of Valentine Pardeaux," I said, squeezing his growing arousal.

"In a way," Wayne replied.

"We are absolutely nothing alike."

"Yes, you are."

"You mean we're both black."

"That has nothing to do with it."

"Sure?" I put his hand on my dick. It was bigger than his. "You know the myth."

"Well . . ." he hedged.

I kissed him. "You taste so good."

"Why do I remind you of Val?"

"You know him?"

"Yeah." I didn't tell him we had just met today. I was curious what he was going to say.

"In the biblical sense?"

"If that's a roundabout way of asking if Val and I met the way you and I did, then the answer is no. If—"

"Hey, hey, hey," he interrupted me.

"What?"

"You talk too much." He kissed me.

"Don't try to change the subject," I said.

He kissed me again.

"But—"

He rolled on top of me and spread my legs a little so that I could feel the impression of him pressed against me.

"Stop that." I patted his ass.

He eased off me but kept his hand around my penis.

"So, why do I remind you of Val?"

He squeezed me affectionately. "Because you're both such bitches."

I pushed him off me. "Fuck you, man." I made my voice hard. I could be butch when I had to.

"The bitch in you turns me on. That untouchable quality is exciting. You're both so hot. So fucking hot and smart and sexy and—"

"Black." I was fucking with him. He didn't seem to be one of those white boys who got off on the skin, the dick, and the virility.

"Val's not that black, so it's not that."

I thought of Valentine Michael Pardeaux. The only thing we had in common was our desire for David. Then I began to wonder. If I reminded Wayne of Val, then on a subconscious level, did he remind me of David?

Even though I had only met David today, I felt that I knew him from his writing. No one could be that far from his creation. I knew his work so I knew him. He was a brilliant writer; Wayne was a brilliant actor. David was articulate, creative, worldly; so was Wayne. David was fine, sexy, virile; so was Wayne. David had been an object of fantasy, a fixation of lust. Wayne was lying next to me, tangible, real, hard and stroking my penis. I closed my eyes. I would not imagine that he was David. I did not need to fantasize about my dream lover. I had a lover right next to me, and what he was doing felt good, soooo gooooo. I lay back and allowed him to jerk me off. We didn't need a rubber for that.

CHAPTER THIRTY-ONE

By the time Patti got up for breakfast, Val had already left for the day. If she had known his routine, she would have realized that he and Lola were out shopping. David was in his room working on *David's Story*. She did not know that. She awoke to an empty house and was still pissed off from the night before. She got up, slipped into her string bikini and went out to the pool. Maybe an early morning swim would clear her mind so that she could develop a game plan that would land her where she wanted to be, in his house, with these people, living his life.

Sitting beside Lola as she tooled down Fairfax to the Farmer's Market, Val leaned his head against the cool glass of the Mercedes window. It was a beautiful day, one for outings with family, friends or lovers. If someone had told him years ago he'd be moaning like a lovesick puppy over the gentle giant who had become his roommate through a mix-up in room assignments, he would have been offended and maybe angry enough to retaliate. But no one had told him then. His feelings for David had sneaked up on him and taken him by surprise. When he had finally gotten past the pleasure they were able to give each other physically and revel in the intangibles, he realized he was in love. Yes, he was helplessly, hopelessly in love with his best friend.

On a purely emotional level, he felt he should be at home defending his territory, staking out David and threatening Patti within an inch of her life. But everything gallant in him told him not to cling and smother his lover. Besides, the clinging vine was not a role he played well. He didn't like jealous, over-possessive types. Before David, he had been in a relationship that had not run its course because his lover loved to drop by unexpectedly, threw fits when he didn't call her back, and got downright silly in public when he even looked at another woman. He had never been like that. He would never be like that. He would not become one of the fawning, overly possessive lovers he detested. Thus resolved, he eased his head away from the cool glass and made himself comfortable in his seat.

"I see you've rejoined the living," Lola cooed, easing her car into a recently vacated parking space. Val was dressed in his "I don't want to be recognized" attire. Lola was in form-fitting jeans and a loose sweater. Her new braids were piled atop her head and her jewelry simple. She wore thick, overly large sunshades. She was speaking to her son in French and moving through the crowd in a whirlwind buying frenzy. To the casual observer, she and Val were just two tourists sampling the tastes and smells of the Farmer's Market. Val loved these brief moments of anonymity when he could move freely through the crowds without concern for his public image and the face he must wear for his audience.

"Really, Valentine, for all the conversation I'm getting from you, I could have come by myself," Lola declared.

"I'm sorry. I was just thinking," Val responded.

"You can't think and talk?"

"Don't be smart."

She threw her head back and laughed. "You're precious." She kissed his cheek.

"I love you."

"I love you too."

Neither one of them saw the camera as an amateur photographer snapped their picture.

By the time Val got home that afternoon, David was still shut in his study, writing. Val knew how involved David got when he was working, so he did not disturb him. He found Patti in the kitchen. She had made a tremendous mess, but the odors wafting from her great many pots smelled delicious. She hadn't bothered to dress. When he saw her, she was barefoot and still clad in her bikini.

"Smells good," Val ventured.

"Here, taste," Patti said then dipped her spoon into the bubbling mass, blew on it to cool it, and held it out to him. He accepted the spicy offering of black-eyed peas, tomatoes, rice and spices, and rolled his eyes in delight.

"You can cook too," he said.

"I can do a lot of things." She winked at him and bumped him with her hip to ease him away from the stove.

"Do you need me to help with anything?"

"No. Sit. Sit." She shooed him to a chair as she began making the salad. As an artist, he could appreciate the graceful curves of her body. As a man, he could appreciate what lay beneath the colorful string. As David's lover, he was consumed by a desire to know everything he could possibly know about her.

"Tell me about yourself, Patti," Val said.

"What do you want to know?" she replied.

"Everything."

"There's nothing to tell."

There had to be something to tell or David would not have chosen her and the fact remained that David had chosen her. David had chosen her and David had chosen him. What did they have in common?

"What's your favorite color?" Val asked her.

"Mauve," she answered. Val's was blue.

"What is your favorite movie?"

"It's a tie between *Car Wash* and *Coolie High.*" Val's favorite movie was *Citizen Kane.*

"What did you want to be when you grew up?"

"Mrs. David E. Lincoln." From the look on Val's face, she knew she had scored a point.

What was Val supposed to say after hearing that? Mrs. David E. Lincoln? Was she even from this planet? Anybody with eyes could see that what she and David had then was not what they have now. Work at the post office or for the city of Dallas in a boring, blue-collar job? Not David. No way. Her expectations for him were well below anything he had for himself. Well below anything Val could think of for him.

"This is really, really good," Val said, indicating the soup. He wasn't going to touch her last statement. No way, no how, unh-uh.

When David finished writing, he was shaking. He saved what he had written and got up from his computer. It was rare that something he wrote touched him so completely. Even when he relayed the horrors of the Timothy Joseph McMahon story, he had been able to detach himself from his creation and remain objective. He was a writer. A creator. Objectivity was a luxury he reveled in. But he knew this last chapter of *David's Story* was Pulitzer caliber. He'd garner at least a nomination.

He poured himself a Scotch, thought better of it, then drank deeply from the bottle. He had always known he was a good writer. Suddenly, he realized he was a great writer. It was a heady feeling to create. It gave him a sense of power and filled him with an exhilaration that was almost sexual. A slight fever burned beneath his skin. His dick was semi-hard. He wanted to scream. He wanted to shout from the rooftops. He wanted Val.

Before he even thought about it, he flipped on the intercom.

"Hey, sexy," David purred into the receiver. "I'm coming downstairs and I want you naked." The intercom system had come with the house. It was one of the few things they had not had to have rewired, revamped and re-built before they moved in. Humming and jubilant over his accomplishment, he followed his nose into the kitchen and stopped dead in his tracks when he saw both Val and Patti at the kitchen table.

Fuck! Fuck. Fuck. Fuck, David thought. He had forgotten all about Patti. The look on his face was priceless when he walked into the kitchen. But he quickly recovered.

"Something smells good," he said as he went over to the stove and sampled from the pot. Ladling himself a big bowl of stew, he sat at the table and faced the two people who had shared the title of being his lover.

David had no idea how he could have been so

fucking stupid. Patti had been a guest in his home, a hovering specter from his past, for more days than he wanted to count. With the completion of his last chapter, he had been so wired that all he wanted to do was celebrate with the one he loved. When he thought of that person, he thought of Val, not Patti. He was too afraid to look her in her eye and tell her.

God, he thought, *I am such a fucking hypocrite.*

PATTI

I did it. I finally did it. I don't know if it was the string bikini or the stew. I didn't give a damn. Davey-Gene had come over the loudspeaker saying he wanted me. He had said it before God and everybody else. Well, he could have me naked in any room in this grand house. As soon as I got him naked, I was going to get him. I was going to do things to that boy that would make him think my pussy was lined in mink. Ain't no way I was getting on that plane and heading back to Dallas, Texas and the post office. I had tasted greatness, and the taste was sweet. I didn't want no more soul food. That was crap poor people ate. I didn't want no more half-stepping. I wanted to live like a queen. So, if he wanted me naked, I would be naked. I just had to figure out how to get rid of Val. It wouldn't do for him to think I was a bad girl. It was going to be hard enough putting him out. But he had so much money, I don't think he'd have a hard time finding somewhere else to stay. After tonight, this would be my house, and it wasn't going to be big enough for me, Davey-Gene and Val. Whoever heard of naming a boy Valentine? White people were a trip.

If Val hadn't been sitting at the table with us, I

would have been all over Davey-Gene. But Val was sitting there, and he was starting to piss me off. There was no need for him to act like he hadn't heard Davey-Gene, but he sat there, eating his Hopping John, acting like he hadn't heard anything. I looked from Davey-Gene to Val and back. I tried to let Davey-Gene know with my eyes that I wanted to be alone with him, but he just didn't get it. I guess I was going to have to stop being subtle and go after what I wanted. And yes, I still wanted DaveyGene.

VAL

Enough. Enough. Enough. I was tired of the pretense. No longer was I going to be an unwilling actor in our little charade. Just because David was suffering from denial, it was no reason for me to continue to encourage this farce. But as I looked from Patti's excited face to David's concerned one, I knew I would keep silent for the rest of Patti's stay. I did not want to be responsible for bursting her bubble or destroying David's image in her eyes. I didn't want to be responsible when the walls of denial came tumbling down— and they would come tumbling down, because even though David didn't want to admit to Patti that he had been talking to me over that intercom system, I knew the truth. He had been talking to me. Me, Valentine, not Patti.

I took no pleasure in watching him squirm. I knew he had gotten us into this mess, he could damn well get us out, but I still didn't like to see him uncomfortable. It was almost painful to watch him try to keep her at bay. It never dawned on me to wonder why she assumed she and David would still get together after so many years. I think I had deluded myself into thinking she had no basis for her assumption that after years, they'd just pick up where they left off. Well, now I know I was wrong.

DAVID

She grabbed my dick! When I raised the last spoon of stew to my mouth, she reached out and grabbed me. Hard. Her nails were sharp. I put the spoon down before my shaking hands betrayed what was going on beneath the table.

My eyes darted to Val. He was concentrating on his Hopping John, no doubt trying to determine which spices Patti had used. I wonder if he knew that the reason there was no meat was not due to some trend toward the new, healthy chic way of eating that included meatless dishes, but because we had been very, very poor and could not afford the luxury of having meat daily.

"This is very good, Patti. It tastes just like Nanna's," I complimented her.

"I learned a lot from your Nanna," she said as she manipulated me beneath the table.

I crossed my legs to keep her from inflicting the duel combination of pleasure and pain. She was so expert with her skilled hand and ultra long nails. This skill she did not learn from my Nanna. I know because I had taught her so long ago what I liked. Since then, she had honed her skills on lovers more daring and imaginative than I had been in my young lust.

"Is it spicy enough for you?" she asked, speaking of more than the Hopping John. She extracted her hand from my body and examined her nails to make sure that I had not broken one in my haste to put a halt to her ministrations.

"It's fine," I said.

"Do you want some more?" she asked.

"No. No. I've had enough." I pushed my bowl away from me. Val got up from the table and cleared away our dishes.

I had been closed up in my study all day, and I hadn't seen my beautiful lover since last night. I wanted so much more than to look at him from across the room while Patti groped me beneath the table. As always, I was awed by how lucky I was to have him. He had on a pair of denim walking shorts, a burnt-orange T-shirt and some hand-sewn leather thongs we had bought in Japan. His hair was pulled back into a ponytail and bound with a thin strip of kente cloth. From his ear hung a dangling, golden X.

He put the lunch dishes in the dishwasher and the remainder of the Hopping John into the refrigerator. Once his back was turned, Patti winked at me and blew me a kiss. I couldn't help but wonder how I had gotten myself into this mess. The sane thing to do was to end this charade and explain to Patti that Val was more than my housemate. But if I confessed that, how could I justify all the sneaking, lying and half-truths that had occurred during her visit? I was damned if I did and damned if I didn't. But I'd be damned if I was going to fuck Patti. I was not going to make that mistake again. I just didn't know how I was going to get her mind off what she thought was our impending tryst.

Val made quick work of the cleanup then turned to face Patti and me.

"I went shopping with Lola this morning," he announced.

"Oh, God," I groaned. "What's the damage?"

"Don't worry. I didn't spend that much," Val said.

"How much is not that much?"

"Not much." Val wiggled his eyebrows and smiled as if he had a secret.

I looked up and noticed Patti noticing the interplay between Val and me. She snorted with disgust into her iced tea. "You two act like you're married," she said.

"When you've lived with each other as long as we have, it's like being married." There. Val had said it without saying it. We were just like a married couple. Patti was just like the other woman. Only in situations like this, the other woman usually doesn't sit, dressed in a string bikini, at the kitchen table.

"What did you buy when you were out shopping?" I asked, trying to take Patti's mind off her last statement.

"I got something for . . ." Val reached into his pocket and pulled out a jewelry box. "You." He presented it to Patti.

"For me?" she asked excitedly.

"For you."

Thank God for Val. My lover. My friend. My savior. As Patti opened the box with shaking fingers, my eyes met Val's over her bent head. I smiled. Val smiled back. Val had scored a point. Inside the box was a gold, diamond and gemstone necklace. It was a chunky, gaudy, elaborate, expensive piece of work. I knew Val, and I knew that as soon as he had seen it, he knew Patti would love it, just as he had known that Kim would love the charm bracelet he had purchased from a little consignment store. The charm bracelet was a delicate golden wisp loaded with intricately carved golden flowers. The bracelet was not nearly as expensive as the necklace, but the bracelet was Kim, and the necklace was obviously Patti.

Val watched with amusement as she preened in front of the reflective surface of the stainless steel refrigerator.

"It's beautiful. Thank you," Patti said as she ran over to Val, threw her arms around his neck and kissed him. It was a purely impulsive gesture meant as a thank you to Val for thinking of her. But Patti was unable to leave it at that. She had had years of conditioning, geared toward soliciting a certain response from men. Given the opportunity to show her appreciation of such an expensive a gift, she would do just that. She rubbed herself against Val, making sure he felt the roundness of her breasts and the suppleness of her shape.

"You're welcome, Patti," my lover said, easing her away from him. He took a seat opposite me at the kitchen table.

"I've got to see what I have to wear with this," she said as she bent down and kissed him on the lips then bounded up the stairs, intent on trying on every outfit she had packed to see which one looked the best with her new gift.

Once alone, Val and I looked at each other and laughed like parents thrilled at seeing their child rip through colorful wrapping paper to the gift inside.

"That was a nice thing you did," I said.

"I'm a nice guy," Val replied.

"Yeah, you are. Come here, nice guy."

"What's in it for me?"

"A surprise."

Val got up from his seat at the table and came to

me. I crooked my finger at Val, indicating that he should get closer. When Val did, I kissed him.

"Where's my surprise?" Val asked me, so I took his hand and placed it over my crotch. "Hmmm," Val mused, "that's a nice surprise." He kissed me again. "Only four more days, David."

"Four more days until what?"

"Four more days until she leaves and we have peace."

"Hallelujah!"

"Hallelujah!" Again we kissed then parted. "What do you have planned for the rest of the day?"

"Well, I really need to write, but I guess I haven't been a good host to Patti."

"You want me to take her off your hands for the rest of the evening?"

"Would you do that for me?"

"I'd do anything for you."

"Anything?"

"Anything."

I eased Val's chair away from the kitchen table and spread my legs in invitation to him. Val got the message. He walked over to me, unsnapped my jeans and lowered my zipper.

"Anything," Val said, reaching into my pants and removing my penis. "Anything." Val knelt and swallowed the whole of me. I threw my head back and sighed with contentment. "Anything."

I reached out my hands and entwined them within Val's hair. It had taken me a while to get used to Val's hair. Of all Val's physical characteristics, his hair was the most white, the most Caucasian.

With skilled tongue and lips, Val manipulated my throbbing erection. He licked the head, caressed the shaft and treasured my maleness. The short, crinkly hairs around my groin tickled Val's nose as he nuzzled at my crotch.

Moaning, I leaned back into my chair to allow Val more access to my body. In the initial moments as Val cherished me, I realized that Patti could have walked through the kitchen door dressed in nothing but the necklace Val had just given her and some dental floss, and I would not have cared. I would not have cared. I would not have cared.

The next thing I knew, Val had taken my muscular thighs and placed them over his shoulders as he put his hands under my hips and pulled me closer for easier access. I was so close to the edge, so close to coming, that I had to make a conscious effort to keep my moans of pleasure from reaching a joyful crescendo. I was so wrapped up in my lover and the pleasure that I was receiving that I almost didn't hear Patti when her voice came over the intercom.

"My necklace is beautiful!" she cooed. "It matches my suede dress, my leather shorts and my almost silk blouse. Thank you. Thank you. Thank you."

We both ignored her. To speak at this time would have been too difficult.

"Hello? Hello?" Patti called. "Damn," she muttered to herself, unaware that we could hear her every word. "Is this thing on?" Again when we did not answer her, she swore into the intercom. "Shit. Here I come."

When I heard her, I tried to push Val away from my swollen crotch, but Val wouldn't budge. He clamped his lips around my penis and hooked his hands into the belt loops of my jeans. I think he wanted her to catch us.

"Val, Val, Val," I moaned, trying to extract myself from Val's sucking mouth. In my mind's eye, I could see Patti leaving the bedroom and walking down the hallway to the stairs. I could imagine her shock, her outrage, her horror, and her disgust as she walked in and saw me straining, sweating, and bucking into my lover's greedy mouth. Yet I could not stop myself. I could not stop before I erupted in a copious, orgasmic flow of love. My lover continued to suckle and extract from me my life's force. "My God. I love you," I managed to say as Val eased my limp member back into my pants.

"I love you too," Val said, in less than a hurry as he kissed me. I could taste myself on Val's lips, salty, strong, and wild.

The clickety-click of Patti's three-inch heels was heard tapping against the Spanish tiles that covered the back stairs leading into the kitchen well before we saw her.

"Zip your pants, David," Val ordered me.

With shaking fingers, I did as my lover instructed. No sooner than Val reached for a bottle of red wine did Patti burst into the kitchen.

In the short time she had been gone, she had dressed in a red suede dress, "come-fuck-me" pumps and her new jewelry. If the dress had a better cut and the shoes, a better quality leather, she would have looked like a thousand bucks.

"Well, how do I look?" she asked.

"Beautiful as ever," I answered automatically.

"Well?" She preened for Val.

He studied her with cool, appraising eyes over the rim of his wine glass. "How would you like to go shopping?" he asked her.

"I'd love to go shopping. I haven't spent any of the money I brought with me," she said.

"You don't have to spend any of it now. Let us treat you to something," I said, reaching into my pocket and extracting my wallet. I took out several crisp $100 bills.

"Come on now, David. She is a guest in our home," Val said as he reached for my wallet and extracted the rest of the cash. He handed the empty wallet back to me. Patti watched the entire transaction, awed by the amount of money that passed from one hand to the other. I don't think Patti picked up on the ease in which Val and I shared. I don't think it was as much of an issue for her as the fact that I had just given Val almost a thousand dollars. It was the amount of money, not the transaction itself that impressed her.

"You two sure know how to treat a guest," she said, wide-eyed.

"We try." Val reached for the keys to the rental car that were hanging on a hook by the door, and ushered Patti through the garage to the parked cars. Once they were gone, I got up from the table and headed toward my study. I had a lot of work to do. I still had a lot of chapters to finish. I couldn't win the Pulitzer sitting at the kitchen table getting blown by my lover.

As I sat in front of my computer and flipped on the screen, I wondered what would have happened if Patti caught us. She would have been shocked, true, but would she have been disgusted? Would she have been offended? Would she have judged, condemned or ran screaming from the room? Would she have still felt about me as she always had, or would I too be placed in that category of faggoty, dickless men she held in such contempt?

Since she would be leaving in four more days, did it really matter? In four days, Patti would once again be relegated to the shadowy world of memory. Her acceptance, denial or rejection of my choice of lover would not be of any significance, tempered by distance. I would not be susceptible to her scrutiny or censor, and I could once again embrace my choices as guiltlessly as I had previously. I did not need the specter of Patticake from my past demanding my attention, affection or dick. With her safely stored away in Dallas, Texas, I would be free to be David E. Lincoln. I didn't have to be Davey-Gene. The persona I surrounded myself with did not allow room for a history like mine. I preferred the trappings of my new life, the ease with which I accepted both Val's and my celebrity status.

Organizing my thoughts so that my reflection on my life, my lovers, my loves did not interfere with *David's Story*, I began to write again.

"Shit," I yelled, frustrated. I pushed myself away from my computer. My writing had been going so well. I had been on a roll, then *Bam!* It was as if a door had been slammed in the face of my creativity. I found myself unable to write. My guess was that it was partially due to stress.

Knowing myself well enough to know that once I lost my edge I wouldn't be able to write again until I recaptured my elusive, creative muse, I got up from my screen and wandered to my gym. Exercise would tire me out, and then I'd take a nap. Maybe after I slept a little, I'd be ready to write again. I hadn't been sleeping well since Patti's arrival and her subsequent early morning raids. Who knows? Maybe in my dazed state, she had captured part of my soul and creativity when she had stolen my sperm.

CHAPTER THIRTY-TWO

*N*ick was a good-looking guy, taller than average, dark and handsome, as the saying goes. He had a body that was built to perfection. Five miles a day and an hour on the Universal weight system in his house saw to that. He had a head full of black as midnight curls, eyes that were expressive and changed colors with his moods and teeth his father, the dentist, had nurtured to perfection. He smiled at the drop of a hat, white teeth shining against the swarthy complexion of his skin, creating a contrast that was breathtaking. He dressed in the height of contemporary fashion and wore his clothes well. He was one of those guys who looked good in silk or denim. He knew it and he exploited it. Nick Shaw was a whore.

Lance yawned, stretched and made himself comfortable on his couch. *Down Went Jonah* was one of his favorite books. When the pressure of his law books got to him, he tossed them aside and pulled a book off his well-stocked bookshelf so that he could momentarily lose himself between the pages of a make-believe world. Books by D. E. Lincoln were the most dog-eared.

Ex-whore, Nick scolded himself as he jogged around the exclusive Turtle Creek section of Dallas, Texas. Rain, shine, snow or hail, Nick ran five miles a day. For years his body had been the instrument of his trade, and he kept it fine-tuned because he never knew when he would be called upon to use it for profit instead of pleasure.

Lance had read *Down Went Jonah* more times than he could remember. He felt a kinship with the main character, Nick Shaw. Had he first read about Nick after meeting David, he would have sworn that David had based Nick on him. But he read *Down Went Jonah* before he met David. David didn't know anything about Lance. He didn't know his profession, ambitions, wants, dreams or desires, yet he mirrored them so well, it was as if when he created Nick, he had been under Lance's skin. He guessed that was part of the reason he was a little in love with David. Settling in, he turned the page.

Oh, he hadn't had to be a whore. His story was nothing like that of streetwalkers performing out of desperation and need. His background was one of privilege.

Like Nick, Lance was a son of privilege coming from a background of privilege. Lance had ruled his destiny. It had not ruled him. The choices he made had not been ones made out of desperation, but instead, desire. Reflecting on this, he found his mind wandering. He wasn't lying on his couch reading any longer. He was fourteen years old, standing in his bedroom window, looking down at Nathaniel Jackson. Just like Nick and Lisa on page 18 of *Down Went Jonah,* their eyes met over a distance. Suddenly, they were the only two people in the universe. Nathaniel Jackson smiled and waved, and fourteen-year-old Lance Dennis fell head over heels in love.

Closing the book, Lance leaned back onto his couch. He'd take a nap. Reading was making him sleepy. As he closed his eyes, he thought of his first love, his first choice, his first conscious decision to travel down the road that led him to this spot, this day, living this life.

He and Nathaniel had met one week later. Nathaniel was bouncing a ball in his backyard. Sweat dripped from his lean body in shiny droplets. Lance was watching from his perch in his room. Drop. Drop. Drop. What he would have given to be a drop of sweat that glistened like black oil in the sunlight as it rolled down Nathaniel's body. Nathaniel suddenly stopped dribbling his ball and turned to face Lance's window.

Lance immediately ducked out of sight.

"You can come down if you want," Nathaniel called to Lance. "I don't bite."

Lance peeked from around the corner that partially obstructed his view of Nathaniel. "Hi," he said, waving weakly.

Although the two houses were on different streets, a bordering alleyway connected the backyards. There wasn't much yard, just enough space for a pool and a basketball hoop in each yard. But since Lance was upstairs in his room, Nathaniel had to almost shout so that Lance could hear him. If the two boys had been in their yards at their respective fences, they could have carried on a conversation in normal tones.

"Why don't you come on down? The gate's open."

Nathaniel extended the invitation then turned and did a perfect nosedive into his pool.

Lance hesitated only a few minutes then went to his backyard. When Nathaniel emerged from the pool, dripping, glistening, and magnificent, Lance stood with his mouth agape.

"Sure did take you a long time to quit looking at me from that window," Nathaniel said.

"Hi," Lance said.

"Hi."

The two boys shook hands. Their eyes met and Lance knew. He was a faggot.

Lance awoke with a jolt. He had drifted off quickly. He shook his head to clear it, got up from the couch and replaced *Down Went Jonah* on his overstocked bookshelf. He had a test in two days. He didn't need to be thinking about Nick Shaw's forays into whoredom or Nathaniel Jackson and the cravings of adolescence. He needed to be thinking about cases and rulings. Donning a pair of horn-rimmed glasses that his vanity only allowed him to wear in his apartment, he studied his law books in earnest.

CHAPTER THIRTY-THREE

Patti and Val spent all of David's money and then some. Afterwards they stopped at a little bistro on Santa Monica for cappuccino. Reflecting on the incident that occurred later, Val realized the entire messy scene could have been avoided. They had been sitting there enjoying the sights and sounds of Santa Monica Boulevard, laughing over their shopping antics, when a little girl approached Val for an autograph.

His first mistake had been signing the autograph for the girl. In doing so, he had drawn attention to himself. No sooner than he had given her a slip of paper and sent her on her way, she was replaced by an elderly woman who had been watching from her table. Val gladly signed her autograph. He was an old pro at this. He smiled and wrote exactly what she asked. When he handed back her autograph book— she was one of those people who carried hers around in her purse—he noticed the line that had formed behind her. He felt a growing apprehension. There was no security or crowd control, and the crowd was getting larger. He signed autograph after autograph.

This was the first time Patti had experienced his fame firsthand. As she watched the growing crowd, she became excited. They wanted him. They worshipped him. They loved him. And because she was with him, they wanted her too. It made her feel powerful and special. She liked that. Who needed David anyway?

There was a flash. Then another. People were taking pictures. Someone shoved a napkin and a pen in her hand. She was tempted to sign it when someone said, "Hey, she's not anybody," and reached over her. The pen and paper were snatched from her grasp. Then she was pushed from behind as people almost crawled over her to get to Val. There were so many people and they were pushing against her. She could barely move. Val stood, attempting to make a gracious exit. It was getting out of control. She stood too, going to follow his lead. But then someone pushed harder. Their table was overturned. She stepped out of the way to keep from falling and ripping her clothes on the overturned furniture. Someone stepped on the overturned table. Then there was a sea of bodies separating her from Val.

"Excuse me," she said, trying to get back to him.

"Wait your turn," someone growled and pushed her aside. She was pushed farther away from Val.

"That's enough," Val said as he tried to get to Patti, but he could not. There were too many people. A flash exploded in his face. The small crowd had turned into a clamoring mob as passing motorists stopped their cars to join the melee. The waiters and waitresses tried their best to restore order but they, too, were ignored and pushed aside. It was getting pretty ugly. All Val's attempts to exit graciously were squelched. He wasn't going to be able to get out of this with his reputation untarnished.

VAL

Damn it! Someone grabbed me by my hair. I felt strands being pulled out. Then I felt a sharp, piercing pain on the side of my face. I reached up to touch my ear and pulled away a bloody finger. Someone had snatched my earring out of my ear! This was too much. Too fucking much. I wasn't signing another goddamn autograph, and I wasn't going to be a punching bag for the masses.

"No. No. No more," I said, pushing the slips of paper away from me. "No," I growled full of indignation. "No more." There was a break in the crowd, and I thought it was because of the look on my face and the change in my attitude. But I was wrong. The crowd parted because there were six of L.A.'s finest pushing through. I had never been so happy to see a cop before.

"Mr. Pardeaux, are you okay?" one of them asked.

"Yes. Yes. I'm fine. But I had a companion." I searched the crowd for Patti.

"I'm over here, Val," she called.

I turned in the direction of her voice and saw not just Patti, but Wayne Carey. He wore sunglasses, a baseball cap and faded jeans, but I knew it was Wayne Carey just the same. With as much dignity as I could muster, I walked toward them.

"You should consider getting bodyguards," Wayne said as he reached out and touched my ear. It was throbbing.

"You called in the cavalry?" I asked.

"Yeah," he replied. We started walking toward my car while the police handled the crowd.

"How did you know?" I asked him.

"I was driving by and saw the crowd. My voyeuristic tendencies got the best of me. There's blood on your shirt," he said.

"It's just a T-shirt."

Patti got into the rented SUV. I didn't know what to say to Wayne. "Thanks . . ." I began. He smiled that famous, million-dollar smile, which was still brilliant despite the disguise.

"Show your appreciation. Have a drink with me tonight," he said.

"I don't know if I'm ready to face another crowd tonight," I said.

"There are places we can go."

"Get in the car, Val. I want to go home," Patti hissed between her teeth.

"I'll call you," Wayne stated.

"Yeah, you do that." I walked around to the driver's side. "But, Wayne," I called, ignoring Patti's hot stare on my cheek.

"It'll just be drinks. Okay?"

"Okay."

I watched him walk to his black Cherokee before I got in the SUV and drove off. On the ride home, Patti sat in angry silence.

David was standing in the kitchen drinking milk from the carton when Patti and I entered from the garage.

"Hey . . ." David was about to voice a guilty greeting. I hated it when he drank from the carton. When he noticed Patti's wild-eyed look, he asked, "What's up?"

Patti went immediately to the refrigerator and got

herself a beer. As she had done when they were kids, she unscrewed the top with her teeth and drank from the bottle. David turned to me for some type of answer, and noticed the drops of blood on my shoulder. He didn't see the small tear in my ear because my hair covered that.

"What the fuck? That looks like blood," he said in a concerned manner.

"It is blood," Patti said, kicking off her heels and gulping at her beer.

"Blood?" David crossed to me and reached to lift my hair and examine my shoulder. He didn't realize it was my ear that was injured.

"It's just a little blood," I said, pulling away from David, indicating Patti with my eyes.

"Let me see," David said as he pushed my hand away and reached for me.

"Jesus, Davey-Gene. It's just a little blood. All they did was grab his earring," Patti spat. She was pissed off. David was paying more attention to me than to her.

"They? They who?" David demanded.

"We stopped for cappuccino," I said, taking the milk carton from David and getting a glass from the cabinet. "A few fans got out of control." I attempted to brush off the incident.

"A few?" Patti asked incredulously.

"Out of control how?" David continued to demand.

"It wasn't that bad," I assured him, pouring a glass of milk.

"What do you call bad?"

"Just overly anxious autograph hounds," I said, handing David the drink.

"There's blood on your shirt," David stressed.

"Just a little."

"They were all over us," Patti explained to David.

"Pushing and grabbing." She threw her hands up, exasperated. "I think you should get a bodyguard like he said."

"Like who said?" David ignored the milk Val handed him.

I tried to intercept. "You know I hate it when you drink out of the carton."

"How bad was it, Val?" David asked again.

"I thought we were going to get trampled until the police came," Patti said, gulping at her beer, totally unaware of the looks I was sending her way.

"The police?" David attempted to keep his voice level so as not to display his concern.

"Wayne Carey called the cops," I said absently as I pulled my shirt over my head. There was an ugly bruise on my shoulder.

"Wayne Carey was there?" David asked.

"He was driving by," I said nonchalantly.

"Driving by?"

"Are you going to repeat everything I say?"

"Until you say something smart, maybe."

Annoyed, I threw my shirt at David. Without missing a beat, David caught it and tossed the crumpled orange mass into the trashcan.

"Come on, guys, it's just a little blood," Patti said as she got the shirt out of the trashcan, put it in the sink and ran cold water on it.

"I can't believe you weren't going to tell me," David said.

"I was going to tell you, David, but you get too worked up."

"Worked up?"

"Yes, worked up. Like now."

"You two are a trip," Patti called from the sink as she scrubbed the T-shirt.

"He should have told me," David said.

The phone rang before Patti could respond to David's heartfelt comment. "Hello," Patti chirped. "Oh, hi, Kim . . . What? Okay. Turn the TV on channel two."

"What?" David said.

"The TV. Kim says turn it on channel two," Patti repeated.

There was a counter-saver 10-inch TV hooked beneath the counter. I flipped it on.

"Oh, God," I groaned, putting my head down on the counter. On the 10-inch screen was a very irate Val. I was looking as angry as David had ever seen me. My eyes blazed, my bearing straight, and my accent clipped.

"No," I screamed. "No more."

The camera angle shifted to a teary-eyed teenager. She had a mouth full of braces and runny mascara.

"And what happened then?" a reporter's voice asked from off screen.

"He pushed me and I fell," the teenager said.

"Did you get your autograph?" the reporter asked.

"No, I didn't," the whimpering teenager said.

The angle shifted to the devastated bistro. There was a shot of the overturned table, broken plates and wasted food.

The reporter, a fresh young woman with a pretty face, was talking to the manager. "Did you have any warning that he was going to set up an autograph booth right here on your property?"

"No. No. There was no warning. We were told nothing. We weren't prepared for that type of crowd. People stopped their cars. Our patrons left their tables. There was a crowd, a large crowd," the manager said in low hysterics.

"And Mr. Pardeaux did nothing to try to disperse this crowd?"

"No. It was like he was getting high off the attention."

"Jesus," I said, flipping off the TV.

"A few fans got out of control? You could have been hurt," David said.

"But I wasn't," I said.

"Did you see that, Kim? They made Val look like a bad guy," I heard Patti say into the phone.

"Why didn't you call me?" David demanded.

"And say what?"

"Say you needed me."

"You know I need you." David and I touched hands gently as lovers do, for the first time not caring that Patti was in the room. But Patti had turned away. She was chatting happily into the phone. Finally, someone was paying her some attention.

It was on every channel. A brief little snippet of entertainment news that made me look like a monster. By 6:00 that evening, *Entertainment Tonight* had run a preview of their show with one segment called "Stars and Their Egos: When Do Their Heads Get Bigger than Their Fame?" By 6:30, I was seething. As a celebrity with an alabaster reputation, I was angry that the masses were so eager to believe the media hype. Suddenly, anybody and everybody who thought they had ever been wronged by me were catching their fifteen minutes of fame by smearing my name on national TV. Frustrated beyond endurance, I finally turned off the TV, grabbed a dog-eared copy of *The Drake Chronicle # 17,* plopped down on the couch and began to read.

Patti was pissed off because no one had mentioned her. She wasn't mistaken for my companion, girlfriend or accomplice. She was nobody. Each time they showed the incident, the camera angle managed to capture me and obscured Patti. Her fifteen minutes of fame had been lost in a crowd scene. She gathered her packages angrily and disappeared up the stairs.

Alone with David, he leaned over the couch and massaged my tense muscles until I drifted into a troubled sleep.

CHAPTER THIRTY-FOUR

Wayne changed clothes three times before he finally settled on a pair of navy blue linen pants and a white raw silk shirt, which had been his original choice and first outfit donned. Once dressed, he put on a pair of Ray-Bans, grabbed his sports jacket and headed toward his car. For his date with Val, he'd drive his Jaguar.

Alone, still unable to write, David had wandered out to the pool. His writing muse was still elusive and maintaining a distance just out of his grasp.

David caught his muse on his fourth lap in the Olympic-sized pool. Not bothering to dry off, he vaulted from the pool and entered the house through the kitchen. He was about to head up the back stairs when the doorbell rang, so he changed direction midstride and went to the door. As he walked through the living room, he noticed that Val was still asleep on the oversized sofa. He looked so peaceful, so untroubled. All David wanted to do was lay down next to his lover and embrace him, make slow, tender love then go upstairs and write his heart out. But he couldn't do that.

"Yes?" David said, opening the door.

"Hi, David. Is Val ready?" Wayne Carey asked.

"Is Val ready?" David repeated dumbly.

"Yes. After his rescue this evening, I told him I'd take him out for a drink or two."

"Sure. Sure. Come in." David stepped aside to allow Wayne the opportunity to enter. "I think Val must have forgotten about those drinks." David walked over to the couch and shook Val awake.

"What? What?" Val mumbled in French.

"Say, you have a guest," David said.

Val sat up rubbing his eyes. "Wayne?"

"Did you forget our—" Wayne caught himself before he said "date."

"Did you forget we were going for drinks?" he finished.

"Yeah, I'm sorry. It seems I did forget." Val stood up and stretched. "Let me change into something appropriate. It won't take long."

"Would you like something to drink, Wayne?" David asked, slipping into his role as host in Val's absence.

"Usually I'd take a beer, but since we're going out for drinks and I'm driving, I'd better hold off."

"Have a seat." David gestured at the paisley chair as he took a seat on the couch. "I didn't know you and Val were such good friends."

"We seem to be running into each other so much lately. it seemed only natural to become more acquainted."

"I see." David leaned back on the couch and put his feet up on the coffee table.

"Been in the pool long?"

"Yeah. Why'd you ask?"

"Raisin toes."

David looked at his feet. "You're right. Sure you don't want that beer?"

"I'm sure."

"If you'll excuse me, I'm going to get one."

Wayne watched as David got up from the couch and disappeared into the kitchen.

WAYNE

I was glad he left me alone. I didn't know how long I could carry out my charade. After all, I was in his house under false pretenses. Everything that was fair in me told me I should announce my intentions and face him like a man, but looking at him sitting on the couch made me hesitate. Call me a coward, but he had two inches and twenty pounds on me, and it was all muscle. Even though David had always been cordial to me, I sensed an underlying current that hinted at a potential for violence. There was an animal magnetism and virility about him that was both frightening and alluring. He was so black, so threatening. How could I compete with that?

"Sure you don't want a beer?" he asked from the doorway.

Damn, he was big. And fine. If I could just get past his blackness—I don't mean his skin color, I mean his "ism," his essence, his blackness that was the all of him—I'd find him sexy. But as it stood, David scared me. My fear of him angered me.

"No. I'm fine," I replied.

He walked back into the room and sat across from me. His muscles rippled as he walked. He didn't seem to care that he was soaking wet. Water rolled off him in rivulets.

"Well," David said, gulping his beer, "I don't have anything else to say, Wayne. Val's the king of small talk."

His comment caught me off guard. I hadn't expected him to mention that he was aware that we hadn't exactly been carrying on a heated conversation. Oddly, it made me at ease. He was human after all.

DAVID

What was I supposed to say to Wayne Carey? I knew him but I didn't know him. We were acquainted but we weren't friends.

"How long have you and Val been living together?" Wayne asked.

"Since college," I answered.

"That's a long time."

"Yes, it is." *What is he getting at?*

"How's your new book coming along?"

Well, he changed the subject. Okay. "Okay, I guess."

"What's it about?"

"Sorry, Wayne. I never talk about anything I'm working on until I finish."

"Not even to Val?"

"You're not Val."

Before I could say something to take the sting out of my words, Val walked in. *Damn.* I had to think it again. *Damn.*

I knew Val well enough to know that he had taken great care in choosing what he was going to wear. After the fiasco of the morning, I was sure that he wanted look as respectable as possible in case there were going to be any cameras around—and there usually were cameras around. He had chosen a double-breasted lightweight Armani summer suit and flat Italian shoes. He wore only a Rolex watch and a simple gold stud in his other ear. He had brushed his hair until the amber highlights reflected the light. His overall look was polished, expensive, powerful and sexy. He was a star, and his look said "celebrity." Together, he and Wayne looked like a million dollars. Two million.

Upon Val's arrival, both Wayne and I stood.

"That was quick," Wayne said. He was impressed and it showed in his voice.

"I didn't want to keep you waiting," Val said.

"Where are you going?" I asked as I walked with them toward the front door.

"I have no idea," Val replied.

"We're going to a quiet, out of the way place I know. Very discreet, very upscale. Very few fans," Wayne said.

"Good," I said.

"You sound like his father," Wayne commented.

"He's not my father," Val stated, and proved it by turning to me and giving me a lover's kiss. It was full-lipped and full of promise.

What the fuck? Val caught me by surprise. Nevertheless, my first instinct was to give in to the feeling. I wanted to give him my tongue and teeth and rub myself against his body. But I couldn't do that with Wayne Carey standing not one foot away and with Patti upstairs. I wasn't that liberated or that free. I didn't know Wayne Carey.

"He knows," Val whispered in my ear, breaking the kiss and hugging my stiffening body. "Ease up, baby. He knows."

I relaxed and let him pull me into a lover's embrace.

"Do I need to douse you two with water?" Wayne asked with a touch of levity.

"No. No. We're fine," Val said as he kissed me again over my protest and squeezed my balls.

I wanted to ask so many questions. I wanted to know what had motivated Val to "come out" now.

"Don't wait up," Val called and smiled at me as he and Wayne headed out the front door.

Don't wait up? Was he crazy? Looking after the two of them, I almost forgot the last chapter of my book was calling me until I heard my muse whispering my name. Filled with questions, I started up the stairs, which had been my original destination until Wayne Carey interrupted. For the second time that day I had completely forgotten about Patti.

VAL

I had wanted to do that for a long, long time. I had wanted to do it long before Wayne Carey stumbled into my life. I wanted to announce to the world that David was mine from the top of his curly head to the tips of his toes. All mine. But of course, I never had. No one had ever seen a display like the one we just put on for Wayne Carey's benefit. I knew I'd have some explaining to do when I got home, but Wayne needed to see what it was he was trying to put asunder.

"Nice car," I said as Wayne opened my door for me.

"I thought you'd like it," he replied.

"I like the Jeep."

"The Jag has leather seats. I thought your ass was too precious for vinyl."

"Damn, Wayne. Do you ever give up?"

"No." He put the car in drive and started down the hill.

CHAPTER THIRTY-FIVE

Lance ran in late. He had overslept. But no one said anything to him as he changed into his costume. When he danced at Marco's, he danced to the top ten hits, preferring pulsing, vibrating beats and costumes that weren't too obstructive. He made enough money in tips from dancing one night a week at Marco's to pay the mortgage on his luxurious two-bedroom split-level townhouse.

He liked to dance. He was good at it. But tonight he wasn't really into it. He had seen Val on TV, and his heart went out to him. He had no doubt that the whole story hadn't been told, and he was curious about what really happened.

As he danced, he realized his opinion of Wayne's infatuation had changed. At first he had found Wayne's near obsession laughable. Then he found it borderline intrusive. How dare Wayne think of Val when they were together? But when he realized that he didn't consider his thinking of David when he was with someone else in the same light, he changed his mind about Wayne.

He angled his body so that a patron could slip a $50 bill into his G-string. The man's hand brushed his flat belly and glided down his thigh, and Lance danced away. If the man wanted more, he'd have to pay more. David, Val and Wayne were forgotten as he danced.

DAVID

My muse sang to me as my fingers raced over the keyboard. It was so easy to get back into the swing of things that I almost forgot about Val and Wayne Carey—almost, but not quite. It was as thoughts of the two of them continued to surface and intertwine themselves within the fabric of *David's Story* that I realized that I was jealous. The realization shocked me and made my fingers pause over the keys. There was no need for jealousy. No need to feel insecure in my relationship. Was there? When I paused to gather my thoughts, Patti came into the study.

Damn. Looking at her, I realized what was meant by breathtaking beauty. On a purely physical level, Patti was a dream fantasy come true, a walking, breathing fantasy love doll. Perfect breasts. Perfect waist. Perfect ass. God, that ass! I had spent so many days on top of that ass, molding, shaping, teasing and tasting that delectable ass. She had on a red, gauzy thing with something like spider webs covering her nipples and her crotch. The pure milk chocolate of her skin showed beneath the transparent red material. She liked red. She looked good in red. Desire hit me like a slap in the face. I crossed my legs, trying to choke my dick. She had done something to her hair. It was piled up on top of her head in a sophisticated style. She had painted her fingernails and her toes, which were the same color, peeked beneath the furry trim on her high-heeled bedroom slippers. I think they were called mules.

"Hey," she said.

"Hey," I replied.

"I slept forever. Where's Val?" She took a seat on the futon and crossed her legs.

"He went out for drinks with Wayne Carey."

"Faggot," she hissed under her breath.

I stopped what I was doing and turned to look at her. "What are you talking about?"

"Wayne Carey is the biggest fag."

"What?"

"Dog, Davey-Gene. You don't know nothing."

"I know a lot, but I didn't know Wayne Carey was a homosexual."

"Ooh, *homosexual?* What a big word for *cocksucker.*"

"You don't know that, Patti. Did you see him suck a cock?"

"No, but I saw him eyeing Val."

"What?"

"That night when we went to that Mexican place. His dick was hard and his tongue was hanging out, but it wasn't for me. Didn't Val tell you any of this?"

"No, Val didn't tell me any of this. Did he tell you?"

"He didn't have to tell me. I can see."

She could see? Why couldn't I? Did Patti have a sixth sense that pointed blatantly to signs of homosexuality? Did her femininity give her insight into the psyche of the homosexual? How did she know Wayne Carey liked men? How could she know that but not know about me? Was it because I didn't like men, but rather, I liked one man? Did that throw her sensor off?

"You don't know for sure," I began, refusing to believe Wayne Carey was gay just from her say-so.

"Ask Val. Ask Val, Davey-Gene."

"I think I will." If Wayne truly liked Val, how was I supposed to handle this?

"I didn't mean to make you upset."

"I'm not upset," I lied. I was upset. If Wayne Carey was gay, that explained a lot, an awful lot. That kiss was for Wayne's benefit.

"I didn't mean to make you mad," she said again and got up. I watched her walk toward me. She swayed with a sensual, womanly movement. Her nipples peeked from behind her intricately designed web as she stood behind me. She began to rub my shoulders. "Your neck is tight." Her voice was like dripping honey. My head was filled with conflicting emotions and thoughts.

Wayne Carey. Wayne Carey, gay? I thought of the gay guy at the youth center. He was a guy I wouldn't mind allowing into my circle of friends. We had a lot in common, a love of good literature and basketball. His gayness didn't unite us. Or did it?

Her hands worked at the tight muscles in my neck and shoulders. My dick didn't seem to have conflicting thoughts. It knew Patti's touch, the smell of her perfume, dark, heavy and clinging, Aromatics. The tip of her tongue as it grazed my ear was sexy, stimulating and mysterious. My dick throbbed hard, heavy and strong between my legs. Was I such a weak man? Was I so devoid of character that I could allow myself to slip into the old and familiar rhythms even as I thought of my lover in the arms of another man?

"You like that, huh?" Patti whispered.

"I like very much." *Didn't I say, "Let's be friends"? Who was I trying to fool?*

She continued to rub my shoulders then slowly, ever so gently, she crossed in front of me and kneeled at my feet. The sight of a woman subjugated on her knees had never done anything for me until now. I felt powerful, omnipotent. I felt like a king. I was a king with a big dick.

"You have nice feet, David." She picked up one of my feet and massaged it.

Of course I had nice feet. Wasn't it just last week that Val and I sat facing each other in the tub, giving each other pedicures? Is that the kind of thing faggots did?

She rubbed, stroked and bent my toes. I had no idea my toes were connected to my dick. My voice was breathless. I was aroused.

"You're really famous, aren't you, David?"

"I don't know if I'm all that famous." *What an insane conversation.*

"But Val is."

Why did she keep bringing up Val? "Yes, Val is famous. He was born famous." What was Val doing? Was he, like me, being unfaithful? There were so many ways to cheat and test the bonds of fidelity.

"I've never been with a man whose feet were as perfect as yours. I like feet, Davey-Gene." She sucked my big toe into her mouth. I felt a jolt of electricity travel up my spine.

"What are you doing, Patti?"

"You ask too many questions, Davey-Gene," she said and opened her mouth to encompass all my toes. And I, weak man that I was, and controlled by my dick, lay back on the couch and let Patti do me.

David's Story, Val or Wayne didn't seem all that important anymore.

VAL

I had never seen anything like it, a gentleman's club specializing in all male entertainment. Male waiters, male dancers, male bouncers and an all male clientele that made the Hollywood A-list look like the dregs of society. I saw people I never would have expected to see. And they saw me too. Me and Wayne. And he made sure they knew I was with him. He didn't hug me. He didn't put his arm around me. He walked next to me and put a hand on my lower back. It was a strong, guiding hand that ushered me toward our seats. His simple gesture said it all. It said I was with him. His date. He pulled my chair out for me, ordered for me and treated me like I had always treated my dates. It was different. It was nice. But he wasn't David. Nevertheless, I allowed him to cater to me. I liked it. I liked being treated the way he was treating me.

CHAPTER THIRTY-SIX

"They're fucking, you know," Wayne said out of the blue. Val and Wayne were sitting at a table near the stage. There was an empty bottle of Dom Perignon between them.

"They are not fucking," Val said for the third time.

"Okay. If you say so."

"I say so."

"I love your accent."

"I've always been partial to Southern accents myself."

"Referring, of course, to the Southern gentleman you have at home."

"Most definitely."

"Tell me, Val. Why do you think they aren't fucking?"

"Because David told me they weren't, and I trust David."

Wayne Carey threw his head back and laughed. "Val, Val, Valentine. Didn't anyone ever tell you not to trust a man?"

"Are you included in that assessment?"

"Most assuredly."

This time Val laughed. Despite Wayne's blatant flirtatious and outrageous behavior, Val was having a grand time. Wayne was a character indeed.

WAYNE

The lights went down, the music came up and then I saw him, Lance. Shit! Of course I had thought of Lance before I decided to bring Val to Marco's, but Lance and I had an understanding. I wasn't a son-of-a-bitch who callously ignored Lance's feelings. It was true that I had taken into consideration the fact that he was not fulfilling fantasies this night. But I had not known that he would be dancing. It seems that I didn't know everything about Lance. I knew he moaned deliciously when his shoulder blades were licked. I knew his body arched gloriously when he came, and I knew I found him appealing, but he wasn't Val. No, he wasn't Val. Shifting in my seat so that I was comfortable enough to enjoy the show, I watched Lance dance. He danced beautifully and gracefully. He was such an exhibitionist. He was getting off on watching me watch him. His penis, that beautiful instrument that curved slightly to the left, beckoned to me, but I ignored it because I was with Val, and Val did not know about Lance and me. Val did not know that just one day earlier, Lance and I had been together.

Watching Lance dance made me think of his body undulating beneath mine. He had tired me out and made me weak. Some time later, I had awakened to the smell of perking coffee and frying bacon. I thought I was in the wrong house. I hardly ever had breakfast and rarely awoke before noon if I wasn't working. When I opened my eyes, I noticed that it was 7:55 A.M. Groaning, I rolled over and covered my head with my pillow.

"Good morning," Lance said.

I peeked from beneath my pillow and saw Lance coming toward me with a tray loaded with goodies. "Don't tell me you're a morning person," I groaned.

"I am."

I moved over to allow Lance to place the breakfast tray across my hips. "You cook too." I leaned over to kiss him.

But he averted his face so that my lips brushed his cheek. "Morning breath," he said, wrinkling his nose.

"Okay. Okay." I got up and disappeared into the bathroom to brush my teeth.

"Better now?" I asked him, blowing my breath in his face when I came back into the room.

"I don't know. Is it?"

I kissed him. He tasted of mint and sunshine.

"Much better."

I crawled over him and sat in the middle of the bed with my bounty. He had prepared crispy bacon, Belgian waffles, a bowl of fruit and a pot of black coffee.

"I don't think I'm going to let you go anytime soon." I sighed, digging into my breakfast. He was pleased with himself as he captured a piece of bacon from my tray. "I could get used to this."

"You need someone to take care of you."

"Are you proposing?" I asked, amused.

"I'm just making an observation."

"I enjoyed last night," I said, turning serious to let him know that I didn't think of our time together as whore and john.

"I'm sure you did."

The sex had been good. Touching. Enjoyable. "No, I'm serious," I said.

"Come on, Wayne. I had a good time. You had a good time. No need to confess undying love."

"I wasn't going to confess my undying love; I just wanted to say thanks."

"You're welcome."

I moved my tray from my lap, leaned over and kissed him. "You're welcome too."

"You taste so much better," he teased me.

I crawled on top of him. We necked like teenagers. I could taste the essence of him. He tasted like mystery. I could smell the freshness of his skin from his early morning shower. He smelled like soap and an earthy cologne that was beckoning. Beneath me, he moaned and opened his mouth to my probing tongue.

While we were engaging in our early morning love play the phone rang. I was going to ignore it, but Lance encouraged me to answer it.

"Hello?" I growled into the phone. If it had been anyone but my agent, they would have gotten a piece of my mind, but it was Todd. I had to take the call.

While I was on the phone Lance got dressed. As fate would have it, he was coming out of the bathroom as I hung up the phone. "Hey, where are you going?" I said as I bounded naked from the bed.

"Home," Lance replied.

"Now?"

"Now."

"I thought we were going to . . . you know." I lowered my voice and ran my hand up his arm. He pulled away from me, intent on leaving.

"Did I miss something?" I asked.

He seemed angry. "No."

"Yeah, I missed something. One minute we were doing the belly rub, the next minute you were up like a shot and dressed. Either I still have morning breath or I did or said something to tick you off."

"The belly rub?" he said, grabbing his bag. It was a leather satchel shaped like a saddlebag. He carried his law books in it and occasionally a toothbrush, clean shirt and change of underwear. I knew because I had peeked into it.

"I'm from the South," I continued. "We say things like 'doing the belly rub' and 'bumping uglies' when we talk about the sex act—what did you expect?"

"I expect you to eat your breakfast then go out and buy me something incredibly expensive, preferably off Rodeo Drive, then do whatever you do while your show is on hiatus."

"What are you going to do?"

"I'm going to study, work out and go to work." He meant he would be going to Marco's.

"Oh."

"Oh."

I leaned over and kissed him. "You'll be working tonight."

"Yes."

I kissed him again. "Tomorrow?"

"No work tomorrow."

Yes, I remembered that conversation, so I guess he didn't consider dancing to be work. As I watched him now, with Val by my side, I felt like he was working. He was working the crowd into a frenzy.

VAL

I knew who he was immediately. We had just met. How could I forget him? I wondered what Kim would say if she knew he danced in such a place. "Told you so"?

Watching him dance, there was nothing about him that screamed "faggot" like Patti and Kim had said. He was very masculine. He dominated the stage. What he lacked in technique, he more than made up for with showmanship. It was as I was watching him with a dancer's eye and appraising him with a dancer's knowledge, feeling my skill superior to his with a dancer's pride, that I became aware of Wayne watching me watch Lance.

"What do you think?" Wayne asked me.

"I think he puts on a good show," I replied.

"You ain't seen nothing yet."

I watched as Wayne made an almost imperceptible motion with his finger. Seen by only Lance and myself, it nevertheless accomplished what a handful of $100 bills could not do for the gentleman sitting to our left. Lance stepped from the stage onto our table. His movements were graceful, pantherlike. I watched as he undulated, performing as if for only us two, a simulation of the sex acts. Though this was all new to me, raw, different, I found it shamefully erotic playing the role of voyeur.

Then he held out his hand to me. The tease. I shook my head no. I wanted to watch, not participate. I had to maintain my illusion of anonymity. Again he held out his hand to me. Again I declined. Not daunted in the least, he offered his hand to Wayne. If I expected Wayne to decline, I was wrong. Throwing caution to the wind, Wayne Carey, America's heartthrob, joined Lance on the table. There was an audible gasp from the crowd. There were so many whispers of disbelief it sounded like a mild roar.

I watched as Lance led Wayne into a pantomimed simulation of foreplay that led to an orgasmic, feigned climax. Then he turned his back to Wayne and bent from his waist, offering his muscular ass. It was as he offered that delectable ass for penetration that I had an epiphany. He had done that before and with Wayne. He offered himself with the familiarity that a lover would, just as I did for David and as David did for me. Then I realized that Lance reminded me of David. The way he cocked his head, the way he walked, and that glorious, glorious skin. He was as dark as David, but much too flamboyant to have a nature like my lover's. Suddenly, I missed David as much as one person could miss another. I missed his smile. I missed his touch. I missed having him rub my feet. I wanted to call David. My cell had lost reception as soon as we entered Marco's. Ignoring the show that was taking place just a few feet from me, I excused myself from the table and headed for the pay phone.

WAYNE

I don't know what came over me. It was as if I had gone insane and blacked out for a few minutes. When I came to, I was poised in a position of power and dominance, a sexual position. I looked down at Lance, noting his position of submission and look of desire, and I looked out at the room, seeing faces filled with longing, lust and admiration of my performance. But when I looked to my table and saw it empty, I realized that Val was not one of the ones who had envied my position. His absence made me wonder if he had even seen me as I performed what a good therapist would call mutual exhibitionist masturbation. Though I was and had remained dressed throughout the performance, I was as hard as if we had actually been involved in sexual foreplay.

I stepped gingerly from the tabletop and took my seat. My dick was extremely sensitive. The slightest touch, including that of the cotton of my briefs pressing against it, had me about to lose my composure. I could not remember ever having been this aroused. I could not remember having been this hard. I felt like, if I didn't get relief soon, I would lose my mind. I looked again for Val. When I didn't see him, I started for the bathroom. Each tortured step was an exercise in endurance.

I remembered a snatch of dialogue I spouted in one of my earlier movies, in which my female co-star, Gina Ritchie, yelled at me, "All men think with their dicks." I had answered, "Not me, baby. My dick thinks for me." How true, how true, I thought as I continued toward the bathroom. The movie was *Lonesome Coyote,* about a private investigator living in Vegas who walked a thin line between the ethical and criminal. Gina had won a best supporting actress nomination for that one. I wondered how the Academy would feel if they knew America's newest darling was a dyke. Maybe the same way they would feel if they knew I was queer. I was perverted too. Only a pervert would be leaning against the cool tiles of a bathroom stall as he relieved himself of sexual tension. I came in a wad of toilet paper, as I had done as a teenager so my mother would not be able to find the evidence that I flushed down the toilet.

"Pervert," I called myself again as I washed my hands and headed back into the bar.

LANCE

When the stage lights went down, I gathered my clothes from the stage floor and beat a hasty retreat. I figured I'd go to my room, shower, change, count my money and have a drink or two with Wayne and Val. Wayne would pay, of course.

It was when I was walking through the lobby that I saw Val. I stopped long enough to put on my robe. I had seen him get up from the table, but I had no idea where he had gone. He had just hung up the guest phone. The look on his face said it all. David. I realized as I looked at him that I was seeing a side of him that wasn't readily available to the general public. I saw Valentine vulnerable.

"Hi," I said as I approached him.

"Hello," he replied. It was like watching the muscles of his face collapse and re-form into the public mask he wore for the cameras, flawlessly handsome but guarded. "You put on an interesting show here."

"I've been told that." Out of the corner of my eye, I saw one of my regulars, Judge Neilson. He liked to wear red lipstick, fishnet pantyhose and three-inch heels when he blew me. He never kept me longer than an hour, and he always tipped $500. He would never approach me as long as I stood talking to Val.

"Excuse me," I said to Val. I crossed over to the judge. "Hello, Judge."

"Hi, my boy," he said. He was a very dignified man. He didn't look sixty-three. He was one of the most respected judges in the state. His wife was a notorious socialite, forever cropping up in the newspaper society columns. He had three sons, each one just as dignified. Each as straight as they thought he was.

"I'm in room fifty-nine tonight. The door is unlocked," I told him.

"Have you thought of everything?"

"Yes, I have. There's a bottle of champagne chilling and I've gotten some CDs of Tommy Dorsey."

"Good boy." He never called me Lance. "Did you get the"—He looked both ways and lowered his voice, even though we were the only two people who could hear our conversation—"you know . . . ," meaning his fishnet pantyhose, cherry bomb lipstick and high-heeled shoes. He'd die before he got caught purchasing those items.

"Of course." I always kept a supply in my room.

"Good, good. I'll see you in—" He glanced at his watch.

"Ten minutes."

"Ten?"

"Ten," I assured him.

"Good, good. Which room?"

"Fifty-nine." It was always room fifty-nine, but I always had to tell him so that he could pretend it wasn't prearranged.

He walked off with a smile on his face that reminded me of a kid who was on his way to his favorite hideout to play with his favorite toy.

I turned back to Val, but he wasn't there. I assumed he went back to the table with Wayne. I'd join them later. The judge only took fifteen minutes. It was an easy $1,200, considering my cut of the fee and my tip.

VAL

There were a lot of reasons that could have accounted for David not picking up the phone. I refused to believe, as Wayne would have me do, that Patti and David were fucking like rabbits.

It was dark in the bar, but I had no problem finding my way back to our table. Wayne was sitting not four feet from the stage, so the track lights illuminated his handsome face. But it was not the face I desired. I could enjoy Wayne's company. I could be flattered by his adoration, but I could not allow myself to start a journey with him that would take me down the road I had traveled with David. I pulled out my chair and sat down. Another dancer had taken Lance's place, but he had neither Lance's grace nor Lance's finesse.

"I thought you had run away," Wayne said with a smile as I joined him. I saw that he had taken the opportunity to order another bottle of wine.

"No. I went to make a phone call," I said.

"He didn't answer, huh?"

"Yes, he answered," I lied.

"Liar." He looked me dead in my face. I sighed. He was right. No need for the charade.

"No, he didn't answer."

"Tell me, Val. What do you see in David?"

"Why?"

"I'm curious." He sipped from his wine.

"David is sensitive, kind and funny."

"I'm sensitive, kind and funny."

"David is supportive, independent, ambitious."

"Good traits for a man to have."

"David is talented, strong, virile."

"He's a paragon of virtue."

"David is great in bed."

"I am too. Let me prove it. I want you, Val. I've wanted you for a long time."

"Wayne, I told you I'm not going to sleep with you."

"Unless he sleeps with her. Which is what he's doing right now."

I sighed with exasperation. "You never give up, do you?"

"No."

"I love David."

"Does David love you?"

"Yes." I did not hesitate.

"Val, look . . . don't think I'm a shit. I'm not. I'm a nice guy. I'm a funny guy."

"You're a persistent guy."

He laughed and the laughter traveled to his eyes. I think if I liked men, I could be entranced by those eyes. I could be hypnotized by that laugh. He was compelling.

"Yes, I am persistent. Would you like to dance? Come on. One dance. Let me die a happy man."

I relented. "Okay. One dance."

Except for the time that I had danced with Wayne at Heathcliffs, I rarely got to dance with someone other than Kim. David was a little uncomfortable dancing with me. We held hands, we cuddled, and we kissed. But we rarely danced. As I danced with Wayne, I realized I missed it. The dancing.

At first, there was an awkward moment because we both wanted to lead.

"I defer to the more talented man," Wayne said.

I held him to keep him from bowing to me, the clown. And I led. The song that was playing was "Sweetest Taboo" by Sade.

Wayne insisted on singing in my ear. He had a good voice.

Then I remembered that I had heard him sing in *Lonesome Coyote*.

The dance floor was full. No one seemed surprised to see me. What did that mean?

"You're a million miles away," Wayne said.

"I'm right here."

"Your body is right here, but your mind is at home with David."

"No, my mind is on Dwight Kelly."

Dwight Kelly, heavyweight boxer, future contender for the heavyweight championship of the world, sat at the bar, wearing a red silk dress and a shoulder-length wig. His record was 23–0.

"Yes, Dwight has problems." Wayne sighed.

"He's wearing a dress."

"And an ugly dress, too."

"He's looking this way."

"Well, stop laughing. I don't want to have to defend your honor. I make a lot of money with this face looking just like this."

"And it's a nice face."

"That's the first time you said I was handsome."

"I never said you were handsome."

"You said I had a nice face. I know what you meant."

I laughed. I was having a good time.

"Can I kiss you?" Wayne asked.

"I'd rather you did not."

"Okay," he said then kissed me.

It was a sweet kiss, the kind you get on a first date when you're sixteen. It was a touch of the lips, soft, desirable, nondemanding.

"I thought I told you 'I'd rather you did not.' "

"But you didn't say no," he said and twirled me onto the dance floor with much aplomb.

LANCE

I came. It was easy. I just closed my eyes and thought of David. David's lips, David's tongue, David's mouth on my dick, sucking me, kissing me, making me come. Afterwards I showered, changed into street clothes and started for the bar where I had last seen Val and Wayne.

DAVID

I came. I didn't have to think about anything but the sensation. With my eyes closed and the lights out, Patti's mouth was just a mouth, a sucking, pulsating mouth, sensual, sexy and successful.

PATTI

I was running out of time and ideas. So when David came, I swallowed. Goddamn it, I swallowed and I pretended I liked it.

VAL

After our dance, Wayne ushered me back to our table. There were too many emotions twirling around in my head. I found myself experiencing twinges of desire that confused and upset me. I did not want to feel desire for Wayne but I did. He was so appealing, so compelling that he touched the side of me I usually reserved for special occasions. Occasions when there were no cameras and I was with people I cared about. He touched my childlike, laughing side that David always saw before Patti arrived. He touched a part of me I had reserved for David.

"What do you want to do now?" Wayne asked me.

"I think it's time for me to go home," I answered.

He glanced at his watch. "It's still early."

"I really need to go home."

"Okay, Val. Do you want to finish your drink?"

"I think I've had enough."

"Mind if I finish mine?"

"No, go ahead." I watched as he finished his beer.

"Come on, let's go."

There was a moment of awkwardness when Wayne pulled his Jaguar up to the front of David's and my house.

"You know I want to kiss you, don't you?" Wayne said.

"Yes," I replied.

"How do you feel about that?"

"I think you're a really nice guy."

"Wait." Wayne took my hand. "Before you give me the 'I-want-to-be-friends' speech, I want you to think about tonight. Think about how I feel about you."

"Wayne," I began.

"Think about the fun. Think about the good times. And after you think about all this, promise to give me a chance."

"Why are you making this so difficult, Wayne? I think you're a cool guy, really, but David is and will always be my true love."

"I'd settle for great sex."

"Goodnight, Wayne."

"Goodnight, Valentine."

I got out of the car and started for the front door, but Wayne stopped me.

"Val?" he called.

I turned.

"I had a good time, Val."

"Me too, Wayne," I said as I disappeared into the house.

DAVID

Our bedroom window overlooked the circular drive-way in front of our house. I saw them pull up. I had just gotten out of the shower. Patti had drifted back to her bedroom. She had a look on her face that said she was sated. She had come three times, once from my tongue, once with my finger and once with her own. Our genitalia had not touched; nevertheless, I'm sure Val would split hairs. I had still been unfaithful. It was the most heinous way you could be unfaithful. I had been unfaithful in my house. It was the house I shared with my lover. Oh, the audacity, the nerve, the weakness of Man, or rather the weakness of this one man. I had not seen Patti in years, but I had thought of her. We had too much history for me not to think of her on occasion. Her character influenced my writing. She embodied the soul of Bexar Street. She was a link in the chain of *David's Story*. But that didn't mean I had to play with her pussy and make her come.

Damn, it was cold in the room. I had not put on any clothes. I stood naked in front of the window. I saw Val. I saw Wayne. I saw Wayne lean over as if he were going to kiss Val. I saw Val politely move away. But Val had not seen me with my head between Patti's legs. God. God. God. All I had to do was set the clock back six days and forget my trip to Dallas. If I could erase my indiscretion with Patti, everything would be okay.

I threw back the covers of my bed and placed myself between the sheets. The cool cotton completely covered the offending member that now lay meek and limp between my legs. There was a tap on my door. I knew it was Val. Patti never would have respected the sanctity of a closed door. He stood facing me with his back to the door.

"Hello, David," he said.

"Hello, Val," I replied.

He reached behind him and locked the door. "Where's Patti?"

"In her room."

"Good." He crossed over to the foot of the bed and began to take off his clothes. "I'd hate for her to walk in while I was making love to you."

"Oh, you're going to be making love to me?"

"Yes."

I watched as he completely undressed. I had written in *Cake Walk* that men were visual creatures, stimulated by nude bodies, lines, shapes and movement. Val stimulated me. Was it love or an insatiable hunger for sex? Was I a sex addict? Would that explain it?

"Move over," he said.

I slid over so that Val could crawl in next to me.

"I've missed you." Val kissed me.

Could he taste her on my lips? Could he smell her womanly scent beneath the saddle soap I liked to bathe with? "I've missed you too," I replied.

We kissed. God, how I loved him. He had bought

me the saddle soap. He said he liked the way it smelled on me. I bathed with it to please him. He wore Polo to please me.

He climbed on top of me, aligning our bodies chest to chest, hipbone to hipbone. Our dicks pressed against each other. Val ran his hand down the side of my body. He was wooing me, making love to me.

"Wait a minute," he said as he got up off me and crossed to the portable CD player we kept in the bedroom.

I rubbed my dick while I watched his muscles ripple as he bent to get the Luther Vandross, Peabo Bryson and James Ingram CDs—lovemaking music.

Once he had started "A House is Not a Home," he turned to me with a triumphant grin on his face. Val could be debonair when he wanted to be. He walked slowly toward me, allowing me to view and appreciate his body, his gait. Slowly, he crawled onto the bed.

I spread my legs so that I could cradle his precious body close to my soul.

VAL

I felt guilty as sin. But I hadn't done anything. I let Wayne kiss me, that's all. But even the kiss was a slip into indiscretion. Who was I trying to fool? It was more than the kiss. It was the fact that I danced with him. What is a dance but foreplay while clothed? I had let him caress me, hold me, try to climb into my head and make me forget about David, the one I loved. I had sinned, if not with my body, then with my thoughts. On the ride home, I had allowed myself to picture me with Wayne, naked, writhing, fucking, and I had gotten hard. My mouth said no, no, no, but my body had betrayed me by responding to him. So, in order to cleanse my betraying flesh of its indiscretion, I had to immerse myself with my love. I had to bury myself deep within him so that I could be cleansed.

I made love to David, slow, tender, precious love. I placed my lover's thighs over my shoulders and delved into David's depths. Flesh on flesh, soul to soul, our silhouettes were glorious as they were caught in coitus. David shifted his weight so that I could continue to love him deeply and passionately. Our bodies were taut, their muscles strained, their ecstasy intense.

"I'm so hard, man. So fucking hard," David moaned, his hands tightening into fists. The sheet was caught between his fingers.

I didn't say anything. I couldn't. I was too busy pump-, pump-, pumping away. Then I was coming. And coming, and coming. Once I did come, I collapsed against David. The sweat from his body anointed me with proof of his love.

David didn't stop. David was still hard. A thin sheen leaked down his shaft. His manhood was coated with desire, hard with unspent release.

I surrounded all of him with my hand and stroked him to readiness. Once I had him bucking beneath me, he increased his strokes until the two of us were covered with evidence of David's love.

Sated. Sticky. Pressed together, groin to buttock, chest to back. Hands clasped while we lay like spoons, Patti was momentarily forgotten. So was Wayne as my lover and I reveled in our union.

"I love you, David."

"I love you too, Val."

I kissed David's shoulder. It was easy because I was behind him. There was so much I wanted to say to him, and I could feel that there was so much he, too, wanted to say to me.

Before this day, we would have just said whatever was on our minds. But this day had brought about changes. Even though we had just made glorious love, little secrets lay between us, separating us from the honesty we usually shared.

LANCE

There were four bars at Marco's. They weren't in either one of them. Neither were they in the club, on the dance floor or in any of the three restaurants. I didn't entertain the thought that they had checked into one of the rooms. It was too early for that. Wayne was trying to woo Val, and you never pushed too hard when you were trying to be impressive. It seemed I had missed them. Oh, well. I decided to gather my things and head home. I had a test tomorrow.

CHAPTER THIRTY-SEVEN

Val left David's room in the wee hours of the morning, well before sunrise. He did it voluntarily, without argument. His compliance was an act of attrition for what he thought a grave transgression. David watched him go and wanted to call out to him, but did not.

It was after 7:00 A.M. when David decided he couldn't take any more. He couldn't remain like prey, trapped in his room, awaiting the arrival of the predator. Only this predator would not devour him with teeth, tongue and mandible. Oh, no. She would stalk him and woo him and seduce him. She would play with him like a cat would a mouse. The tables were turned. She was in control. He was the victim. Lying naked in his bed made him defenseless against the song she sang. She was a siren.

Gathering his defenses, he went to the shower. She would not find him naked, awaiting her. He would be dressed. He would be ready. The layer of clothing would be just one more defense against her seductive assault.

WAYNE

After I delivered Val into the arms of David, I went home expecting to dream the dream of infatuation with billowing clouds, gentle sex and unconscious thrusts of my hips against my bed, producing my second self-induced orgasm of the night. But that's not what happened. I got home, stripped, crawled between the covers and realized I wasn't able to sleep. I tossed. I turned. I tried to jerk off. Nothing worked. Then I reached for the phone. I wanted to call Val, but I would not. If Val ever were to come to me willingly, I would not allow the fact that I had once caused trouble between him and David to be a negative thing between us. So, instead of calling Val, I called Lance. He answered on the fourth ring. There were two lines in his house, one for customers and one for friends. I used the latter. I hoped I had made the right choice.

"Hi. I hoped you were at home," I said to Lance.

"I just got in," he replied. He didn't seem surprised to hear from me.

"What are you doing?" I asked.

"Do you want to come over?"

"No."

"What do you want?"

"I want to talk."

"Oh?" His voice changed. It sounded deeper, sexier.

"What are you doing?" I asked again.

"I'm just getting out of these tight jeans."

I could picture him taking off his pants. I could see the definition of muscular legs and slim hips as they emerged from the clinging designer material.

"What are you doing?" he asked me.

"Just lying here."

"What are you wearing?"

"My birthday suit."

There was a pause on the other line. "Put your hand on your dick."

"What?"

"Wrap your hand around your dick. Stroke it softly."

"Are you crazy?"

"Are you doing it?"

"No."

"Do it."

"What are you doing?"

"I'm playing with my dick." He laughed, his voice low and throaty.

"Is it hard?" I had never participated in this type of sex play. It was mildly erotic, lying in my dark room, rubbing my dick and listening to him describe how I should hold it and caress it and make it hard.

"I don't know what to make of you," Lance said.

"Don't make anything of me. Just make me come," I said with a sigh.

"How do I do that?"

"Talk to me."

"And say what?" he asked.

"Tell me your dick is hard."

"My dick is hard."

"Tell me you can see it big and swollen, throbbing and shining as it slides in and out of my mouth."

"It's big and swollen and throbbing. I can see it shine as it slides in and out of your mouth."

"How does that make you feel?" I wanted to know.

"Good."

"It's better than good."

"Yes, better than good."

"Tell me what you'd do to me if you had me there with you."

"I'd fuck you."

"How?"

"You know how."

"Tell me."

"I'd bend you over and spread those luscious cheeks. I'd hold that precious ass in my hand and plunge into you. I'd lick your shoulder blades and stick my tongue in your ear. I'd tell you how much I loved doing what I was doing."

"You love doing it to me, baby?" I growled.

"Yes, I do."

"Well, I love it when you do it to me. What are you doing now?"

"I've taken off all my clothes and gotten into the bathtub. I'm holding the phone in one hand and my dick in the other. It's slippery with soap. The top of my head is poking up through the bubbles. It's so hard it's turned purple. When I come, it's going to shoot straight up into the air, and little drops of come are going to fall back into the water like milky raindrops."

That did it. I came. A copious outpouring of semen erupted from the head of my penis and overflowed, running down my shaft and covering my hand.

"Goooooooood!" I groaned. It had been so good. It was like I had been with someone.

"Was it good for you?" he asked with a chuckle.

"Damn good." I sighed.

"Good. I like a satisfied customer."

"What are you talking about?"

"Don't worry, doll. It'll be a nice, discreet charge on your Visa. Or is it your Master Card we have on file?"

The dawn of awakening; a sliver of knowledge eased into my euphoria-filled brain. Had I inadvertently dialed the business line connected in Lance's house? It was a blow to my overgrown ego that Lance could get me off so skillfully, so easily, so lovingly, so professionally. I reached for the business card he gave me the last time we were together. I kept it on my nightstand. *Lance Dennis, Personal Consultant.* It was a plain white card with raised gold letters. There was a number for his room at Marco's—of course, all calls went through the receptionist first—and a number for his business line at home. He had written in his home number for me. I had called the wrong number. Shit.

"How much is this going to set me back?" I said.

"You can afford it. I read *Entertainment Weekly.*"

My salary had been reported in last week's edition as $225,000 per episode.

"And did that little dance at Marco's cost me too?"

"You bet your sweet ass."

"*¿Cuánto más?*"

"*Mucho dinero.*"

"You speak Spanish?"

"Fluently."

"What else do you speak?"

"Look, Wayne, why don't you let me call you, or you can call me back on the other line this time."

He was laughing at me.

"It's not the money," I stressed. I could afford his services. It was important to me he knew that.

"I know it's not the money."

"Then what is it?" *Does he have someone else holding?*

"I want you to know that I really do like you."

"Good. I'd hate to think it was just the money."

"It's not the money."

"Good." I hung up and he called me back on my phone.

PATTI

That boy could eat some pussy. He did it just right. He used just enough teeth and tongue. When it got real good to me, he used his fingers, those nice, man fingers with blunt nails, strong digits; skilled lover's fingers and hands. But he didn't use his dick. That son-of-a-bitch kept his nine-inch dick to his goddamn self. But I still got off—"once, twice, three times a lady." I had wrapped my long legs around that boy's head and came. And came and came. Let's just see if I'd be going back to Dallas.

KIM

I was an attractive woman, educated and independent. I could have any man I wanted, except for the one I had set my sights on.

Val surprised me with a breakfast invitation. We were at a little cafe on Melrose that was secluded and chic. Unlike the chaos Val had experienced during his last outing with Patti, this one was more successful because the management staff secured safe passage for its celebrity clientele.

He had appeared on my doorstep, looking like a

wounded puppy and just screaming for a little tender loving care. Looking across the table at him now as he picked at his omelet, I realized he was hurting. I also realized there was nothing I could do. Every time I tried to solicit some positive response from him, I was unsuccessful. Obviously, something he wanted was nothing I had to offer.

Our relationship had changed. We were no longer ignorant of the attraction that hovered beneath the surface of our friendship. Phrases like "I love you" and terms of endearment like "darling," "love" and "baby" did not pass between us as readily as they had before, and were blatantly absent during our meal. When Val looked into my eyes, I felt as though he was seeing the sister he never had, not the lover he could have.

"I love you, Kim." I could tell that he meant it when he reached across the table and took my hand. "But I am in love with someone else."

He meant that too. I felt as if he had dropped me—*hard*. Val never dropped me. In the years that we danced together, he had never let me go. There was a first for everything.

VAL

If I had met Kim before I met David, I would have been lying between her spread legs, losing myself in her inviting flesh. But I met David first. His fragrance was more sweet than any I had smelled, and his song more alluring than any I had heard. I knew how Kim felt about me. It both saddened and distressed me. I did not want to hurt her, but by the nature of my admission, I had. Kim could be for me what David was, only if there were no David. So, friends we were, and friends we would remain. Forever. Amen.

KIM

Val left me at my door with a kiss on the forehead and a brotherly pat on my back. It had all changed. I saw it in his eyes and felt it in his touch. Even though he had not said it, there would be no more shared kisses at his kitchen table with the taste of chocolate bittersweet on our tongues. No more pressing bodies, even accidentally, when I was wet with desire instead of sweat, in anticipation of feeling his sinew and muscle against my body. The rejection was gentle, the pain tolerable, and the embarrassment not so sharp. Damn, I was still a little in love with him. But I would get over it. I had to, or I wouldn't be able to keep dancing with him. And I wanted my career more than I wanted to pursue a one-sided love affair. Besides, any man who could take that "hoochie ho" over me, well, he might not be the one I need. So, just like that, I accepted the rejection. It was over. Done.

DAVID

I sat in front of a blank computer screen for nearly an hour before the muse of inspiration sneaked up behind me and tapped me on the shoulder. My problems with Patti were forgotten as I once again delved into *David's Story*.

"You don't have to go."

"I want to go."

"You lie. You lie. You lie."

"No, I really want to go."

"Liar."

Micah and Aaron sat in the front seat of Micah's car. They were parked in the alley outside the large warehouse Leslie Martin used as a combination gallery, studio and house. The alley was filled with cars, most of them limousines, Jaguars and Mercedes. Nevertheless, Micah's vintage Thunderbird fit right in. There was a party going on. Loud music filled the alleyway. Leslie Martin was an artist and a very successful one. His work, which had set the art world on its ear, had been described as everything from provocative to pornographic. He was one of Aaron's clients. Micah hated Leslie Martin . . .

"Shit." I deleted what I had written without even rereading it. It was crap. I flipped back to the last two pages, reread them, and once again tackled *David's Story*. It was too early for me to dismiss the conversation with my muse as the desperate attempt to occupy myself so that I would not have to face Patti. Armed in my attire of jeans and T-shirt, I would not be easy prey in the light of day, as I had been in the half-dressed, ultra sexual cover of nightfall.

As an art buyer for a large corporation, Aaron traveled in a circle that was very unlike what Micah had seen and been apart of as a policeman. But Micah was no longer a policeman, and Aaron's efforts to indoctrinate his lover into his world met with resistance.

"What kind of party is it?" Micah asked as he and Aaron pulled his vintage Thunderbird into a parking space next to a Rolls.

"A celebration kind of party," Aaron answered.

"Oh. That tells me a lot."

"Look, Micah. Go in with an open mind and you'll have a good time."

"I've got the feeling you're trying to prepare me for something," Micah groaned.

"I'm just trying to prepare you for a good time."

"Yeah. Yeah. Yeah." Micah feigned reluctance as he followed Aaron into the large warehouse that Leslie Martin used as a combination gallery, studio and house. Leslie Martin was a very successful artist. His provocative work had set the art world on its ear with reactions ranging from the alarmed to the outraged to the excited. Heralded as everything from thought provoking to pornographic, it was sometimes called trash instead of art, nevertheless, it was expensive, trendy and selling like hotcakes. His least expensive piece was a painting of a partially dressed transvestite holding a bouquet as he walked down the aisle toward marital bliss. It had sold for $17,000.

As part owner in a trendy upscale gallery, Aaron had handled Leslie Martin's last exhibit. The party was to celebrate the first time in the history of Upscale Trend, which was the name of Aaron's gallery, that all the paintings in one exhibit had sold, from the miniature nude pregnant woman dressed in a nun's black-and-white cap to the blown-up photograph of a penis captured in the midst of ejaculation. The gallery's commission had been $67,000. Even though Micah feigned reluctance, he was filled with curiosity about the people Aaron spent so much time with.

"Fuck!" I couldn't write anymore. I stopped typing and pushed myself away from the computer. I had never considered myself a coward, but as I sat hiding out in my room, doing what cowards did and feeling how I'm sure cowards felt, I realized that until I faced

Patti in the daylight, I would remain as a coward, a prisoner in my own home.

PATTI

I went to the TV room. I stretched out on the chaise lounge and picked up a copy of one of David's books, *Down Went Jonah*. I had never seen it. I had never heard of it. I didn't know what it was about. I had just learned a long time ago that if you wanted a man, you better make him think you were interested in the things he was interested in.

I touched at the tears as they rolled from my eyes, and I closed the book shut on my lap. I felt like I should stand up and testify because my life had been changed as surely as if there had been a "laying on" of hands.

Until I picked up David's book, I didn't read. Books were for smart people, and I didn't have to be smart because I was pretty and fine. But suddenly, pretty and fine didn't mean anything, and I wished I hadn't always had this ass or these tits. Maybe if I had been ugly or fat or " 'flicted," I would have had to be smart and I would have read beautiful stories and dreamed of far away places. But I wasn't ugly or fat or "'flicted." And I had this ass and these tits, and so I hadn't known that words written on paper could be as beautiful as an old hymn sung on Sunday morning. I did know, though, how to work my assets to my advantage.

I put the book back on the shelf. I put on my tightest jeans and made sure my nipples could be seen through my T-shirt. I had only been smart since this morning. I had had this ass and these tits forever.

DAVID

What is hotter than hot? What is sexier than sexy? Whatever it is, Patti was all that. She was nipple, aureole, fleshy breast, short crinkly hairs, pouting lips, clinging, sticky insides. There was a gossamer thread that connected our genitalia, transcending the boundaries of flesh. There was a psychic connection forged by the loss of virginity and shared strawberry sodas on a hill behind an old clapboard store that sold greasy French fries in paper sno-cone cups with ketchup diluted with pickle juice. I had no memory of Patti that did not include the manipulation and stimulation of my dick. I had nothing to draw on that did not include sex. So, where could we go when our beginning was so traumatized? What could we do when all I thought of when I saw her was sex?

"Hey, Davey-Gene," she purred as she crossed over to me. I could see the outline of her nipples and the cleft at the junction of her thighs. I could close my eyes and draw her breasts, her ass, and her inviting, hairy lips. I could not draw her face.

"What are you doing?"

I had left my computer and lounged on the futon. An empty bottle of J&B lay on its side near me. "Nothing," I said, my tongue heavy in my mouth.

She stretched out sensually next to me. Her legs were long, shapely, big, black girl's legs that I had had wrapped around my hips like a good pair of jeans and around my ears as she had lain screaming her passion into the otherwise empty house.

I wanted to touch her. I wanted to be able to lie next to her and talk without touching her. I wanted to ask about all the years between our beginning and now. I wanted to talk about being a cop, getting shot and writing books. I wanted to talk about college. I wanted to talk about Val. I wanted to talk about me and Val. I wanted to talk about the secret that had been made dirty because it was a secret. But I would not talk about any of that because Patti and I did not talk. Patti and I fucked.

"I'm so glad I came out here Davey-Gene. So glad," she said, snuggling close to me and throwing her leg over my hips.

I didn't say anything.

"I'm glad I got to see you again." She crawled on top of me.

I did nothing. If I continued to lay there and let her have her way with me, it would have ended as all our sessions did, in a sweaty, sexually fulfilling encounter that left me ashamed. I shifted so that her weight did not press against my erection. I did not need that piece of flesh between us. Its singlemindedness and sole purpose was to undermine my integrity.

"What's that?" She reached down and encompassed me. "Oh, yes. You are glad to see me."

It would be so easy to allow her to jerk me off. It would be so easy to allow her to have sex with me. But that would be the coward's way out. And I had resolved to not remain a coward in my house. I felt my erection begin to subside as she straddled me. Finally, my dick had learned what my heart had always known. Patti was not Val.

PATTI

It had never happened to me. Never. When I got a man hard, he stayed that way. At first, I did not know what to do, but my mama didn't birth no fool. So, I shimmied down David's body and took his soft self into my mouth. He put his hands on my head like he was trying to push me away, but I wasn't having it. I clamped down hard with my lips and just grazed his dick with my teeth so that he'd know I meant business.

"Oh, Patti." He moaned, and I knew I was doing everything right. Soon I could get whatever I wanted. The best way to keep a man soft was to get him hard.

DAVID

I meant to push Patti away from me. I meant to speak with my tongue the truth that my flesh knew. I meant for there to be no more mendacity in this house. I meant to tell Patti of me and Val. I meant so many things, but forgot them as soon as she engulfed me with her inviting wetness. I forgot what I needed to say. All I could say was, "Look-a-here, look-a-here, look-a-here."

VAL

She was sucking his dick. David's dick. My dick. I knew it as intimately as I did my own.

"Not too hard. He likes light pressure around the head," I said, taking perverse pleasure in startling them both.

"Oh, shit!" David said as he jumped up so fast that I'm sure he bruised himself on the roof of her mouth.

"Damn it, Davey," she yelled as she fell to the floor onto her pretty rump.

"Val, let me explain," David began as he tried to walk toward me and push himself back into his jeans at the same time.

"Baby, please . . ." He grabbed my arm.

"Fuck you, man." All I could think of was that Wayne was right. I pulled away from him.

"Val, wait, please."

I turned to him and pushed him into the wall. There was a loud thump as he hit it with great force.

"Baby, it didn't mean anything."

"Then why did you do it?" I shouted.

"It was just sex."

"It's never just sex when feelings are involved." I had four more stairs to go, when he grabbed me again. I did not want him to touch me. I turned with a dancer's grace and a boxer's sureness and put all I had behind the punch.

"Goddamn it, Val." He grabbed his nose. There was blood.

"Let me see." I hated myself for caring.

"Fuck!" he muttered as I led him to the downstairs bathroom. He sat passively on the stool while I took a cold towel and pressed it against his face. "I think you broke my nose."

I had. It was already swelling. I didn't say anything, but continued to clean him up. He put his hands on my hips and pulled me between his spread legs while I doctored him. I had trusted David with my heart. I had trusted David with my soul. I had trusted David with my secrets. I should not have trusted him with Patti.

When I finished, I threw the towel in the sink.

"Val . . ." He placed his head against my stomach and held me with all the love and pain that he possessed.

I wanted to tell him it was okay. I wanted to tell

him that I understood. But I could not. I did not understand. I wasn't that big. All I could see was her sucking his dick and him, lying back, eyes closed, mouth agape, liking it.

"Val . . ." he said again.

"Fuck you, man." I pushed him off me and headed for my car. I did not answer as he called after me.

PATTI

Cocksucker! Faggot! I was so mad I couldn't think straight. I grabbed my suitcase and just started throwing shit in it. I got all my stuff plus all the stuff Val and I bought with David's money. Just thinking about all that money made me sick. All that fucking money! All of it, and I wasn't going to get a penny of it because I didn't have nothing he wanted. Nothing. No wonder he couldn't get it up for me. My Davey-Gene had turned into a fucking faggot. No man had ever left me willingly. No wonder he couldn't get it up.

I threw off my robe and stood before the full-length mirror to study my body. There was nothing wrong with me. Nothing. The problem was that he wanted a dick instead of a pussy. So it wasn't me. No. No. No. He was the one with the fucking problem. It was him that was all screwed up, not me; I still had it going on.

DAVID

I took the stairs two at a time. The time for confrontation was upon me, and I dreaded it. I found her in the bedroom, packing her things.

"Patti . . ." I began.

She slammed her suitcase shut and turned to me with such hatred in her eyes that I was forced to take a step backwards.

"You see this?"—She cupped her breasts—"Or this?"—She ran her hand over her ass—"How could you choose him over me?"

"I love Val," I confessed without hesitation.

"Don't say that."

"I do."

"Queer." She punched me. "Cocksucker! Punk! Sissy!"

I tried to protect my face from her tirade of insults and punches. "Please," I said, grabbing at her flaying fists. "Stop it. Just stop it." I held her hands behind her back.

"Let go of me. I don't want you to touch me, you fuckin' faggot."

I let her go.

She turned her back to me as she began to dress. "I don't know you anymore. I just don't know you. David? David E. Lincoln? D.E. Lincoln? I don't know any of those people. I know Davey-Gene, but the Davey-Gene I know don't suck no dick."

I wanted to grab and shake her. I wanted to hold her and cry on her shoulder. I wanted to scream. I wanted to whisper. I wanted to confess. I wanted to deny. I wanted it to be as it had been between us when we had been Davey-Gene and Patticake forever, but it would never be that way ever again because we weren't Davey-Gene and Patticake forever. We were David and Patricia. The children who had spent a joyous youth filled with discovery of sex and pleasure had grown into adults with lives that revolved around other things besides a momentary gratification of the flesh. I needed to talk about the here and now, where I had landed after taking a path that led far away from the projects, poverty and redundancy.

I had looked at her and seen what I wanted to see. The picture wasn't accurate. She still called me Davey-Gene. Where could we go from here?

I watched silently as she packed her bags. She would not let me help her, screaming and throwing things at me when I got close to her. She wouldn't let me talk to her because whenever I opened my mouth, she covered her ears.

I stood and watched silently as she gathered her things and waited on the cab.

When the cab arrived, I didn't know what we looked like, me with my broken nose and blood-splattered sweatshirt, she in her three-inch heels, orange leather hot pants and pink-and-orange tank top. To the cab driver's credit, he put her bags in the car without a word. When I approached him to give him money, he cringed as if he expected me to hit him, even though I looked liked the victim, so I threw a hundred dollars on the front seat of his cab and told him to get her to LAX.

When they drove away, I closed the door on Patti, the cab driver and a part of my life that would have to be examined later when I was no longer weary. I walked up the stairs to our room and ran a hot bath. I needed to be prepared when Val came home. I knew he was coming. I just didn't know when.

CHAPTER THIRTY-EIGHT

For the second time in less than a week, Wayne awakened to the smell of frying bacon and brewing coffee and knew he wasn't alone. Yawning and stretching, he walked naked into the bathroom. He peed, washed his hands, brushed his teeth and wandered into the kitchen.

Lance sat at the kitchen table. He had done something to his hair. His braids were piled atop his head like an intricately woven crown. An open book lay before him. He wore horn-rimmed glasses and gnawed on a pencil. His look was studious, the air about him confident.

Looking at Lance as he studied, Wayne was once again struck by an overwhelming feeling of déjà vu. Lance looked as if he belonged in Wayne's kitchen. He shook his head as if clearing away the picture of Lance at his table. A relationship with Lance was not what he was looking for. He had set his sights on Val. He was getting closer to Val. He wanted Val. Val, not Lance. But the practical side of him said, "If you

can't have the one you love, love the one you have."
The one he had was Lance.

LANCE

At first I didn't know why I hadn't left after the
sex, which was my custom. But looking at him as he
walked into the kitchen, I knew why. I was starting to
like him. It was getting to be more than sex.

"Morning," I said.

"Morning," he responded, grabbing a piece of
bacon, pouring himself a cup of coffee and then sitting opposite me. His nakedness didn't bother me. It
seemed natural. My being in his house also seemed
natural. I didn't like that. This was not what I had
planned.

WAYNE

"I didn't know you wore glasses." I put my feet in
Lance's lap.

"Only to read," Lance said.

"You know what they say."

"What is that?"

"Men don't make passes at boys in glasses."

Lance grimaced. "Droll, Wayne. Very droll." He
reached for his coffee, took a sip and grimaced.
"Ugh . . . cold."

I got up and poured him a hot cup of coffee. "How
do you take it?" I asked, my hand hovering near the
sugar.

"Black like me."

"No, not like you." I handed him the coffee. "There's

a little purple-like plums and a little red-like cinnamon under your skin." I rubbed my knuckles down his cheek. "If it were just black, there would be no character, no soul."

Our eyes met.

LANCE

Yep, that's why I hadn't left. He said things like that that were so damn poetic.

WAYNE

Shit. I think I was starting to like him.

LANCE

Of course, I let him fuck me.

WAYNE

We didn't fuck; we made love. I didn't think of Val.

CHAPTER THIRTY-NINE

Val didn't give Wayne the opportunity to respond. As soon as he opened his door, Val was all over him. He kissed him fiercely, and just to make sure Wayne knew what was going on, he rubbed his crotch for emphasis.

"Whoa," Wayne said, detangling himself from Val. "Who are you?"

"You know who I am," Val said as he kissed Wayne's nose and walked past him into Wayne's house.

"Seems to me you've been telling me in not so many words to fuck off."

"It wasn't me."

"Looked like you."

"It was an imposter." Val took a seat on the couch.

"What's going on, Val?" Wayne followed and sat opposite him.

"You were right, you know."

"I'm always right. What was I right about?"

"David and Patti."

Wayne didn't know what to say. "I didn't want to be right, Val."

"I didn't want you to be right."

"Let me get you a beer. Or would you rather have wine?"

"Beer is fine."

Val watched as Wayne disappeared into the kitchen. He was dressed in faded 501's that hung low on his hips. He returned quickly with two long-neck beers. There was a trail of fine hairs covering his chest and disappearing into a well-groomed V at the open waistband of his jeans.

Val took the beer gratefully and said, "Thanks."

Again, Wayne sat facing Val. He too drank from his beer and accepted the companionable silence that existed between them.

Once he had finished his beer, Val crooked his finger at Wayne, beckoning him nearer.

Wayne raised an eyebrow at Val's silent request. "You've got to be kidding."

"Don't you want me still?"

"I think I'll always want you."

"Well?"

"Why did you come to me, Val?"

"Does it matter?"

"I think it does."

"Because."

"Because why?"

"Because I said if he sleeps with her, I'll sleep with you."

"Unh-uh. Not good enough."

"Okay, because no matter what I say or how I have acted previously, I am and always have been very attracted to you."

"Much better." Wayne smiled and took a swig from his beer. "So, Val, it's a sex thing?"

"Yes, Wayne, it's a sex thing."

" 'A sex thing,' " Wayne repeated, drinking from his beer. "Okay, I can handle that." He stood and held his hand out to Val. "Can you?"

"Yes, I can." Val took Wayne's hand and walked with him into his bedroom.

"Open your mouth. I want to taste you when I kiss you," Wayne said against Val's lips. They were lying in Wayne's king-sized bed. They were both still partially dressed. Val had lost his linen shirt somewhere between the living room and Wayne's bed. Wayne had unfastened the last button on his jeans.

Val parted his lips, and Wayne's tongue darted into his mouth. As they kissed, Wayne ran his hand down Val's body, caressing his belly and tickling his navel. "Ticklish?" he asked.

"No, you?"

"No." Wayne's wandering hand entered the fly of Val's shorts and cupped his balls, feeling the weight of his penis. "Um, I like that." He kissed his way down Val's body, pulling his shorts with him. Once he had Val naked, he stood at the foot of the bed and looked at his prize. "Damn, I think I'm looking at perfection." He eased his jeans down his legs.

As Wayne undressed, Val propped himself up on his elbows and watched. "Turn around," Val ordered.

"Why?" Wayne asked, although he did as he was instructed, posing and flexing for Val's benefit.

Val let out a low wolf whistle. "Nice ass."

"Are you an 'ass' man?" Wayne crawled back into the bed.

"I am now." Val rolled on top of Wayne and nipped his ass cheek.

"Don't stop."

Laughing, Val covered Wayne's muscular ass with kisses.

"I like that."

"I knew you would." Val began to blaze a trail of kisses up Wayne's spine. He licked his shoulder blades and rubbed himself against Wayne's ass. Although he was finding their encounter pleasurable, he was only semi-erect.

Wayne rolled onto his back and pulled Val on top of him. "What do you like?"

"I like it all."

"Good." Wayne kissed Val's chin and licked his neck. "You taste like tangerines."

"It's the soap David bought me for my birthday when we were in Milan. It's all natural."

Wayne kissed Val.

"David's ticklish, you know," Val said, rolling onto his back, taking Wayne with him.

Wayne straddled Val's body easily and captured Val's hands with his. "What's my name?" he asked.

"What are you talking about?"

"My name, what is it?"

"It's Wayne."

"Right. Wayne, not David. Got it?"

"Got it."

"Good." Wayne ran a finger down Val's body to a nipple and encircled it. "You're so hot." He leaned down and kissed Val's nipple. "So very hot." He stretched out on top of Val, aligning their bodies. "Can you feel how much I want you?"

"Are you going to talk all night?"

"Yep." Wayne ran his hand down Val's body.

"You're silly."

"You're sexy." Wayne kissed Val.

"You're hard."

"You're not." Wayne eased off Val.

"What are you doing?"

"I'm going to put on my pants, make a pot of coffee and help you figure out what you're going to do," Wayne said, getting up.

"Wait a minute. Let me get this straight. You don't want me?" Val asked, sitting up in bed, a look of disbelief on his face.

"Oh, I want you; you don't want me."

"Wayne—"

"Maybe some other time, Val. Some other day."

"But—"

"No buts. I already think I need my head examined."

"Wayne?"

"Get up. You'll love me in the morning."

"I think I'm starting to love you now."

"Damn, Val. I didn't want to be friends."

"You're really a nice guy, Wayne."

"Yeah, yeah, yeah." Wayne pulled on his jeans and headed into his kitchen.

Wayne made a pot of Godiva International coffee and listened to Val pour his heart out to him. And in the telling of their story, Val's and David's, Wayne became what he did not want to become, Val's friend, not his lover.

VAL

We were not going to have sex. We couldn't have sex. We were becoming friends. He made coffee for me and rubbed my feet and led me to his guest bedroom. He didn't try to make love to me. He didn't pressure me. He just became my friend. And I wouldn't fuck my friends, either Kim or Wayne. I could only fuck David, that son-of-a-bitch. I was glad I broke his goddamn nose. I should have kicked him in the balls.

CHAPTER FORTY

Lance was arriving as Val was leaving. The two men met on the walkway leading into Wayne's house. Lance raised an eyebrow. Val suppressed a nervous, amused smile.

"Hi," Lance said.

"Hi," Val responded. They sized each other up. "I slept in the guest room."

"I didn't ask."

"But you wanted to."

Lance laughed. "Yeah, I wanted to."

The two men shook hands. As Val started toward his car, he stopped and called to Lance. "Lance?"

Lance paused with his hand on the doorknob. "Yeah, Val?"

"He really is a nice guy."

"I know."

"He deserves a nice guy."

"I know. That's why I'm here." He waved to Val and disappeared into Wayne's house.

* * *

Aaron sat at the vanity and stared at his reflection. What he saw was a good-looking man, full-lipped, somber-eyed, well-groomed and handsome.

"I, Aaron Bovia," he said, "am a homosexual."

There. He had finally said it, and the walls had not come tumbling down around his head. He felt refreshed, renewed and reborn. He had shed the lie as he had shed his previous life. Mendacity was no longer an unwanted friend overstaying his welcome and contaminating the air with lies, half-truths and deception.

"What are you grinning at?" Micah asked from the doorway of their bedroom. He was dressed in black leather slacks and a denim shirt. His big feet were encased in cowboy boots and he looked good enough to eat. Aaron, who had always been more liberated than Micah in all things, could admit that without recrimination.

"Nothing," Aaron said.

"Nothing, huh?" Micah crossed the room and stood over Aaron.

"Sure?" Aaron patted Micah's hand.

"Good, let's go." He kissed his lover's ear. Aaron stood. He was dressed in a well-tailored silk suit. The raw material felt good against his skin.

"We look good together."

"Yeah, we do."

They were taking a big step, the two of them, exchanging vows as would a "normal" couple. But what was normal? Did being a member of the majority make it right? No. At least not for Micah and Aaron. The time for conformity had long since passed.

"Mick?"

"Yeah?"

"I just wanted to say I love you," Aaron said.

"I love you too." Micah took Aaron into his arms and kissed him deeply. Then hand in hand they headed toward their ceremony. Together they were. Together they would remain. What God had joined in love, let no man put asunder. Amen.

David's fingers paused over the keyboard before he typed *The End.* The storybook ending was a cop-out, trite and predictable. But Micah and Aaron needed a happy ending because Micah and Aaron were David and Val.

David turned off his computer and wandered into the room that Val had used while Patti was staying with them. He began to move all of Val's things back into their room. After that, he dozed off to sleep, waiting, waiting for his lover.

He awakened to the sound of the shower running and knew Val had come home. He had fallen asleep atop the covers while he waited for Val. The sound of the shower was reassuring and frightening. He didn't know what to say, but he knew what to do. He stripped out of his Calvin Klein's and padded to the shower.

David had been sleeping when Val walked in. Val wanted to hug him. He wanted to kiss him. He wanted to yell at him. He wanted to kick him in the balls. Instead, he pulled off his clothes and got in the shower. The water felt good against his skin. It was cleansing and refreshing.

Through the steam he saw David come in. His dick swayed as he walked. Even unaroused he was huge. He had the black man's burden, a big dick and the responsibilities of it.

Their master bath had been built to Val's specifications. The shower was twice as large as a normal shower and very deep. There was no shower curtain. There was no need. David stepped into the shower. He didn't say anything. He just came up behind Val.

There was enough room. They could get clean without touching. Arms, legs, hips, thighs and buttocks had no reason to fight for space in the overly large shower. David's erection grew. He did not try to hide it from Val.

"The water is too hot," was the first thing David said, praying that Val would remember.

"This is my morning ritual. I'm just tolerating you," Val replied.

He did. He did remember. Val adjusted the water temperature.

"Give me the soap," David said, leading Val down the road to remembrance. "Turn around. I'll wash your back."

Although their roles had been switched, Val did as he was told. He turned to allow David the opportunity to wash his back. Smooth hands, soapy and wet, glided over his skin.

"That feels good," Val said.

"Uh-huh."

David had not planned on seducing Val. Val had planned on being seduced by David. As it was in the beginning, it is now and ever shall be. David and Val forever, together, Amen.

Slowly, David's hands traveled over Val's body, soaping under arms, chest and thighs. Val's penis had developed a mind of its own. Throbbing and straining for release, it pointed toward his navel. He didn't ask David if he knew what he was doing. David knew. David's hands slowly glided from Val's thighs to his ass. They soaped, caressed and separated cheeks gently, oh so gently. The tip of a soapy finger grazed Val's opening and was replaced by a tongue, a knowing, loving tongue that asked for forgiveness with every kiss and caress.

They continued down this road because it was the only way they could go. This journey had to be made. There was nowhere else for David and Val to go, so when Val turned to David, David did the only thing he could do. Faced with Val's penis, David's mouth opened and swallowed the whole of Val, who was big, bigger than life, big with wanting David and only David. Not Wayne, not Kim. Only David. So when Val came, he braced himself against the walls of the shower and poured his seed into David's mouth. And David swallowed because it was meant to be. Afterwards, the only sounds in the room were those of their heavy breathing, running water and David's tears dropping.

"Forgive me," he cried. "Forgive me."

And all Val could say was, "I do."